my perfect sister

my
perfect
sister

PENNY BATCHELOR

Red Door

Published by RedDoor

www.reddoorpress.co.uk

ISBN 978-1-913062-27-9

A CIP catalogue record for this book is available from the British Library

Cover design: Emily Courdelle

Typesetting: Jen Parker, Fuzzy Flamingo

Printed and bound in Denmark by Nørhaven

*For the Batchelor gang: Mum, Dad, Paul, Anna, Tom and Nic;
and my husband Chris*

Thursday 4th May 1989. 4.15 p.m.

Out in the garden Annie enjoyed the feel of the sun on her skin in the dappled afternoon sunlight, relishing casting off her red gingham dress and lying down on the grass in the back garden playing horizontal starfish. The grass tickled her as she moved her legs and arms sideways in tandem, pretending she was floating in the sea; a feared creature of the big, wide ocean. Free to float away to a desert island.

The school day was over. Above her head a cabbage white butterfly flapped its wings, teasing her by flying back and forth almost rhythmically towards her nose but never quite trusting to land. Annie giggled with delight and opened her mouth, pretending to swallow the butterfly in one. It flew away towards the fence separating their garden from next door and disappeared into the pink blossom on a tree.

Annie bathed in the warmth of the sun against her skin and started to doze, dreaming about chocolate ice cream. Perhaps her mummy would take her to the corner shop to buy one when she got out of bed. All would be well with the world.

Suddenly a shadow covered the sun, cooling her face, causing her to wake up and sit bolt upright.

'Oh!' she said, startled. 'It's you.'

~ 1 ~

2014

I stand in my childhood bedroom, though little remains of what it used to be. On the walls where in my teenage years I had Blu-Tacked Nirvana and Oasis posters there's now pale blue wallpaper with a small, white, peony pattern. The old cider-stained taupe carpet has gone, replaced by a dark blue plush version. Instead of my vanity table placed against the side wall there's a modern sewing machine on a stand, surrounded by neat, stacked plastic boxes containing threads and fabric. Lots of flowers and pink. Everything has a place and is rigidly in it.

The pencil marks on the door frame recording my height over the years have been emulsioned over. A white flat-pack wardrobe stands where my old wooden one used to be. Inside are empty hangers, the kind bought in a multipack, not plastic ones taken from high street shops on a Saturday afternoon shopping trip. No cast-off underwear destined for the laundry lounges on the floor. The childhood books I left behind are long gone, as is the small bookcase. Only the single bed remains as a remnant from what the room once was to testify that I slept here. Even that, pushed up against the back wall instead of jutting out into the room, is covered in a patchwork quilt no doubt sewn by my mother to show her crafting skills off to guests.

If she ever has any.

This is not my room anymore; it's the spare bedroom. In fact, it's as if I never was here, as if I didn't exist.

On the contrary, it is Gemma who probably doesn't exist, but you wouldn't know it by looking in 'her' room. I shut the spare room door behind me and push open the brown door with a pottery multi-coloured 'Gemma' sign still stuck on it. Behind that door is a lost world, a museum piece from a distant decade that should be covered Miss Haversham-style in dust and cobwebs but is as spick and span as if it were cleaned yesterday.

No doubt it was.

Presents lie on the floor next to the bed where her shoe collection used to be – one for each birthday and Christmas she has been gone. For goodness' sake. Does Mother think Gemma is going to come back from the dead and open them?

Her pop posters still line the walls, her lipsticks, mascara and eyeliner neatly sit on the dressing table below its mirror (I hate to think of the bacteria on them), and from the back of her dressing table chair hangs her mini-rucksack, the black one she took out with her when meeting her friends. Scruffy, the mangy fluffy dog Mother said Gemma was given as a baby, guards her pillow. It's the same bed linen, purple with white swirls that she once slept in, but freshly washed and ironed. This is a sanitised teenage girl's bedroom, without the smell of perfume, freshly-washed hair, sweaty cast-off clothes or a cup of once warm coffee. Without breath. Without life.

I look at the pinboard resting on top of the desk. There

are photos pinned there, photos I haven't seen for all those years I've been away. Photos from a real camera, the kind where you point, shoot and don't know what the picture will turn out like until it comes back from the developer's. In the middle of one faded rectangle Gemma smiles at the camera, her dark brown hair pulled back in a ponytail, her eyes laughing at something the photographer must have said. She is in the park, I think. The evening light dances on her cheekbones, striped pink in that eighties fashion; her cut-off T-shirt shows off a tanned midriff above a pair of pale blue ripped jeans; she's raising her arms in the air as if to say this is mine. This is all mine.

The other photos show a mixture of permed girls and mulleted boys in a variety of fading situations: someone's house, the park again, and one where they wear white school shirts with fat, short ties. She smiles out from the pictures, frozen at sixteen.

As I turn to leave I notice another picture at the bottom left-hand corner, one of my parents looking much younger, sitting on the step outside the front of this house. Mother is curled up on Father's knee and they are smiling for the camera, their happy faces belying what I can remember from my childhood. I peer closer inquisitively then remove the pin and pull the photo away from the board. The corner of another photo had covered part of the image. I take a sharp breath when I see which part hasn't been viewed by the world for twenty-four years. Here the colours are bright and stand out next to their muted neighbours.

To the right of Father, a real-life gap of about twenty centimetres away, there's a little girl with a ginger ponytail and a brown pinafore dress looking the other away, not part of this cosy family scene. Me.

Gemma must have taken it.

I hear the front door close softly.

Occasionally I think that if she weren't already dead I'd want to kill Gemma myself.

~ 2 ~

I close the bedroom door quietly and walk to the stairs. The old swirly red and green stair carpet has gone, replaced by a dark beige industrial one, the practical kind that won't show up the dirt. I remember as a young girl sitting on the stair third from top, rubbing my face against the carpet, half-closing my eyes and watching the red and green dance together millimetres from my eyelashes whilst a policewoman spoke to my parents in voices muted by the closed kitchen door. Every ten seconds or so loud sobs punctuated the mumbling. 'Stay upstairs until I say so,' my father had said, ushering me into my bedroom. Time passed, was it minutes or hours? A minute can feel like millennia to a young child.

I'd ventured as far as the stairs but no further, as if there was an invisible barrier holding me back, fixing my eyes on the carpet pattern. There I'd stayed until Father came to get me and told me I had to have an early night. You see, that's what I remember from my childhood, not picnics, birthday parties or trips to the park but the police coming round when my sister didn't return home and the pervading shadow it cast everywhere. Except that shadow, that gloom, that tiptoeing around death never left. I did instead.

When I walked out of the red front door for the last

time I may have lived on this planet for a month longer than Gemma ever did. I left at soon as the bell had rung on my final day at school and didn't come back, ever, to this house.

I returned from Leeds over a decade later to see my father in hospital after his stroke, and although she had left the message on my mobile to let me know which hospital he was in I hovered in the darkest recess of the corridor until my mother had left. A dying man's bedside isn't the place for a row, or more likely the silent treatment. My mother is more passive-aggressive than the dramatic argumentative type.

The smell of the disinfectant stuck with me, pinning itself to my recollection of the day. Whenever there's that scent in the air I think of my decaying father. He couldn't talk well but squeezed my hand and a tear ran down his cheek; he then pulled on my arm, gesturing that he wanted to tell me something. I bent down to his level, so close that I could feel his shallow breaths on my ear.

'Forgive your mum,' he said. Thirty seconds passed whilst he drew upon some more energy to speak his final words to me. 'She loves you, she just couldn't show it. Look after her when I'm gone. Please.'

I smiled at him, a wide smile that didn't stretch to my eyes, and nodded – a panacea for the dying. Like hell I'd keep my fake promise. His last words to me were about her, not some words of love and wisdom for me. He'd been the buffer between me and her, but even on his deathbed he took her side. What about me, I wanted to scream. What about me?

Nine days later I went to the church funeral but skipped the pub buffet and reminiscences about what a decent bloke he was by old colleagues, neighbours and those who wanted a free lunch. Instead I went home, got drunk and remembered Father in my own way as the quiet, smallish man who tried, but never quite hard enough. Did I love him? I think so. But I can't say that his passing made much of a difference to my life, it now being so far removed from the bad old days.

And yet, despite all my remonstrances, here I am at 22 Greville Road, the place I'd swore I'd never return to.

With great sadness and faint hope I pat my back jeans pocket where my mobile is. It hasn't vibrated and there's still no text or voice message from Shaun begging me to come home. Or rather back to his home – the one he asked me to leave in no uncertain terms after what I did, the situation he couldn't understand and I won't bring myself to think about.

Greville Road is now the only semblance of a home I have left.

That's how low I've sunk.

I walk down the stairs, steadying myself for the inevitable moment when I'll come face to face with my mother for the first time in, how long? I've lost count. In fact, I never bothered to start counting: far away from here, living a different life, I didn't have to think about facing up to what I'd spent so long running away from, being the left over one, the daughter who was still around, a stark reminder to them that their wonderful, beautiful, preferred Gemma was not. How could I possibly ever live up to the memory of a dead saint?

My childhood key, the bronze one with the stripy plastic cover at the top 'to show you this is the key to home,' Father had said, still worked and when I arrived she was out. So they hadn't changed the locks, but then that was probably nothing to do with me. Mother will have kept the locks the same just in case Gemma turns up with her key, a bunch of flowers, a husband, family and a dashing tale to tell about what she's been up to since that summer day when she never came home.

Downstairs now, I walk into the kitchen, which is still the same and looking none the better for it. Mother is standing at the sink with her back to me making a cup of tea. The noise of the kettle may have covered my footsteps.

'Hi,' I say a bit louder than necessary, steeling myself. Why am I nervous? Should I have agreed to come here at all?

She turns around, balancing a tea bag on the end of a teaspoon. If this had been another situation it would have almost been comic.

'Oh Annie…' she says, her words tailoring off to a soft silence. The first thing I notice is that her knitted cardigan is hanging off her once plump frame in swathes. She looks like a child dressing up in adults' clothes. She is pulling the edges of her right sleeve with her left hand: fidgeting, twisting, rubbing. Her eyes, surrounded by a panda bear's black rings, seem to have sunk into her skull, whilst her crumpled skin is stark white, almost translucent, criss-crossed by red, angry veins in a spider's web fashion. Her once golden-brown hair is now grey and cropped shortly to her head. She is gaunt, haggard and shrivelled.

I gasp in shock, and then cough to try to cover up my initial bad-mannered reaction. I hadn't expected it to be true, I'd assumed that her wheedling pleas were just a manipulative pretence to guilt trip me into returning and the reason I could give for heeding them.

Mother really did have cancer. Or rather cancer had eaten her up and was preparing to spit her out, used and desiccated, into the grave.

~ 3 ~

What do you say to a woman you haven't seen in well over a decade and now appears to be dying in front of your eyes? My answer is biscuits. I ask mother if she has any to go with the tea and jump up to the kettle to busy myself making my own cup. Whilst the steam rises from the kettle, I wash up the few dirty plates lying in tepid water in the sink. Even the crockery with its chintz pattern, now amazingly back in fashion, is the same I ate and drank from as a child and, although slightly chipped, it has worn better than mother has.

'There's a packet of digestives in the tin,' she informs me. I don't have to ask where the tin is; it's to the left of the bread bin in the same place as it was in my childhood. I take a couple and carry my hot cup of tea. It is only when I sit down opposite Mother that I notice the mug I picked up from the draining board. It is white with slight enamel cracks and the words 'Gemma's mug' written in pink on the side. I clench my fingers around the handle until they turn white.

'Thank you for coming. I didn't know whether you would. I am glad you did.' Mother's eyes stare at me then dart away as if scorched.

I pause for just a bit longer than is natural to think of something to say. 'That's OK. What's, um, your diagnosis?'

I put the mug down on the table a little too heavily and a small pool of brown liquid splashes on to the table. At home I would have left it but here instinct tells me to leap up and fetch a piece of kitchen roll to mop it up with in case it leaves a stain.

'Ahem.' She coughs and gestures towards the cork mat covered with a view of the Lake District. I duly oblige and cover Coniston Water up with the bottom of Gemma's mug.

She gets straight to the point but doesn't look me in the eye when she says, 'I have stage three kidney cancer and a secondary tumour that I need chemotherapy for. The doctor removed the kidney in an operation.'

What do you say to that?

She takes another sip of her tea before carrying on. 'Aunty Lena, I mean Elaine, has been taking me to the hospital for treatment but her Den isn't so well now and she can't always spare the time.'

'What about Reg? Does he still live next door?' Reg, his wife and son who is a few years older than me lived on the other side of our semi-detached house when I was a child. He had been a kind man, if a little too fond of foot-stomping country music that penetrated through our dividing wall.

Mother pulls her cardigan more tightly around her. 'Reg is drunk most days. I doubt he's able to drive a car and if he was I wouldn't get in it.' She is very disapproving of alcohol is my mother, only stooping to sipping a gin and tonic at Christmas and birthdays. At least she can't blame the cancer on booze.

'Karen?'

'She left him about ten years ago. Reg is on his own now.'

I know what I ought to say. 'Well I've got my car. I can take you to the hospital. When is your next appointment?'

'In a couple of days' time. Thank you.' She places a wizened hand on top of mine and it takes all my forbearance not to snatch it away. Mother doesn't do affection, I barely remember any hugs and kisses, caresses or tenderness. Even when I was a little girl and she washed my hair she'd brush it through not with warmth but with ruthless efficiency. I'd wail as she pulled out the knots. When I turned six she took me to the hairdresser and told her to cut it short in a practical, no-nonsense style. I cried for days at the loss of my bunches.

The last time I lived in this house mother spent most of her time lying down in her blacked-out bedroom, free from the sunshine, life's responsibilities and me. Breakfast was Father's job. She might deign us with her presence after school, but the chip shop and the pizza takeaway did jolly good business from our house on the days she stayed upstairs until I learned how to cook pasta and stir fry for Father and me. We never knew which days those would be.

Aunty Lena, Mother's best friend, usually picked me up from primary school, walked me home and saw me safely inside before she returned to her own house to keep an eye on Uncle Den. His leg never got better after being severed in an accident down the mine. 'I've worked so long underground that I turned into a mole,' he'd say to make me laugh, sticking his front teeth out and shutting his eyes to a black chink.

'You know where I am, come and knock on the door if you need me,' Aunty Lena implored every time she dropped me off from school with a smile, before walking back down the path and shutting the gate behind her ample bottom. She only lived a few doors down the street and I was used to making that short journey along the cracked pavement. There were twenty-five pavement slabs between our houses and I was so proud the day when I first managed to hop on each slab, counting them as I went along. I smile at the memory.

'How are Aunty Lena and Uncle Den?'

'Den can't leave the house now. Elaine's bearing up. She said she'd pop round tomorrow to see you.'

'I'd like that,' I say with genuine enthusiasm. Aunty Lena had been the nearest thing I'd had to a mother. I forwarded my address to her when I moved to Leeds but as the years passed any Christmas cards and letters she may have sent were left unanswered in that first house share because I'd moved on, crafting out my new life. I still kept the same mobile number though, hence mother dearest calling when she wanted something from me.

'Did you think that about seeing me again? You've stayed away so many years, Annie.'

Here we go.

I think about my answer before I reply. 'I'm sorry you've got cancer.' It is the truth and the most I can give her. There, for today, she lets it lie and moves the conversation on to the ingredients for a shepherd's pie she has in the fridge. I offer to make it whilst she goes upstairs for a nap. She's tired, she says, a side effect of the medication.

She always did have an excuse to shut herself away in her bedroom.

Whilst mother is upstairs I feverishly chop up the onion

13

and carrot with a sharp knife, slicing them to smithereens. After I put the meal in the oven I wash up, scrubbing, foaming and rinsing to rid the mugs and pans of their inner brown stains. When I reach for the tea-towel with one hand, the mug I'd used slips through my other wet hand and smashes on the floor.

Whoops.

I quickly sweep up the pieces and dump them in the bin, destined for the dustbin lorry and landfill, buried and never seen again.

Dinner passes in relative silence with comments about the state of the weather, it is unusually cold for this time of year, and the meal is followed by two hours of soap operas and dramas Mother follows on the television. I am glad for the diversion, to be able to sit not talking yet staring at a box. The only time my phone vibrates is when delivering a text from my bank telling me I have nearly reached my overdraft limit.

I lie still in the homogenous spare room single bed that night, as usual awake for much longer than I should be, recalling my secret childhood dream, the one thing that comforted me deep in the night when everyone else was asleep, but rest didn't come to me. If I'd told anyone they would have tarnished it by laughing and thinking it childish and silly. I know it is. I've known it ever since I was a little girl and first thought it, a few nights after the police came and our house went cold but my secret kept me warm. Since then I've updated it and embellished it, holding it tight in the darkest hours.

I used to daydream that I was adopted and my real

parents were longing to find me. Or perhaps I was swapped as a newborn in the hospital and they'd only just found out that who they thought was their daughter was actually a cuckoo in the nest and the true birth daughter of a bland, lower-middle class couple, the father now long dead. My real parents, whether I was adopted or swapped in the maternity ward, would be hiring lawyers and petitioning their MP: fighting to find me, to hold me in their arms. Mum would be called something like Margaret, Mags to her good friends. She'd have reddish cheeks, a short bob turning grey, a smile that shines past her lips into her eyes and a little middle-aged spread – won't we all in our mid-fifties? – but the sort that comes from good home cooking and lots of long Sunday lunches with red wine and friends who love her for who she is. Dad would always do the washing up. He'd tease Mum about her cooking but secretly was proud of her, pleased that out of all his friends' wives Margaret was the most friendly, the best cook, and the happiest. Dad, called something like Fred, would have a tanned face from hours on the golf course. Margaret would make fun of his addiction to the nineteenth hole, but she'd like the social life that came with the golf club and wouldn't want a husband who stayed at home under her feet all the time. They'd have retired early because Fred had a decent job in industry and got a good pension payout. Some of their free time they spent holidaying at their caravan in the Lake District.

Yet the hole in their life, the empty place at their dinner table, would be me. Margaret and Fred wouldn't have any other children. Oh how they'd long to find me and make their family complete. This is not my life. I was not meant to be thirty, single, jobless and back at my childhood home, nursing a woman who only matches the definition of the word 'mother' in the biological sense.

Every few hours I hear her shuffle to the bathroom, flush the chain then return to her bed. No noise comes from Gemma's room, bar the sound of a creaking heating pipe. I don't really remember when it ever did, what it was like when she was alive and loud, playing music and shrieking with friends in the way that teenage girls do. Or did Gemma ever do that? I didn't, not in this house.

I was five when she never came back from school. When a police search failed to find her, and no one responded to my parents' television pleas; her case was quietly placed on the back burner, lacking enough evidence to pursue it further. If she had run away there was no trace of her, but Father swore that to leave without telling them was completely out of her character. Her purse was never found, although she hadn't taken a change of clothes, her building society pass books or anything of value when she went to school that day. The police case is still open but there is an assumption that Gemma is dead and her killer unknown.

The majority of what I remember doesn't actually come from my own memory, it has been pieced together by things I've learned later on: snippets of conversations; overheard whispers; a police report I sneakily took from father's desk and read; a photo album that was brought out on every family occasion to remember Gemma as Mary in the school nativity play (thank goodness my parents didn't own a video camera – can you imagine me having to sit through home movies of her again and again?), Gemma in her Brownie uniform,

Gemma performing in a ballet show (the only after-school activity I ever had was trying to cook beans on toast myself when I was so hungry that my stomach rumbled out loud) and blowing out the candles on her sixteenth birthday cake. If I try to picture her face it's one of those photos that appears in my imagination, stuck in time forever in a split second.

When I try really hard to think of her, screwing my eyes up tightly to take me back to the young me (hell, I hardly remember even being five) it's more a series of impressions rather than visualisations of her that come to me. The floral scent of a body spray mixed with the throaty cough of inhaled hairspray; noise around the house, something that absented itself since her disappearance; a body much bigger than mine but not quite yet a grown-up; and an intermingled sense of longing and fear when thinking about being around her. I don't remember though her being the type of big sister who doted on the newborn and played second mum. No cosy, huggy, family set-up here.

The morning light is fighting to come through the thin curtains of the spare room. From my mother's room I hear the calming low mumbling of a talk radio station but no sign of life.

Downstairs I'm once again on my own in this museum of a house. I'm staggered by how, despite my bedroom's makeover, little else has changed since I was a girl. Yes, the TV is now a flatscreen and the old yellow kettle with a farmhouse pattern on the side has been replaced by a shiny chrome version, but the sofa, most of the carpets, the wallpaper, the pictures, in fact all the basics you see when you walk through the front door, are the same. Perhaps the paintwork has been touched up but I doubt it has since Father died because I never knew my mother to do DIY or pay for a handyperson to do it for her. The house reminds me of an elderly lady dressed in her one best outfit that went out of fashion thirty years ago and is pulling at the waist and bust.

The only thing I can find to eat in the cupboards is bread. There's a little bit of milk left but the freezer is bare. I make a mental note to go to a supermarket today and replenish the stocks – surely mother should be eating healthy, fresh food in her condition? My bank account is, however, as empty as the cupboards themselves and I've nothing to top it up with. Suddenly the stark reality of my situation hits me. I own nothing but my car, and even that was bought with a loan. The place I used to call home belongs to Shaun and he doesn't want me back. I only have clothes and a few personal items to call my own. My whole life fits into two measly, battered suitcases that I bought in a rush two days ago from the local charity shop. Even the suitcases are second hand.

I feel tears building up behind my eyes and a prickling situation in my nose. I blink the tears fiercely away before they come. I have done enough crying over him. I will not waste any more tears mourning his lack of understanding and compassion over what I did. I must harden my heart, for where has love ever got me? Stuck back in 22 Greville Road that's where, with a sick woman and a mausoleum to a dead sister.

The vibration of my mobile phone puts an end to my maudlin thoughts. I breathe quickly until I look at the screen: it's not Shaun, it's Priti. I quickly press the green 'accept call' button.

'Annie, where the hell are you? It's been ages!' she greets me buoyantly, as loud as her effusive personality and colourful sari dress sense. Immediately I sigh with relief. I might not have money, a boyfriend or a life but I still have a friend on my side.

'Priti! It's so good to hear from you. I know, I know I should have called. It hasn't been the best of weeks. How are you?' What strange conversational formalities we English go through before knuckling down to what we really want to say.

'Never mind me, what about you? Mark told me you and Shaun have split up and you've moved out. Where are you? Are you OK?'

I pause, wanting to let it all out but I know if I do it will be hard to put the cork back in to the emotional bottle.

'Well,' I giggle slightly nervously, 'I've been better. Um, yes, Shaun and I have split up and he kicked me out. Is it only a fortnight ago that I last saw you, that wine night down the pub?'

'Sounds like you could do with a bottle now.'

Priti knows me well. We met at a company I temped at eight years ago, a dull as dishwater telemarketing job that saw me sworn at down the phone on average fifteen times a day (I did the maths in an effort not to take the vehement strangers too personally) and we clicked immediately. She sat opposite me in her little pod, with her headphones on, pulling grimaces as her lilting accent poured sweet nothings about double-glazing into the phone's receiver. That little act of rebellion brightened up the repetitive day and soon, when the supervisor wasn't walking round our section, we struck up a competition to see who could pull the worst face whilst waxing lyrical about the product we had to cold sell. The trouble was I found it hard not to laugh, and one particularly boring Tuesday I found myself letting out a snort of hilarity when Priti attempted to stick her pointed tongue up her left nostril, lamentably at the same time the customer was telling me that she could do with some double-glazed patio doors for her back room because her grandson had run into the old one, concussed himself and now possessed a permanent scar on his forehead that had required seven stitches. However unfortunate that was for the boy it was even more so for me because my line manager so happened to be listening in on my performance at that point. Back to the temping agency the next day I went. My friendship with Priti, however, has lasted longer than any subsequent jobs. It was through her friend Mark that I met Shaun, them having been school friends who never moved away from their hometown and still hanging around with the same crowd.

'What happened?' Priti presses. 'And where are you? Do you want to meet up?'

'Well… you'll never believe this. I'm staying with my mother.'

I move the telephone earpiece away from my ear to temper the high-pitched laugh that screeched out of it.

'Yeah right, seriously, where are you?'

'At my mother's.'

Stunned silence.

'God you must be desperate. Are things really that bad? You told me you never wanted to see her ever again.' Priti isn't one for subtlety or euphemisms.

'I wish you could stay with me but with Tamwar's brother still hogging our sofa-bed there's no room. You really don't want to sleep in the same room as him Annie, he's disgusting. Snores like a pig and the room needs airing for hours once he's out, only for him to do it all again the next night. And he hasn't yet grasped the concept of tidying and washing up. He left his dirty underwear all over the bathroom floor until I threatened Tamwar with divorce.'

I get the picture. I can't stay with her, not that I was angling for it. Living with a happily-married couple would not be best for my emotional state of mind at the moment.

Priti continues: 'What happened with Shaun, Annie, have you split up for good?'

'Looks like it. He threw me out and I haven't heard from him since.'

'Why?'

'It's a long story.' My voice begins to quiver so I shut up.

'*He* threw *you* out?'

'Yes, why do you say that?'

'It's just that, well, Mark also said that Shaun has been, er, quite close to another woman recently. Some blonde slapper. He only said this to me last night or I would have told you already.'

'What?'

'Shaun was down the pub with her last night and they were together. From what the slapper was saying they hadn't recently met. I'm sorry Annie, he's a shit. Shaun the Shit.'

So after everything he said, and all the blame he piled on me for what I did, getting rid of me was what he wanted all along.

The tears come down my face in torrents, turning my

nose into a snivelling mess. How could I have spent two years with a man about whom I'd obviously known so little and meant even less to?

'Oh Annie, I shouldn't have told you over the phone, I'm sorry, so sorry… foot in mouth syndrome again.'

In the corner of my eye, amidst my sobs and sniffles, I see the shadow of my mother shuffle into the room, look at me, hesitate, then walk straight out again.

'Can I see you at the weekend, Annie? I could come and stay a night. What you need is pizza, Prosecco and Priti.'

I think of the spare bed in Gemma's museum that serves as an untouched memorial. Fat chance I'd have of mother letting Priti sleep there. It'd probably finish her off.

'Yes, that would be great.' The tears stop now and my eyes sting sorely. 'I don't think you can stop here though I'm afraid. There's only my sister's old room.'

'The sister who died? Don't worry, I'll find a B&B. Tamwar will be happy having a lad's night in with his brother.'

'Yes, that's her. It'll be really great to see you.'

'What about your job?'

'I was made redundant last week. They didn't give me any notice. Bit of a double whammy.'

'Oh hell. Poor you… is it strange being back with your mother?'

'She's got cancer. She rang and left a message on my phone asking me to come back and help her. It was the only option I had.'

'Cancer? That's rough. I wouldn't wish that on anyone. We'll find you another option. Trust me. Onward and upwards.'

'Gemma's room's still untouched. It's like a museum,' I tell her.

'Annie, I don't think you ever said, what happened to your sister?'

I take a deep breath and stare at the bland painting on the wall of a Victorian gentleman and lady promenading on the beach, seemingly without care or artifice.

'I don't know. Nobody does. She just never came back. That's all I've known since I was a little child. Gemma went to school but didn't return home.'

'It's the not knowing that must be so difficult for you.'

'Well, she's dead. It's obvious. Gemma hasn't been heard of or seen since 1989. She must be dead. You can't fake a whole adult life.'

'Could she have killed herself?'

That shocks me. 'Well, I've never thought of that. Why would she want to? I think the police worked on the lines that she had been abducted.'

'It's fascinating. Don't you ever wonder what was going through her head, what she was thinking, what did actually happen to her?'

'No. I'm sick of hearing about her. She was all that was talked about until I left home.'

A pregnant pause. 'That's a bit harsh, isn't it?'

Priti's not mincing her words today.

'I guess so. I didn't really ever know her,' I reply, slightly tersely. 'What you don't know, you don't miss.'

'It must have been rough for you growing up in the shadow of that,' backtracks Priti. 'Hey, there might be something in her room, something that the police missed?'

She always did like murder mystery dramas on the television. I'm more of a reality TV fan myself.

I hear someone on the other end of the line calling Priti's name. 'Look, I've got to get back to work now, I'll call you soon to make the arrangements for Saturday. Take care Annie; don't let Shaun the Shit get you down. Love you.'

She hangs up. I walk through to the front room where mother is immersed in mind-numbing daytime television.

'Morning,' I say, with fake cheer.

'Good morning Annie. I hope you slept well.'

'Not too bad. Can I get you anything?'

'I shall make myself some toast, thank you, now you're out of the kitchen. And – I just wanted to ask – are you alright? You seemed a little upset earlier.'

A little?

'Annie, the cancer treatment has a good chance of working you know.' She gives me a little smile.

She thinks I was crying about her.

'Right. That's good. There's not much food in, I was thinking of popping out to stock up and buy something for dinner.'

'Thank you, Annie.'

I pause, feeling like a naughty teenager. 'It's just that I haven't got much cash on me...'

She stares at me with the same old disapproving eyes. 'You can take a twenty-pound note from my purse. It's in my handbag hanging on the bannister.'

Talk about feeling like a fourteen-year-old again asking for dinner money.

'Thanks.'

She sits back in her chair.

'I'll be back before Aunty Lena comes.'

I walk upstairs to put my trainers on and grab my handbag. On the landing I push the door of Gemma's room open slightly and peer in, wondering if that place does, as Priti says, hold any secrets.

My phone interrupts my reverie. Shaun's name is on the screen.

I immediately press the 'call reject' button.

~ 4 ~

Aunty Lena, or Elaine as she bids me to call her now I'm no longer a child bound by social etiquette or the inability to pronounce the word Elaine properly, sweeps me into her arms and holds me so tight as if she thinks I'm really a mirage that will slip through her fingers. Her bosom is bigger, her hair greyer, the twinkle lines around her mouth more pronounced and she walks with a conspicuous drag on her right hip, but she still has the same huge heart, infectious kindness and marked enthusiasm for other people's business. I feel my breath release and my spine relax as she kisses me on my cheek and I see the delight in her face. How long has it been since someone was so pleased to see me? Surely not as long as I suddenly think. Since our second or third date Shaun never seemed that pleased to see me, not even post-coitally when he would get out of bed to go to the bathroom or, more usually, turn over and commence snoring within sixty seconds. Perhaps he knew he'd hooked me, so he didn't feel he had to try like the first time he came over to me at the party and offered to make me one of his own-recipe cocktails. Then his eyes shone when I said yes – I didn't like the vodka, coke and orange concoction he handed me in a cracked plastic cup but I drank it to keep talking to him, enjoying his patter and the slight hint of nervousness emanating from his stubbly good looks. I felt power, the delight that this stranger wanted me and the heady anticipation that the feeling was mutual.

'Look at you!' Elaine cries, putting one arm round my shoulder and steering me towards my mother's sofa, urging me to sit down then grasping my hands within hers.

'How beautiful you are. You hardly look any older than when you were a teenager.'

Perhaps she is developing cataracts.

'Now I want to know everything, what have you been doing, what do you do for a living, do you have, oh what do they say, a "significant other"?'

Elaine winks at me and my heart warms at her exuberance whilst I chuckle at her attempt at political correctness and openness to the possibility of my being gay. Mother is perched on the end of the well-worn leather armchair, which was always Father's seat. She looks so small in it and is eyeing me beadily; the homosexual reference having gone way over her head.

'My boyfriend and I broke up not long ago,' I reply. 'I was working in a call centre but was made redundant… no, I'm joking, I'm really an international supermodel. You won't have seen pictures of me because I mainly work in Brazil.' Elaine always brings out the mischievousness side in me and she throws her head back and laughs, but Mother looks confused, her expression as if to say 'what *you*, a model? You're five foot three! What is the world coming to?'

'Oh Annie, how I've missed you.' Elaine beams and I smile back. Then it hits me – this is what a mother should be like. Someone who enjoys your company and wants to be with you. The smile I give her comes from the heart and not the teeth.

'Cup of tea, Elaine?' Mother says, ending the moment.

'You rest, I'll go and make a pot,' Elaine replies. I follow her into the kitchen to help.

Elaine scoops me into her arms again and I linger, enjoying the moment of being held and her delight at seeing me.

'You're all grown up. A bit on the thin side though, have you been eating properly?'

'Of course, chips, pizza… takeaways…' I reply with a chuckle.

Elaine fakes a look of horror as she fills the kettle with water from the tap and switches it on.

'How long are you back for? I hope you're going to stay for a while. For your mum's sake, for my sake, maybe for your sake too.'

'What do you mean?' I take a teaspoon out of the top drawer and take the milk carton out of the fridge.

'Sometimes it's good to come home. To make peace with the past.'

The kettle boils and I put a teabag into each of the three mugs.

'Not using the teapot?'

I start to sigh until I see the twinkle in Elaine's eyes and realise she's teasing me. I laugh back.

'You better make sure your mum doesn't catch you – you and these new-fangled city ways of making a cuppa!'

'In the city you don't have a cuppa, you order a flat white to go,' I replied with a knowing nod of the head.

'Well you're not in Leeds now. Mine's milk no sugar. I gave up because of the diabetes risk.'

'Very sensible.'

'So how long are you back for?'

'I don't know. For a while. I guess I'll see how Mother's treatment pans out.' I don't say "until she dies", although the way Mother looks now I do think it and also that it may not be too long.

'It's so good of you to come back, Annie,' says Elaine. 'Your mum didn't think you would when I suggested it. I'm proud of you. I know it can't be easy for you coming back here what with everything that went on.'

I don't know why but my stomach and maybe something internal near my heart lurched. 'You suggested it? So it wasn't her idea?'

Elaine put her palm on my shoulder. 'She thought it was a brilliant idea. It's just that she's still holding on to the past...'

'I know,' I cut in. 'I've noticed.' I roll my eyes and Elaine raises her eyebrows in agreement.

'It was hard for you as a child. Hard for your mum as well. She's not a well woman, Annie. Thank you so much for coming home.'

I feel a slight sense of guilt at not telling Elaine the real reason I'm here, which I quickly trample down with my new-found knowledge that it wasn't even my mother's idea to contact me in the first place.

'I can take her to the hospital appointments in my car.'

'She'll really appreciate that. Are there any old friends you can get in touch with whilst you're here? I want to see lots of you, obviously, but you don't want to be stuck with a couple of old women the whole time.'

'You're not old!' I laugh.

'I'm not young either!'

I pour the boiling water into the mugs and stir them one at a time.

'Actually a friend from the city is coming to visit at the weekend. Priti. You'll like her, she's lots of fun.'

'You're pretty too. Don't put yourself down!'

I chuckle at the semantic mix-up. 'No, her name is Priti with two Is – she's of Indian heritage.'

'Ah. Lovely name. I look forward to meeting her.' Elaine takes the teabag out of her mug and adds a splash of milk. I put one sugar in Mother's and leave mine black then spoon the teabags into the bin.

'When's she arriving?'

'Sometime after lunch I think.'

'Your mum and I often go to the pictures on a Saturday afternoon. I'll ask her to stay over at mine, then you and Priti can have some space when she visits.'

'Thanks, Aunty Lena,' I say, and I mean it, I really do. Elaine just seems to know what is right without being asked.

'Can't see Mother allowing Priti to stay in the *spare room* though.' I raise my eyebrows to emphasise my deadpan humour. Instead of laughing, Elaine just looks sad, her eyes misting over with the weight of the past.

'Yours has been the spare room,' she replied. 'Granted, the *other* bedroom could have done with clearing out years ago but it's difficult, it's a delicate situation with your mum.' She pauses, seemingly to choose her words carefully, and takes my cold left hand in her warm right one.

'Annie, I do worry about you, you know, having had to grow up with all this. Please try and understand, though, that your mum is doing the best she can. It might not seem enough but she is trying. She's never been strong... I mean you coming back is a godsend. She thought she'd lost you too.'

With this Elaine pulls me into a hug, but instead of greedily relaxing into it as before I tense slightly, pushing her away.

'Tell me she wouldn't prefer Gemma coming back instead of me,' I say with a touch of petulance, pushing my chin-length bob back behind my ears defiantly.

'No Annie, no, get that thought straight out of your head. We don't know what happened to Gemma but she's not coming back. You're here, flesh and blood, your mum loves you very much, as do I. You and Gemma are two completely different people. She looked out for you, you know. Please don't be bitter, don't let the past spoil your future. You were too young to have to go through the loss of your sister and too young when you left home...'

Am I bitter? Am I competing with a ghost? Something inside of me snaps and I feel my eyes go hot, my throat constrict and tears threaten to appear. But I won't cry. I've done far too much of that recently. Instead I question Elaine. 'Gemma looked out for me?' That's not something I remember.

'She did. When you were a young child it wasn't easy for your mum. If you ever have children you'll find out what it's like.'

I blanche at the word 'if' and give a brief thought to a baby that could have been but never will be.

'I'm back because she has cancer, not for some sort of emotional reunion.'

'Like I said, I'm so glad you're here. And your mum is too. Give it time.' Elaine squeezes my arm in solidarity.

We carry the mugs through to the lounge and the three of us make small talk, or rather Aunt Lena and Mother do: who has got married, had a child (or three), got divorced or moved away since I was last here.

Quite frankly, I couldn't care less.

Mother's first hospital appointment is two days later. I spend my time until then keeping busy with my mobile switched off. For someone who has always had a distinct aversion to rubber gloves and a bottle of bleach I find a strange sort of bodily and mental comfort in cleaning the house, removing months' old grime and seeing the place look as clean as it ever can be considering its age. With each scrub I wipe my mind and obliterate the thoughts that want to wage war in my psyche.

In the corner of the kitchen I free a wasp from a spider's web although it's obviously dead already. I throw the wasp out of the window and scour the tiles until no trace of the death trap is left. I bleach, wash, mop and vacuum throughout the day until hunger and a need for the loo make me stop.

In the evening, keen to avoid yet another soap opera, I pace the streets of my childhood. The television blares from Reg's house through the rotting open window. The outside of his house can't have been painted for well over a decade, nor has the front garden been tended. Weeds snake into the holes between the cement and bricks; the recycling box left out for the council overflows with glass: wine, vodka and beer bottles, and a slit in a black sack of rubbish spills its fetid contents onto what was once the front lawn.

A bang from up above causes me to stop and see where it came from. I think it was the shutting of the upstairs window. A man, almost ghost-like, as thin as Mother, with haggard eyes and a bulbous nose looks out at me, keeping eye contact for longer than is usually polite. He's staring, not observing. I assume this is Reg, although he no longer looks like the youngish man he was. With a shiver I turn to walk on and increase my pace. It's times like these I wish I had a dog with me – a companion, a bodyguard, a reason to be walking the streets after working hours.

The neighbourhood and parade of shops have at the same time changed a lot since my youth yet also not at all. Kids still hang out around the chip shop, although the bank branch and phone box have gone and the video rental store is now a beauty salon offering lasers and fillers. The pub on the crossroads at the end of our road is still called The Phoenix but now boasts a food menu outside and a kerfuffle of smokers crowding at the doorway having a cheeky cigarette. The small park nearby is practically the same, although the creaky swings and slides have been replaced with brightly-painted new ones and have some sort of rubber matting underneath to stop children falling on their backsides onto the concrete like I used to do. Huddled on the bench are some young teenagers passing round what looks to be a plastic bottle of beer or cider. Only their haircuts and coat designs contradict the feeling that I've gone back in time to the 1990s. It's a cool, brisk evening, one that has seen the death throes of summer and is welcoming autumn's chillier grip.

Walking back, I quicken my pace past Reg's house. There's no light on in his windows anymore but I still feel distinctly uncomfortable, as if he's peering through his filthy curtains watching me go by. Holding my keys firmly in my fist I run the last few metres to the front door of Mother's house and quickly let myself in.

The hospital appointment doesn't get off to the best start. There's nowhere to park near the entrance – I make a mental note to get hold of the forms to apply for a blue disabled parking badge for Mother – so I drop her off and, after a couple of circuits followed by numerous other tired-looking drivers in the same boat, I finally find a space in the car park's back of beyond next to a clamped, rusty old banger. When I run to the entrance Mother is not there so I follow the signs and make my way to the chemotherapy day unit, which, I instantly notice, has a pleasant floral scent different from the antiseptic stench of the corridors. Mother's there in the waiting room, chatting to a smartly-dressed woman wearing a brightly-patterned headscarf. She's probably in her forties, although with her drawn, washed-out features it's hard to tell.

'Annie, this is Mel,' says Mother. The woman, Mel, smiles a radiant smile that changes all of her features and I catch a glimpse of the person behind the cancer.

'Hi,' I say, giving a small wave.

'Mel and I have had our chemo at the same time before. She's gets through a novel every time and then passes them on to me if they're any good.

'What are you reading today?' I ask.

'P.G. Wodehouse. *Thank you, Jeeves.* I'm working through his back catalogue.'

'I hear her laughing away and always want to know what the funny parts are,' says Mother. She's smiling with her friend.

A nurse comes out and greets us all. 'You ready to get this party started?'

I'm quite taken aback by the jocularity of it all, as if we were all about to go on a pub crawl. Not that my mother has probably ever been on one.

'This is my daughter, Annie. Annie, this is Una, the nurse here.'

I had rather gathered that – the unflattering dress and black lace up shoes had given the game away.

'Annie, hi, your mum has told me a lot about you.' Una shakes my hand then smooths a loose stray of her tied up afro hair back into place with a kirby-grip.

'I'll take these two lovely ladies through to the ward and then would you like me to talk you through what we do here?'

Good point, I didn't have a clue what to expect. I hadn't directly asked Mother and when it did once come up in conversation, a discussion about how many hours I needed to pay for in the car park, she'd muttered something about sitting in a chair for a few hours and it not being too much trouble.

Mother and Mel have their blood tested first to check that it's safe for them to have the chemo. They choose armchairs next to each other to sit in for the treatment. Rather than looking away when the cannula is inserted in Mother's hand I'm fascinated by the skill with which Una does it, although I do let out a childish snort when she says, 'you may feel a small prick'.

I've felt one a few times myself.

When the drip begins to transfer its bagged contents into the two women's veins I start to feel awkward and out of place. Other patients have relatives there to chat or hold their hands but Mel and Mother seem perfectly content discussing the punchlines from *Jeeves and Wooster*.

'Do either of you need anything?' I ask, hovering in the background. They already have a jug of water and a hot drink each on a table next to their chairs. Mel has brought in some rice crackers to nibble on to quell any nausea she says, in case the anti-sickness medication they've already taken doesn't work.

'They're fine, aren't you?' says Una, bustling up behind and checking the IVs.

Mother and Mel are hooked up to chemotherapy drips. They certainly don't look fine to me.

'I've got time for a quick break, do you want a stroll with me to the vending machine? It's chocolate time already,' Una asks me.

'Yes, you go Annie. Nothing to do here. I'm not going anywhere!' Mother jokes. She jokes! What has Una put in that drip? Vodka? Nitrous oxide?!

I follow Una through the double doors out of the ward, along the corridor, up a flight of stairs and then along to the vending machine replete with every kind of chocolate bar and crisp packet you could ever want. I plump for ready salted whilst Una gets her cocoa fix, slapping the machine to ensure it stumps up her change. She says nice things about Mother: what a lovely lady she is and how she appears to be coping well with the treatment. She probably says she same thing about every patient.

'Appears is the operative word though,' she goes on. 'We only see patients' hospital faces, not how they're managing at home. How's she doing? Is she eating well, keeping warm, staying free from stress?'

'I only came back a few days ago. We're not close… but I'm making sure she eats healthily, not that she eats a great deal really.'

'And you? How are you coping? You've moved back in with your mum, yes? That's a big life change for you.' She takes another bite of her chocolate bar. 'What people tend to forget is that cancer doesn't only affect the person who has got it, it has an impact on the whole family.'

'I'm taking it as it comes really.' I feel a pang of guilt at what Una thinks is my great sacrifice.

'It's all you can do but remember that there are people you can talk to. There are leaflets on the ward about support groups for people whose loved ones have cancer. And if you want to ask me anything when I'm around then feel free.'

'Thanks,' I reply, then cut to the chase. 'How long, erm, what I mean is, will she get better?'

'There are no guarantees. You need to talk to her oncologist. What I can say is that she appears to be responding well to treatment and many people in her position do recover and have a good ten or twenty years left.'

'Right, thanks.' I feel relieved, then strange for sensing that emotion.

'So carry on with your life as normally as you can. What do you do?' Una puts the last two chocolate squares in her mouth and throws the wrapper into the bin.

'Call centre work usually. I've temped a lot. I was made redundant from my last job.'

'Rough. Are you looking for another one?'

'I'll need to soon,' I admit. 'My purse has moths flying out of it.'

'Tell me about it! Once my salary goes in it nearly all goes straight out again in bills and my student loan. Listen, I don't know if you've thought about healthcare assistant work but I know they're always looking for people to join the bank here. It's zero hours contract work but there are lots of shifts for people who they can call on at the last minute.'

'What does it involve?'

'Bedpans, feeding people, helping them wash, that sort of thing. You get training.'

'Sounds better than most of the call centre jobs I've done. I'm sick of being shouted at on the telephone.'

'Give it a whirl, I'll find the HR number for you before you go home.'

As we walk back to the ward our conversation changes to her plans to see her boyfriend after her shift and I tell her a funny story about one night I was supposed to see Shaun early on in our relationship but turned up to the wrong restaurant not realising there were two of the same Italian chain in the city. I feel myself relaxing.

Back on the ward there are a couple of new patients. Mel has dozed off. I make small talk with Mother and tell her about the healthcare assistant job. She says it's worth finding out more and I agree. I think I'd enjoy working with people. Briefly the thought goes through my head of what Gemma would have done for a job if she were here. Investment banker? Hot-shot lawyer? Super-clever Gemma was set to go on to do A levels – I'm sure she wouldn't be slopping out bedpans for a living. My jaw clenches. There she is in my head, her angelic face smiling out from the photograph. She'd be doing something far, far better than me. Montage-like I remember the policeman knocking at the door; silence followed by sobbing; mother's bedroom door always firmly shut; no one bothering to notice where *I* was.

I rush to the ladies to throw up, purging my acrid bitterness down the loo.

At least I know it's not morning sickness.

~ 6 ~

The Phoenix pub is beginning to empty of underage chancers who have most likely moved on to the town centre for a livelier scene now the time is approaching 9 p.m. Priti arrived late in the afternoon. I met her at the nearby B&B that was cheap but not very cheerful, where she checked in, dropped off her bag and I then took her on a swift walking tour of my old manor to make the most of the dying sunshine.

Inevitably the walk ended at the pub where we order a two for one burgers meal deal and a bottle of Pinot Grigio between us with a glass of water each as an afterthought. She tells me all about her brother-in-law's latest misdemeanours and I laugh heartily, the wine going to my head a bit. I'm enjoying having fun with my good friend.

'Look,' says Priti after a story about a pair of skid-marked boxers being left on the floor in the bathroom, 'at the bar, second from left. He keeps looking at you. Salt and pepper hair, blue long-sleeved T-shirt.'

I do the well-worn routine of pretending to look in my bag whilst cricking my neck to get a sneaky look. Priti laughs at my feeble attempts at being discreet. Her cackle grabs the man's attention and he looks our way with amused eyes. Caught. I could look guiltily away but instead grab the mettle, smile briefly back and down more than a modicum from my glass.

The man in question seems friendly enough, if somewhat older than my usual type. His short hair is mostly grey with a smattering of white at the temples. I'd say there's a lot average about him: average height, about 5'11"; average build, neither skinny nor fat but with the tiny beginnings of a beer belly; averagely dressed, wearing the jeans and long-sleeved T-shirt combo that's the casual uniform for most men in early middle age on a weekend. What stands out are his eyes: openly friendly, dark brown and twinkling with a hint of mischievousness as if to say, 'come on, talk to me, I dare you'.

I always did love a dare as my school exclusion record will testify. A challenge to press the fire alarm button to get the class out of double French ended up with me sitting at home for a week before I was allowed to go back. Not going to school was a gift rather than a punishment and I spent that week under house arrest, although my sleeping mother wouldn't have been aware if I'd hitch-hiked to Land's End for the whole week and didn't return. It was my father who told me that it wasn't the teachers he was worried about, it was me, because I had let myself down. No arguing, no slapping, no histrionics, just him looking sad. There was too much sadness in our house already, so I spent that week batch-cooking lovely dinners to eat when he came home from work and to stockpile in the freezer for the future. I got through most of the *Delia Smith's Complete Cookery Course* book from the library. With every successful moussaka, coq au vin and toad in the hole, I felt a sense of achievement I'd never experienced at school.

'Do you think he'll come over? He's alright isn't he, for an older bloke,' smiles Priti.

'It's a bit too soon, isn't it?' I reply.

'You know what they say, to get over a man you have to get under another one,' she winks. I groan at the well-worn cliché.

Despite her dirty jokes, Priti is rather conservative. She swears hers wasn't an arranged marriage but her parents had been casually organising for her and Tamwar to 'accidentally' meet at family parties for months until cupid's arrow struck and they became an item. Priti belittles Tamwar sometimes and likes nothing better than to roll her eyes whilst she recites his annoying habits but deep down I know they have a strong love, the kind of which I've never felt. Never felt yet, I hope. My theory is that she likes to feel she's in control because the depth of her feeling for Tamwar frightens her. Although she's part of a tight-knit family she doesn't like to rely on other people. One late, blurry night she admitted she'd be lost if anything ever happened to him. That's something she doesn't usually like to admit, even to herself.

'Women don't need men. They're just useful now and then,' I say. Priti widens her eyes at me. I turn. The man has approached our table.

'So men are useful for putting up shelves and unblocking the sink?' he says playfully. 'Is this the 1950s?'

I smile with embarrassment at having been overheard in the middle of a private conversation but can't think of anything witty to reply. There follows an uncomfortable silence.

He breaks it by offering his hand to me and then to

Priti to shake. 'I'm Gareth. I think we may have met before actually. Can I get you ladies another drink?'

'More Pinot would be gratefully accepted, thank you,' simpers Priti and I shoot a warning glance at her. I want to spend time with her tonight, not feel obliged to make conversation with some random man because he's bought me a drink.

'Would you like to join us?' I kick Priti under the table but she carries on smiling and doesn't retract her offer.

'Yes, I'd like that if you both don't mind. I don't want to interrupt a girls' night.'

'Are you not here with anyone?' I ask, hoping he'll take the hint.

'My mate and his missus,' he replies, pointing his head towards a smartly-dressed couple at the bar. They can cope without me for a bit. I'll get the drinks in.'

I take the chance to admonish Priti. 'Relax!' she replies. 'Be open to new experiences. If he's a plonker at least he'll give us something to laugh about later on. Free booze, Annie, free booze!'

The man returns carrying two glasses of wine (250ml I notice, he's not a skinflint – or is he trying to get us drunk?) in one hand and a bottle of premium beer in another. He puts them down on the table, avoiding the beermats, God love him, and takes a seat in between us.

'I'm Priti and this is my wonderful friend Annie. I've got a free evening pass away from my husband and am visiting her this weekend.'

Priti has laid her cards straight out on the table. See what I mean about being conservative? She talks the talk but perish the thought that any man would think she's single and try to hit on her.

'I'm Gareth. Sorry, I told you that already.' A small, rather endearing blush flushes his cheeks. I get the feeling he doesn't regularly chat up women.

'Annie, I think we've met before, though you were a child then. Your sister, is she, was she, Gemma? You look like her – your face, I mean, not your hair colour.'

Talk about puncturing the mood like a pin bursting a balloon.

I look down at my glass. 'Yes.'

'I thought so, I was at school with her, a couple of years below. I knew her from the school orchestra. I came around your house a few times to practice a tricky part – she was first violin, I was second. Sorry, I'm gabbling on.' Then he adds, 'I'm sorry she hasn't been found yet.'

Once again, I can't think of anything to say. Gemma's ubiquitous smiling celluloid face swims in my subconscious. Priti sees my discomposure and swiftly takes over, although I rather suspect that the mention of Gemma has piqued her interest.

'Did you know Gemma well?' she asks.

'Not that well; if it weren't for the orchestra she wouldn't have noticed me. Girls don't tend to hang around with boys two years their junior. She was a lovely girl though and took time to help me practice. I'll never forget that.'

'You got children yourself, Gareth?' Priti's now getting down to the nitty gritty. I've already clocked her looking at his left hand to see the absence of a wedding ring. That doesn't mean anything though, some men don't like to wear them or he could have taken it off before coming out.

'No, I was married for ten years but we didn't have any kids. Divorced two years ago.'

We all take a gulp of our drinks in unison.

'I, I don't remember Gemma that much,' I say, inquisitiveness taking me over. 'I was only little when she, she... Anyway, you said she was kind, what else was she like? I've always had the feeling she was perfect.'

Gareth looks at me as if he doesn't know what to say. 'Well, like I said I didn't know her very well, but she was always kind to me. I think she was quite academic and had lots of friends although she wasn't in the cool group – the kids who bunked off and went smoking, clubbing and drinking. She got teased sometimes I think because she got good grades. I once saw another kid calling her a swot because she'd done well in her mocks. I don't think she cared though. She made some jibe about the boy having a small penis.'

Priti and I snorted with laughter. This anecdote certainly broke the tension. Making jokes about small penises (or is that penii or penes)? That's my kind of man.

The chat continues amiably. Gareth says he hasn't seen me around here before and I tell him I've recently moved back to look after my mother. He's a supermarket manager, sick of aisles of baked beans, and hopes to retrain as a lawyer. In the evenings and weekends he's studying for a law degree with the Open University. Tonight he's out to celebrate his friend Mo's birthday, the chap sporting the expensive-looking clothes at the bar. He's known Mo for years from working at the supermarket. Priti buys another round.

Talking about Gemma feels both wrong and strangely appealing. I've only ever heard my parents and Aunty Lena's side of the story. Perhaps she wasn't so perfect after all; would I have liked her if she'd lived to adulthood? Could we have even become friends?

When there's a lull in the conversation about whether wine or beer is better and our favourite comedy catchphrases, Priti blurts out the question that's on the tip of my tongue before I get the chance to.

'Have you any idea what might have happened to Gemma?' she asks Gareth.

'No, it was so long ago.' He takes another swig from his beer bottle and starts fiddling with the beer mat, peeling off bits into soft, white shards.

'I remember the police came to the school to talk to her friends and her teachers but I wasn't interviewed. I think the feeling was that she'd run away. There were rumours that she was worried about taking her GCSEs and that she wasn't happy at home. When weeks passed and she didn't turn up the gossip was that she must have been murdered. Sorry to be so brutal, Annie.'

Priti presses him further. 'Was there anything out of the ordinary you'd noticed about her? Any friends, boyfriends we don't know about?'

'Again, it was all so long ago and I wasn't close to her. She never confided anything to me. As well as having a group of girlfriends she seemed to be as thick as thieves with a bloke called Mike who played the trumpet in the orchestra. I think they were in the same form.'

It's getting late now and I simultaneously feel tired and stimulated by the alcohol. I down my untouched tap water in one.

'It'd be nice to see you again if you'd like to, Annie?' says Gareth. Time has swiftly passed and his friends are glancing over as if they want to leave. 'Can I take your number?'

I hesitate and ponder whether to give him a false one but then realise I'm far too old for those games. Gareth seems nice and one date won't hurt. At least it will show Shaun I'm moving on – I'm sure it will get back to him via Priti and Mark.

I punch my number into Gareth's phone and he sends me a text to give me his.

'I'll call you,' he says. 'Do you like Indian? Italian?'

'Italian,' I reply with a smile. Priti is practically bursting over with excitement at the thought of my going on a date. I can imagine her galloping in a hat towards the finishing line two years too soon and boasting that it was her who brought the happy couple together.

'Perfect. Italian it is.' Gareth shakes our hands again and gives me a peck on the cheek. 'Good to meet you, Priti.' He turns to walk back to his friends then stops and turns back.

'I don't know if you know this and it's probably not relevant, but a boy who was in Gemma's form was sent to prison a couple of years ago. I don't know whether Gemma had much to do with him at school. Toby Smith his name is. He went down for attempted murder of his wife. It was a big scandal around here.' With that he walks off to the bar.

Could Toby have had something to do with Gemma's disappearance? Was he always violent? Priti buys another bottle of wine, to go, from the bar. 'Is your mum staying at your Aunty's?' she asks. I nod. 'Then let's go back to your house for a bit. It's time for us to look in Gemma's room. Maybe there are some letters or a diary? We can see if there's any mention of Toby.'

I'm too drunk to protest.

If I'd been reading *Jane Eyre* recently, I'd be rather perturbed by the gothic creaks and thuds emanating from Gemma's room; but knowing that Mother wouldn't have invested any money in the upkeep of the house, I put the groans down to the death rattles of the central heating system.

Priti and I are in Gemma's museum, swigging out of the rather disgusting bottle of wine, the type you only drink when you're too pissed already to care what it tastes like, and are about to start our Famous Five-style hunt for clues.

Being in this place with Priti has taken the edge off my resentment of Gemma's bedroom still being here, mausoleum-like. Maybe it will be a blessing and not the curse I took it to be. Thanks to the wine the whole situation seems rather funny.

Priti seems sure she's going to find something that will solve the whole mystery, as if my life is a one-hour television drama with only five minutes to go before the denouement.

Instead of turning the main light on and announcing what we're doing to the whole street, we've put on the 1980s bright yellow bendy side lamp and are swathed in its shadows. Priti is sitting on the immaculately-pressed duvet cover, now crinkled, and the wine bottle is on the bedside table. I'm cross-legged on the floor wondering where to begin. Despite myself, I've fetched some toilet roll from the loo to act as a coaster for the bottle and warn Priti not to spill it over the bed. Somehow, that would just feel wrong, although the wicked side of me would quite relish trashing the place.

Priti is gabbling on enthusiastically, gesticulating wildly with her arms to make her not-quite-so-coherent points. I'm long gone from being sober and that certainly helps with following her train of thought. She's trying to decipher what happened to Gemma, as if being in her bedroom will imbue her with her spirit. Thank goodness she hasn't suggested a Ouija board.

'So Gemma's disappearance. What are the possibilities?' she says, rustling in her handbag, pulling out a biro and a bank-letter-looking sheet of A4 paper, which she then turns over and begins scribbling on, drawing outlandish spirals first to get the pen to work.

She thinks this is some kind of game, like the murder mystery dinner party I once went along to, playing the character of a Russian down-at-heel princess called Svetlana. She didn't do the deed; the whole scenario was so complicated that none of us really cared who did after the second course. This was a bloodless fantasy crime where we all got to safely go home and sleep guilt-free in our own beds.

That said, I drunkenly play along with Priti, joining in for the ride.

Priti continues. 'Possibility number one – Gemma is still alive. The police ruled out Gemma running away but could she have done? She only had her school bag with her and nothing else had gone from her room here. No change of clothes, money… but surely if she did run off you'd have heard about her by now? To be hiding all this time and not let your family know. That's just cruel…'

I nod. The room seems to be slightly spinning. The floor definitely isn't horizontal.

'Unless she was running *from* something.'

'Like what?'

'Was she scared of someone and didn't want them to know where she'd gone? Your dad, erm, he didn't did he, he wasn't too *fond* of Gemma?'

'You mean was he a kiddy fiddler? No!' That suggestion sobers me up a bit. Father may have been a bit useless as a parent but he never, ever, would do anything like that.

'Sorry, had to ask, the police would have done. It could have been a possibility.' Priti takes another glug from the wine bottle, narrowly missing spilling a bit on the precious carpet as she waves her arm around again. I know that *Prime Suspect* is one of her favourite vintage police TV shows and think that she fancies herself as the Asian Helen Mirren. Not the Asian Miss Marple, of course, because she wouldn't want the grey, curly perm and twinset.

'So, your dad's ruled out. Now you've never got on with your mum. Could she be the reason why Gemma might have left?'

I think of how I stayed away from the parental home all those years. She certainly was the reason why I didn't come back for so long.

'I don't think so. Gemma was in the middle of her GCSEs when she went missing. Passing would have been her ticket out of here. She could have gone to sixth form college somewhere else.' I pause in thought. 'I suppose she could have found the pressure too much, but that still leaves the question of how could she have disappeared off the grid for so long.'

'OK. On to possibility number two.' Priti scribbles again on the piece of paper. 'Accidental death. Run over by a bus? Drug overdose?' Now Priti has moved her televisual crime influences on to *Breaking Bad*.

'If she'd been run over by a bus or topped herself her body would have been found, wouldn't it?'

'Good point. We'll rule out suicide and a fatal accident. So on to possibility number three.'

Priti lowered her voice conspiratorially. 'Murder. She was either murdered the day she disappeared or snatched and killed later.' We take it in turns to swig out of the bottle, which is now sorely depleted.

'You missed one out,' I said. 'Abducted by aliens.'

We burst into laughter. My stomach turns over and there's a sickly taste in my mouth. I don't know if it's caused by the wine or the thought, the real, raw, visceral thought of a person being murdered. Would she have suffered? What would it be like to be terrified for your life? It suddenly hits me that Gemma was a living, breathing human being, not just a face in a photograph or a name constantly deified on a never-ending loop.

I crawl to the desk and pull myself up until my eyes are level with the photo-clad pinboard that riled me so much less than a week ago. Gemma's face is still there, hogging the attention, frozen in its sixteen-year-old prettiness. I pull a picture away, the savage motion creating a tear from where the pin was to the side of the photograph. There's now a gash from her earlobe.

'That's her?' Priti asks, taking the photo from me.

'Yes. That's her. Saint Gemma.'

'She was just a kid, Annie. Why are you so angry with her? It's as if you blame her for dying.'

I turn on her. 'What's it got to do with you, Priti? You grew up with all your family. I had a shit childhood. This house was a morgue with everything revolving around Gemma, Gemma, Gemma. Mother banged on all the time about how wonderful Gemma was but did she come to my school plays or assemblies? No! She slept through them. I didn't exist. Can you blame me for resenting Gemma – she can never do anything wrong, can she, she's dead. She'll always be unliveable up to and what am I? A failure. A thirty-year-old failure.'

I've worn myself out with my rant.

Priti doesn't take this personally. She puts her arm around me and gently pulls me to sit next to her on the bed then passes me the bottle, telling me to swig. I have the last mouthful, the one that old wives' tales say is fifty per cent spit.

'You're not a failure. You are a beautiful, intelligent woman who has been through a very hard time. I can't imagine coping with everything you've been through.' She gives me a cuddle. I nestle my forehead in her shoulder. Just for a moment I want to soak into her confident skin and believe her. I'm not used to talking about my past.

'Your mum must have been pretty ill if she stayed in

54

bed all that time. And having to grow up not knowing what happened to your sister, that's awful. You were far too young to experience such a loss and its effects on your family. Maybe you should talk to your mother about it, find out how she felt and why she neglected you so much.' Priti looks me in the eye with a hint of sadness to dispense some tough love. 'You're not a child now, though, Annie. You can make your own future… you said earlier about doing some bank healthcare assistant work.' I'd filled in the online application form this morning. 'Maybe that could lead to a career, not just rubbish, mindless telesales work like I still do. I'd love a proper job, one where I actually enjoy going there every day. And you've got a date! A night out with gorgeous Gareth!'

'He might not call.'

'His loss if he doesn't, but I bet he will. He seems keen. Don't compare yourself to Gemma. You're two different people and you can't even remember what she was really like. Look at this photo.' Priti waves Gemma's torn picture in front of my face. 'She was just a teenager. A hormonal teenager who will have had the same feelings and made the same mistakes that we all did at that age. There's no reason to think she disappeared on purpose. She didn't do it to spite you. What happened wasn't her fault, the poor girl. She was just a kid. It's her abductor you should be angry with, not her.'

She rocks me from side to side for a minute then I break apart. I look at Gemma's photo again. Where previously I saw pride and arrogance I now see a youthful vulnerability in her unlined face, her slight frame and the brown ponytail it would be so easy to pull to yank her head back and lay bare her white throat.

'If you can find out the truth then you can lay her to rest, but maybe you'll never know. You've got to move on. You *need* to move on.'

'Easier said than done. I wish I were someone else, Priti, and had a fresh start.'

'This is your fresh start, sweetheart.' Priti takes my hand and squeezes it. 'You've lived with your mum for nearly a week now and she's not so bad, is she? Talk to her. Find out more about Gemma. I'll help you.'

'Back to the possibilities then. But if the police haven't found out what happened then I don't know how we can.' An urge to go to the loo hits me. Even after all that has happened, life's basics still carry on regardless.

'We can but try.' I let go of Priti's hand and give her a thankful smile that I hope conveys that she's the oasis in my loneliness.

'I have to say, though, I wouldn't put any money on the abducted by aliens theory.' I try to lighten the mood, which has become dark enough to hit too close to home. A car alarm goes off outside – five piercing loud beeps until it stops abruptly, breaking the tension.

'The aliens were your idea!' Priti carries on. 'If Gemma was murdered, who could it be? What about this Toby guy? If he's capable of attempting to murder his wife, could he have hurt Gemma when he was a teenager? Did they know each other well? Perhaps they were seeing each other on the sly? Maybe you can track down her friend Mike that Gareth mentioned. He might know. Are the police still investigating Gemma's case? I wonder if anyone has told them about the Toby link?'

'I don't know. Sorry, I've got to dash to the loo.'

'OK, I'll go downstairs, drink some water then call a cab. We can talk more tomorrow.'

On my return from the bathroom I see the wine bottle is on its side on the floor dripping the last of its sugary contents onto the carpet. It's white wine, so it won't stain, but I'll still know the drops were there.

Priti's taxi soon arrives. I walk her to the car and promise to meet her for brunch in about eight hours' time. We hug and she tells me to believe in myself before nearly tripping into the car in her red three-inch heels.

There are no streetlights on, thanks to council cutbacks, and, when the headlights of the cab have disappeared around the corner, the only illumination of the street is the low glow emanating through the curtains of Gemma's room. It lures me back in the house. With Priti gone, my solitariness hits me. There's no warm body of Shaun to climb in next to and hold, or housemates to watch late-night TV with. I'm on my own in the house, as I am in life. With this unsettling thought, I'm unwilling to go to bed straightaway, so I go back upstairs to Gemma's room, straighten the duvet cover, put the wine bottle in the hall to take out for recycling and pin the photo back on the board. The tear is barely noticeable.

I run my fingertip over the photo of Gemma and her friends in the park. Next to Gemma, looking away from the camera, is a shaggy-haired blond boy with a strong chin and heightened cheekbones. Peering closer, although the colours on the photograph have faded, I think that he has black eyeliner on. He's wearing a baggy black T-shirt with the band The Cure's logo on it, a pair of stonewashed jeans and white trainers. It seems that something just out of frame has caught his eye. I think how these days what with digital photography and the ability to instantly take multiple shots that this image would never have passed the first cut, never mind have been printed out.

On the right of Gemma is a tall boy with the skinniness of a youth who has yet to fill out his fast-growing frame. He has shortly-cropped light brown curls and is lounging on the bench with his jean-clad legs spread widely and a hand resting on each of his knees. Although he is faced towards the camera, his eyes point towards Gemma in a shy fashion, smiling like he's responding to something funny she has just said. His clothes, brown trousers and a long-sleeved checked shirt that are dated to modern eyes, mark him out as being less fashion conscious or tribal than the other boy. They're the sort of thing I imagine his mum may have bought him from M&S.

Standing to the right of the bench is a plump girl wearing Dr. Martens lace-up ankle boots, a long black billowing skirt and a white top with what looks like cartoon Dalmatians on the front that she has styled by pulling some of the material over a thick turquoise belt loosely belted around her waist. Her frizzy, permed hair reaches just below shoulder-length and she's blowing a kiss to the camera with her frosty-pink-painted lips.

Who are these people? Could any of the boys be Mike or Toby? Or did either of them have the job of being behind the camera that day?

Priti and I had not disturbed any of the room's contents nor, despite what we'd hastily planned, rummaged around for hidden clues. The dressing table the pinboard leans on has three drawers. I take a chance and quickly open them but they're empty. Nothing's there, no tell-tale letters, personal diaries or secret confessions waiting to be discovered, only a smattering of dust accompanied by the smell of stale air. There's nothing for me here and there won't be anything to learn in the pile of presents mother left there because she did so after Gemma's disappearance. Time for bed.

I shut Gemma's door, straightening the pottery name sign whose right-hand corner had skewed slightly upwards. There's no reason for Mother to know I've been in if I don't want her to. Right now the idea of talking to her about it seems a step too far if I want to avoid confrontation, which I do. We're tolerating each other well enough so far and seeing as I'm stuck here for the time being I don't want to, and can't face yet, opening old wounds. She's too sick for that, even I can see it. Part of me remembers my father softly stepping around her in case something happened that would drive her to her bed and her tablets even more. He never explained to me, though, why she took medication. It was always a subject left unspoken.

Back in the spare room, now my room again although it feels more like a cheap one-star hotel room, I undress, throwing my clothes on the floor and not bothering to put on any pyjamas. The moment where sleep intercepts consciousness drifts quickly towards me but then the car alarm outside starts shrieking again and I sit bolt upright with a jolt. In front of me, although I can barely see it in the night's gloom, is the chest of drawers that holds my smallish stash of clothes, underwear, make-up and other paraphernalia. A thought hits me. My drawers are messy, as is the top of Gemma's dressing table, which is strewn with lipsticks, mascara, eyeliner and other teenage detritus. Yet if the top of her dressing table is so cluttered then how come there's nothing in the three drawers below? Or rather, what was in there and has since been removed instead of being left to bide its time in the bedroom museum with the rest of Gemma's belongings?

Thursday 4th May 1989. 8.00 a.m.

Diana woke to the sound of the bird singing on the branches of the large oak tree spreading its wings to the heavens in her front garden. Where Frank had slept was now just a cold dent in the mattress. She stretched her arms over it and caressed the sheet, relishing in not having to sleep curtailed, curled to one side, but able to enjoy the freedom of the whole of the cool space to lie in. It was still early – only eight o'clock – she could sleep on, maybe until the girls had gone to school, and slumber in peace without the sound of the kitchen radio, slamming doors and raised voices. Her medication rarely gave her a good night's rest and she longed for the rare morning when she woke refreshed and renewed with a clear head. Today was not one of those days.

From her bedside cabinet, she opened a plastic prescribed bottle and swallowed one of the pills down with a few sips of stale water left over from two nights before. Sweet dreams, she prayed, please come.

Downstairs, Frank, a middle-aged man of a rather unimpressive yet solid height and build, washed up his cereal bowl and processed in his mind the jobs he had to do today at the garage. He felt lucky to work in an industry relatively unaffected by a recession that had pushed so many other businesses to the brink. People might not be buying many new cars any more but the old ones would always need servicing and repairing. His manual work gave him solace in his labour and thoughts, whilst lunchtime banter with his two colleagues and, occasionally a pint in the local, were all he felt he needed for a social life.

Into the kitchen stomped Gemma. Frank's first thought was that she had taken much more care over her hair, swept back in one of those fat orange headband things, and loud make-up than on her school uniform. Her skirt seemed to inch higher by the day and she wore her blue and green striped school tie high and fat over a crumpled blouse. Gemma was responsible for her own washing and ironing and lately she'd decided not to bother. Still, it was exam time around now and Frank thought not to pick her up on it. Doubtless she needed as much time as she could spare to revise, for she was an intelligent girl set to study A levels in the sixth form and then be the first in the family to go to university. Frank puffed with pride at the thought, although he personally didn't see the point of reading books for three years when you could be working with your hands and earning good money. Gemma was better than that, though, she would one day go further than he himself had ever dreamed was possible at her age.

'Dad, Annie's not getting up. She's mucking around to get on my nerves. I can't hang around and wait to take her to school if she doesn't hurry up because I've arranged to meet Mike before classes to revise.' She grabbed a slice of bread from the bread bin on the kitchen work surface and shoved it straight into her mouth, chewing and swallowing quickly before she'd even tasted it. Frank sighed. His boss was usually understanding but there were limits on how many times he could be late because of walking Annie to school. Gemma usually did it, dropping her off early before hot-footing it to her own, occasionally sneaking in at the back door via the playing fields so as not to be marked down late by the beady-eyed prefects. Today, however, Frank knew he had a big job on, a repair that had to be finished for the customer to pick the car up at lunchtime, and he dare not risk taking time out.

There was only one thing for it. Usually Frank shied away from his wife, having decided it was better to organise things himself rather than placing any expectations on her that could be dashed or, even worse, set her off down the road he didn't know if he could cope with her going down again. Truth be told he had become slightly frightened of her illness following its recurrence some months after Annie's birth, and the days when he soothingly reassured his wife that he loved her regardless had long passed. They had settled into a routine where she did whatever it was she did all day in the house – God knows it rarely involved cooking or cleaning – and he did the rest, or rather he and Gemma did the rest. He knew it was a lot to ask a teenager but Frank himself had shouldered the burdens of life early having left school at fifteen to work as an apprentice and provide money for his widowed mother. He certainly wouldn't ask Gemma to give up on her education. Yet Annie did need looking after. Today her mother would have to step up and do her fair share, for there was no other alternative. After taking a deep breath, he called her name up the stairs then braced himself for a reply.

$\sim 8 \sim$

I wake up naked, hungover and cold with the duvet kicked on to the floor, ripped from a dream about being trapped in a locked car stuck on a level crossing with no way to get out. My heart is banging and it takes me a split second to come to and realise where I am. The front door opening and closing has ended my comatose slumber with a bang. Mother is home.

I specifically avoid seeing her, knowing that with the way I'm feeling my fuse is very short. No way do I want to make polite conversation about whichever film she saw and what she had to eat at Aunty Lena's. I quickly wash and dress, washing down two paracetamols with the glass of water I'd thankfully remembered to put by the side of my bed last night, then sneak out of the front door when I hear she's in the kitchen. Lord knows I had enough practice doing this as a teenager.

The walk to the café where I've arranged to meet Priti clears my head. I pass the park where children are already shrieking and playing, kicking their shoes towards infinity on the swing and trying to reach the stars from the climbing frame. Some of the mums chattering on the park bench look a good few years younger than me. The scene makes me smile but I don't feel any urge to take their place.

Priti is already there in the café and is sipping a cappuccino. She looks as bad as I do, not even her glaring red and orange tunic is able to distract from the bags under her eyes and the remnant smear of eyeliner she missed taking off last night. On the wipe-clean table in front of her is her large-screen mobile and she's jabbing away at it with fervour.

In the background some easy listening music fights for precedence over the hubbub of conversation. Nearly all the tables are occupied by brunchers, whether they be families with young children, older couples reading the paper instead of talking to each other, or a handful of people who are rewarding themselves for their morning jog by eating a croissant with extra butter and drinking a double espresso. A balding, smiling barista who is far too jolly for this time in the morning takes my hot chocolate and toast order and offers to bring it to my table. I thank him, copper up some change from my meagre purse, and take the numbered wooden spoon he gives me to where Priti is sitting.

With no make-up on, bar last night's smudges, and her long black hair tied back in a casual bun, she appears younger and gentler than her usual strident day-to-day persona. She's engrossed in her mobile phone and hasn't yet noticed me. Being from Yorkshire I'm not usually one for PDAs but, filled with warm feelings from her words last night, I creep up behind her and give her a hug.

'Morning comrade!' I say as she jumps with fright then turns to see me, her face erupting into a beam at my presence. The beam turns into one of her signature silly faces, sticking her tongue out of the right side of her mouth and narrowing her eyes to convey to me the depth of her hangover.

'Didn't take any pre-emptive paracetamol last night then?'

She slumps her shoulders and pats the chrome chair next to her to indicate for me sit down. 'There weren't any left in my bag. I bought some this morning at the newsagents but they've not kicked in yet. You look as bad as I feel.'

'Haven't had a shower yet. I wanted to avoid Mother and her diatribe about her night out. My hair desperately needs a wash.' I run my fingers through it disdainfully. 'Hey, do you remember back before the smoking ban when we'd stink to high heaven after going to the pub?'

'I still do sometimes if I have a cheeky ciggie in the beer garden. Not often, though, I'd rather smell of wine than an ashtray.'

I nod in recognition. 'You not eating? Mine's on its way.'

Priti shivers in mock horror. 'You having a laugh? I've ordered a full vegetarian English to soak up all the alcohol in my system before I can even contemplate driving home. Look, Annie, I've got something to show you.' She jabs again at her phone and shuffles it along the table until it's under my gaze. 'Toby Smith, I searched online for him. That's him, there, in a news report about his sentencing.'

I pick the phone up and swiftly move my index finger and thumb away from each other to zoom in on the colour image. It's a holiday-type photo of an unremarkable-looking tanned, middle-aged white man with his arm around a younger, more attractive Filipino woman. Both are wearing shorts and T-shirts and are posing on a beach, smiling at the camera and raising their cocktail glasses to the person behind the camera. A similar photo but with different participants probably exists in most couple's social holiday albums. The caption says the couple are Toby Smith and his wife Jasmine.

I squint a bit to make sure but I'm certain it's him, the blonde boy with the eyeliner in Gemma's photograph. Time has fattened him up, added a tattoo to his neck and robbed him of the messy blonde locks but he has the same bud-shaped small mouth, broad forehead and aquiline nose.

'Do you recognise him?' Priti asks, drumming her fingernail extensions on the metal table as she does when she's waiting for something.

'Yes,' I reply excitedly. 'He's in a photo in Gemma's room, one with her and her friends in the park.'

'The park we walked past yesterday?'

'I'm not sure.' I'm only half-listening to what she's saying because I'm trying to concentrate on the news article.

A different member of staff who's not as cheery as the first barista and is all of seventeen brings over our food and my drink in a grump, as if we were asking an unreasonable favour from him. He spills some of my drink in the saucer and grunts 'sorry' before ambling back to the counter in his own time. I tut and give him a death stare behind his back.

Priti tucks in to her breakfast straight away and I take a sip of my hot chocolate, licking off the cocoa sprinkles from the foamy milk with my tongue. It's my ritual. That done, I turn my attention back to the phone.

The article says that Toby Smith was sentenced in Leeds Crown Court to serve twenty years in prison for the attempted murder of his wife Jasmine Smith. He had beaten her so severely in the kitchen of their home that she was lucky, the police say, to have recovered without any lasting brain damage, although she has permanent facial scars. Jasmine Smith was later found by a neighbour and the police arrested Toby Smith that evening at the ferry port in Liverpool. He admitted grievous bodily harm but denied attempted murder, saying that he had been severely provoked by her belittling behaviour. It took the jury just five hours to find him guilty in a unanimous verdict.

Provoked by a few words from a smaller, younger and slighter person to beat her half to death? What planet was this man on? It told me a lot about his character and view of women. Had he always been that way? Was he violent when he was at secondary school? Could he have harmed Gemma if she had fallen out with him or said some words he didn't want to hear?

The article went on to point out that Toby and Jasmine married seven years ago after a swift romance following his holiday in the Philippines. Jasmine moved to the UK where she got a job at the local supermarket and was described as a friendly and efficient worker who always had a smile for her customers. Toby worked as a plumber. One of his co-workers was on the record as saying he wouldn't have thought Toby would be capable of such as crime as he'd never shown any signs of violence and seemed to be happily married to his wife.

The Chief Crown Prosecutor for the region gave a statement: 'Today justice has been done for Jasmine, and her family and friends, although we know that nothing can take away the memory of the horrific ordeal she went through at the hands of her husband. Throughout the trial she has shown great courage and our thoughts are with her as she rebuilds her life.'

Jenny Greene, from the police force's Domestic Abuse Investigation Unit, appealed to anyone who is suffering from domestic abuse or suspects it is happening to someone they know to report it to specially-trained police officers. 'We take this crime incredibly seriously,' she is quoted as saying, 'and want to prosecute offenders well before their behaviour escalates to the level Toby Smith reached. You are not alone. We are here to help.'

When I finish reading, I pass the phone back to Priti, who is halfway through devouring her carb-fest breakfast and has a blob of tomato ketchup on her chin. I point at it and she wipes it away with her finger.

'Nasty, horrible bastard,' I say, revolted by the crime he committed and unable to imagine myself how, if I were Jasmine, I could carry on with everyday life. The thought that Toby Smith would have seen my sister every day at school gives me the jitters. At least he's locked away now and can't hurt another woman. He won't find himself top dog locked up in a high security prison with the scum of the earth to whom violent assaults were something they did before breakfast. I wonder whether two years inside have cowed him or only served to teach him new tricks.

'Are you going to talk to your mum to see if the police are aware of this?' asks Priti.

I guess that Gemma's case is still open – I haven't heard that it's closed – but then again I've been off-grid for so long that I wouldn't have known anyway. The person for me to ask is Aunty Lena. She'll know what the state of play is without me having to bring up the subject with mother.

I tell Priti I'm going to go and talk to her today. She

approves and says that when she's back at home she'll do more online searching to try and track down Mike. Mother doesn't have the internet at home and I'm reliant on my accessing it through my pay as you go mobile. Priti promises to forward any interesting web links to me.

We order a coffee each and then Priti decides she feels well enough to drive back to her flat. She insists I don't need to walk her to her battered old Nissan Micra and says she'll text me to let me know she's home safely. I watch her walk down the street to the nearby car park, attracting more than a few male glances as she holds her now-not-thumping-head high with confidence. It's good to have her on my side.

~9~

I've never been one to have lots of friends: a huge girl gang who are best friends forever through thick, thin and life's hard slaps to the face. My life is not an American sitcom with lots of group hugs and 'I love yous'. It's not that I'm not sociable – quite the opposite – I'm not afraid to talk to strangers and work my way into a group, subtly working out the dynamics including who is Queen Bee and who are the hangers on. I've observed the same pattern everywhere. The worker bees bustle round the queen, feeding her ego until she's ready to fight her alpha rivals until social death, and they last as long as they amuse her, at which point they are replaced by new eager faces, of which I was often one.

Not long after I first moved to Leeds, I joined in with a crowd I'd met through the house share I was living in at the time. It was an amorphous, ever-changing group of those new to the city, whether they were studying, working or escaping from a stultifying life under their parents' roof. People came and went: ex-boyfriends and girlfriends dropped out, on to other pastures and pliant bodies; new lovers were brought along to show off and were sometimes lost to another member of the gang, for this kind of group friendship didn't extend to the loyalty of denying one's individual lusts; a few settled down or moved elsewhere on to better things; one man, a quiet, amiable chap when he was sober but a violent, angry drunk when he wasn't, was last seen being driven by his father to rehab; and a few years ago a round robin email from a party girl I hadn't seen for ages informed me that one of the regulars had thrown herself under an incoming train at Leeds station.

This was a group where you were still alone although you were surrounded by lots of dancing, sweaty, sometimes drug-fuelled people. Texts typed on brick-like Nokia mobile phones, sent by the latest person who aspired to be the hive's king or queen, told us where to meet. If you didn't go, chances were no one would call you up to see if you were alright, unless of course they were your housemate and the rent was due. I could party along with the best of them, charming a crowd and playing the fool, hiding myself in the thick of the Leeds night scene. No one talked deeply about their personal life or went further than saying they'd had a rubbish day at work. The unwritten rule was that we were there to party, your problems were your own and anyone putting a downer on the proceedings would find their mobile stopped beeping.

Looking back now it was crazy really. Starting a fight (as long as it wasn't with anyone in the group), getting arrested, or making a complete fool of yourself by stripping and dancing on the bar tables were perfectly socially acceptable, even encouraged to give us all something to gossip about. Look at Lisa, she shagged her boyfriend's best mate in the club's disabled toilet! There's Callum, he got so drunk he collapsed in the street, vomited all over himself and was stretchered off to hospital to have his stomach pumped whilst we all said what a laugh he was! Yet to sit with a lemonade in a quiet corner trying to tell anyone who would listen why life's clawing, black cloud was shitting all over their head, that was a no-no.

Not that I cared then. I didn't want to be known as the dead girl's sister. I'd broken free of all that – left it back in Greville Road never to be seen again. I reinvented myself as the fun one, the carefree one, the one you'd call because she guaranteed you a good time yet wouldn't try to muscle Queen Bee out of the limelight. I felt no need to be adored for the sake of it. One thing I'd learned from childhood was that I could manage on my own.

Friendships at school were a different matter. In primary school other kids seemed wary of me. When Gemma disappeared, our form teacher – so Aunty Lena later informed me – told the other children when I was absent from class that they should be kind to me because my sister was missing. On my return I didn't know why the others were acting differently at playtime. Some of the girls looked embarrassed when I wanted to join in hopscotch and tag and one rotund boy from another class asked me if my sister was dead. One classmate, Olivia with her oh-so perfect blonde plaits, shouted at him and told him that he had to be nice to me because the teacher said so.

I didn't want anyone to be nice to me because the teacher said so. Plus I didn't want Olivia, who hadn't invited me to her birthday party at the church hall, to stick up for me. Tears welled up at the humiliation. The boy from the other class started to laugh. I kicked him in the shins then pulled hard on Olivia's plaits, pulling out a clump of blonde hair.

After a teacher had pulled me off Olivia, the Head called Father to the school and told him to take me home for the day. Years later, Aunty Lena told me that I escaped exclusion on compassionate grounds. If my sister wasn't missing, they deduced, I wouldn't have behaved that way.

Wrong. The teacher didn't get it that she had caused the situation in the first place. I'd have done the same to any child who treated me like that.

After that, I distanced myself from the other kids. I see now, with an adult's hindsight, that it was because I couldn't trust that others wanted to be friends with me, rather than feeling sorry for me or displaying some pruriently distasteful interest in the police case surrounding my sister. Mother stayed in her bed and never mentioned my having friends over for tea like other children did. Father worked too hard to think about it. I'd have been too embarrassed to bring anyone home anyway, in case they saw Mother wearing her nightie in the mid-afternoon. Ours was not a welcoming house. No 'Thanks for visiting!' mat graced our front door.

Olivia, the plaited princess, made sure her followers didn't talk to me unless they had to. Her parents, I learned well after the event from Aunty Lena again, went down to the school to complain about my 'assault' and, even though I was only five-years-old and my sister was the subject of a massive missing person hunt for Christ's sake, wrote a letter to the school governors 'expressing their displeasure that the school's disciplinary procedures for bullying were not followed in this case'. So then, according to Olivia and co and their parents, I was labelled a bully for the length of my primary school career.

Eventually, I formed an alliance with the other outsiders: Jess, a sweet, kind-hearted girl with a mild learning difficulty whom the others never picked for their team because they complained about her being slow; Ian, a bright, funny boy, small for his age and who used a wheelchair due to having cerebral palsy; and Wayne, who lived with a foster family, wore hand-me-downs and never had the latest toys the other kids talked about at lunch-time. Together at school we were a tight-knit group. We didn't need anyone else and the others didn't want us anyway.

Occasionally, Jess's or Ian's mum, keen to encourage our friendship, would invite us all round for tea after school or for a weekend play-date in the park. With a knowing look that made me feel ashamed of my family, they'd make sure they ferried me around in their car because mine didn't have one. Jess and I would make daisy chains or compete on the swings to see who could kick the highest cloud, whilst Wayne pushed a delighted Ian along the path as fast as he could run. Then we'd all play catch, eat sandwiches and crisps and drink fizzy pop until we felt sick.

I'd forgotten how happy those few but far between outings were. I wonder where Jess, Wayne and Ian are now? Ian went to a different secondary school from me because it was the only one in the borough that had a lift. Wayne and I were mates at secondary school until his mum got out of prison and he moved back in with her in a neighbouring town; and Jess, I have no idea where she is now. After an unhappy couple of terms in secondary school where, if it weren't for me and Wayne, the kids who hadn't grown up with her would have eaten her alive, her parents moved to a different catchment area so she could switch to a mainstream school with a good reputation for including children with learning difficulties.

With those three gone I began to hang around mostly with older kids who didn't remember me from primary school and hadn't any preconceptions of what I was like. I was a walking teenage cliché: smoking behind the bike sheds, drinking in the park, bunking off school and doing whatever I wanted to do, anything rather than do what I was told to do. Life was for living, I thought, even if living it didn't make me feel any happier. Was anyone supposed to like being a teenager anyway? Isn't it a given that it's the worst time of your life?

It was only when I met Priti at work and was introduced to her crowd that I felt I'd found real friends again. Priti was never backwards in coming forwards about her emotions, the silly rows with her family or when she was on her period. At first I felt quite taken aback at the way she never hid what she was feeling, but after time some of her behaviour rubbed off on me and I felt able to break through the glass veneer I'd erected around myself and share what I really thought. 'You've got to tell me something personal about yourself,' I remember her saying to me a fortnight after we met. 'You know that I farted loudly on my first ever date, you owe me one!'

There's only so much I shared with her, though. I couldn't help but think that if she really knew me my phone would stop ringing.

Once the dead girl's sister, always the dead girl's sister.

~ 10 ~

Instead of walking straight home from the café, I make a short detour to Aunty Lena's. As she opens the front door, the mouth-watering smell of roasting beef hits me – my vegetarian phase only lasted six months – and I follow her into the kitchen where she's preparing Sunday dinner. They knocked through their kitchen and dining room when I was a child and since then they've refitted the kitchen with white shaker units and an inbuilt oven. It's the first time I've seen Uncle Den since I've been back. He's sitting in an armchair with his foot up on a small side table, which also has a digital radio on top that's tuned to the *The Archers* omnibus on Radio 4. His lounge chair looks out of place in the kitchen beside the round dinner table but he looks very comfortable there and I imagine that the couple spend a lot of time in that room. At least there he's near the kettle.

I'm shocked at his physical deterioration since I last saw him. He's thinner and more fragile, his neck having acquired three folds of skin and his wrists that were once thick and strong now resembling snappable twigs. Mentally, though, he's right on track and he cracks jokes straight away about what he imagines I got up to in Leeds – bet you left lots of broken hearts there, hey? – and I can tell he's pleased to see me again. The feeling is definitely mutual. Why couldn't he and Lena have been my mum and dad? They didn't have any children of their own. I've never asked why, whether they'd tried for them but weren't blessed by a visit from the stork.

Lena asks me to stay for dinner and, although it smells so tempting, I decline, saying that I ought to get back and make something for Mother. Lena nods approvingly. 'Another time then. Why don't you both come round next Sunday? I'll roast a chicken and make onion gravy.' After general chit chat, during which I learn that the romantic comedy film the night before had been a disappointment with far too much bad language, I fill them in on my discovery. Lena and Den hang on my words once they realise I'm talking about a possible link to Gemma's disappearance.

When I finish, Lena turns the potatoes roasting in the oven, giving herself a minute to ponder what she's just heard. She looks weary for a moment and wrinkles her forehead in thought. 'I did hear about the Toby Jones case, you couldn't miss it with all the publicity, but I didn't know that he was in Gemma's class at school. I don't know either if the police are aware of the connection. He wasn't a suspect at the time.'

'They should have castrated him for what he did to his wife,' adds Den angrily. 'That's a better deterrent to others than prison.'

I smile, remembering Den's non-PC views on dealing with offenders.

'Who would I contact to ask if the police know? At the very least they could interview him again in prison, if anything to rule him out.'

'There was a family liaison officer, you'll be too young to

remember. WPC Hargreaves she was,' says Den. 'Nice lady with the rough job of telling your parents that Gemma still hadn't been found.'

'Yes, but she wasn't that young then, was she, she's probably long gone now, the police get to retire that early,' replies Lena. She lowers her voice a little and says directly to me, 'I don't think your mum knows about the Toby link. Best not mention it unless you have to, eh? She needs to focus on the chemo right now. I doubt she's got the strength to deal with both.'

I nod but feel a flinch of annoyance that yet again Mother is protected in her own little world whilst other people do her dirty work. Then I remember the sight of her hooked up to the drip in hospital and take that thought back.

'Why don't you ring the police station tomorrow, tell them what you know and ask them to investigate it. That's what we pay our taxes for,' says Den.

It's a plan, not much of one, but it's a start. Mother has her next chemo session tomorrow. I'll make an excuse to go to the hospital café during her treatment and ring the police from there. I can't not follow this up: it's like having an itch and needing to scratch it. Someone somewhere knows what happened to Gemma and that person might be Toby. In that instant, I realise that Priti was right last night. I do need to move on. Leaving home didn't work, I'm still trapped in the same cycle of anger and resentment that I hadn't previously realised encased me. If trying to find out more about Gemma and what happened to her is what it takes then that's what I do. I want to break free. I *need* to break free.

After saying my goodbyes and promising to return soon

– Den tells me I must come and watch his favourite daytime quiz show with him – I walk the short distance back to Mother's house. There's no way I can avoid Reg's place unless I walk around the block clockwise and approach Mother's from the other direction. That'd be daft and besides I've been out long enough today. It is lunch-time and I need to check that Mother is eating properly and taking her medication.

I'm nearly past his house and am so tantalisingly close to the gate when Reg's front door opens and he calls me. 'Annie? I thought you were back.' I'm too near to pretend not to have heard him.

It's the second time today that I'm shocked by the appearance of a figure from my childhood. Like Mother, he is bordering on skeletal in his face and arms, but unlike her his stomach is distended as if he were seven months pregnant. His hair is grey and in need of a wash and cut, his nose resembles a bulbous red strawberry and there are age spots dotted randomly on his yellow-tinged face that's also lined with broken capillaries.

'Sorry, I'm in a rush,' I say, turning to carry on to my front door, when he interrupts me and says he wants to talk.

There's no way I'm going in his house. I walk towards him, making sure I'm not within his arm's reach, but I can't avoid the stench of a blend of alcohol and body odour exuding from him. 'I really can't stop. I need to make lunch for Mother.'

'Is she why you're back?' he asks. I can't work out whether it's a comment or accusation.

'Yes. I'm back until her cancer appointments are over.'

'She's got cancer? I didn't know.' He looks startled.

'Well, did you ever ask? She does live right next to you.' Immediately I curse myself for saying that in case he takes me up on the offer and wants to pop over for a coffee. There's something about him I really don't like. His presence unnerves me. Reg is a different man from the line-dancing, friendly neighbour I knew in my early childhood. Come to think of it, I saw very little of him in my teens. I think he rarely came next door then.

'I don't get out much.'

I bet he makes it out alright to the off-licence.

'Are you OK?' he asks. I really don't have the time or patience for idle conversation.

'Fine, thank you. I really have to go.'

'I'm sorry about your mum,' he says. I start walking but he opens his mouth again. 'Remember to tell her that, Annie. Remember to tell her that I'm sorry.'

~ 11 ~

It's Monday afternoon and Mother is once again sitting in a plastic-covered armchair hooked up to a drip under Una's supervision. This time Mel isn't there and Mother is quieter, deciding not to chat with the other patients but instead focus on the television in the corner of the room that's tuned to a daytime panel show. She didn't eat much of the sausage and mash I cooked yesterday and spent a while in the bathroom in the evening pretending not to throw up. Today I've brought rice crackers. She hasn't admitted it but I can tell that the nausea caused by the treatment is really getting to her.

I'm sitting on an orange plastic chair next to her – there's not even any lip service to make visitors comfortable – and I can feel my thighs going numb where they press down on the lip of the seat. I can't bear to watch the mindless TV programme and wouldn't be able to concentrate on it anyway what with rehearsing in my mind what to say to the police when I can slip away and make the call.

Una comes over and asks how we both are. Mother thanks her for telling me about the healthcare assistant job and I add the caveat that though I've applied I haven't heard back yet and don't have much relevant experience.

'The ability to cope with blood, urine and faeces is what

you need,' Una counsels, checking Mother's pulse as she talks. 'Some people don't last a week. If you can deal with violent vomiting then they'll snap you up. No one wants the work these days because of the low pay. Why clean up other people's mess when you can pull pints in a bar for the same wage and earn tips on top? Yet they still expect the NHS to be there when they get sick.'

It occurs to me that Una would get on well with Uncle Den.

'I did think about being a nurse when I was in primary school but, you know, my exam results weren't good and I left school at sixteen.'

'It's not too late to train. There's an access to higher education course specialising in healthcare at the local college. After that you can apply to do a nursing degree. We often have their students in on work placement. I'm a whizz at spotting who'll last the course. How a trainee treats a patient on the job matters much more in my mind than a piece of paper with an exam grade,' she winks.

Temperature taken and approved, Una puts a blue inflatable band around the top of Mother's arm that isn't attached to the drip and presses a button. The band inflates and, with a hissing sound, deflates slowly accompanied by beeps on the machine. 'Your blood pressure is fine, Mrs Towcester. Do you need anything?'

I offer Mother the rice crackers and she takes one, nibbling at it like a reticent mouse.

'I'm OK, thank you, Una. I'm feeling a little tired and might try to have, what do they call it? A power nap.'

Una smiles and moves on to the next patient. That's

my cue to exit the ward, go to the loo (all this tea drinking has its effects) and head for the hospital's brightly-coloured but sterile-feeling Women's Royal Voluntary Service café – thankfully overpriced American coffee chains haven't yet wormed their way into this hospital. I haven't a clue if it smells of disinfectant because my senses have adjusted to the hospital's environment.

So as not to look out of place, I buy a hot chocolate from the vending machine in the corner and take a seat at one of the spare tables. Shoving the empty cup and plate left over from the last person to the side, I pull out the local police station's number from my jeans pocket, where I'd stored it this morning for safekeeping, and dial.

Nerves hit me. What if they think I'm bonkers calling them about this? Am I wasting their time? I recall Den's words yesterday, that the police are paid to investigate crimes. It's their job. That calms me down; they have to take me seriously.

When I explain why I'm calling, the man who answered the phone puts me on hold for a few minutes. There are rhythmic beeps in my ear that let me know he hasn't cut me off. Eventually, another man's voice, one with a more ingrained Yorkshire accent, comes on the line and introduces himself as Detective Inspector Dave Glass. 'Annie, isn't it, what can I do for you?' His tone is friendly enough. 'You've been put through to me because I worked here when the investigation into Gemma's disappearance went on.'

'Thank you for speaking to me. I've got something to report regarding Gemma's case. A classmate of Gemma's, Toby Smith, went to prison two years ago for attempted murder of his wife. It seems a bit of a coincidence to me. I'd like the police to interview him and see if he was violent to Gemma.'

There's a pause on the line.

'Well, thanks for letting us know, Annie. I remember the Smith case very well, although I wasn't on that team. That man is definitely a nasty piece of work and offenders who commit such a brutal crime usually do have a history of violence. But I'm sorry to say that, what with our stretched resources, we can't re-open the investigation into Gemma's disappearance unless we have strong new evidence.'

I sigh. 'Isn't it enough that Toby Smith was in the same form as Gemma and was her friend? I've got a photo with them both in it.'

'I get where you're coming from, I really do. Red tape doesn't work that way, though. My advice is to go to a solicitor and get them to write to the Chief Commissioner stating what you've told me and ask for it to be investigated. The bosses take official letters much more seriously, sadly, than a grieving relative.'

I don't know any solicitors, having never had any need for one.

'I shouldn't really say this, and don't tell anyone I did, but it might be worth you adding that you're prepared to go to the press. Those at the top hate bad PR. They won't want it dragged up in the papers that they've failed to solve the disappearance and ignored a tip-off from the family.'

'Thank you. I'll do that.'

'No problem. You did the right thing to call. Contact me again if you find out anything else. When you've sent the letter I'll do my best to lean on my DCI.'

It wasn't what I was hoping for but at least DI Glass hadn't turned me down flat.

Taking another sip from the appalling hot chocolate that was clearly made not with milk but powder and water, I log onto the internet and search for local solicitors. There are a number of solicitor firms listed, all with the same kind of name: Blah Blah, Blah & Blah, and I haven't got a clue who to try. I mentally discard those who say they specialise in family law, divorces and no-win no-fee compensation claims and then scan those who are left. Suddenly one name based in my home town jumps out at me: Wilson & Zedda. Zedda was my school friend Ian's surname. His great-grandfather emigrated at the age of sixteen from Italy to Glasgow to work in an ice cream parlour; the sweet dessert at that time was growing in popularity in the city. Ian couldn't speak a word of Italian but always supported Italy in the World Cup after England had been knocked out.

I press the web link on my phone and a corporate-looking website appears. On the homepage there's a description of the firm's services, a paragraph blurb about their ethos and a stock photo of a smiling middle-aged couple waving a will document. Ignoring these, I click on the 'about us' button where there's a list of Wilson & Zedda's employees accompanied by head and shoulder photos.

There he is. Ian Zedda. Older, slightly plumper, but still unmistakably my old friend. His biography says that he graduated with a law degree from Newcastle University and stayed there to do the legal practice course and a Masters specialising in human rights. After working for an international firm in The City for four years he relocated back to Yorkshire where he founded his own practice not that long ago with his wife, Jennifer Wilson. I go to her biography and learn that she also studied at Newcastle University and her specialism is criminal law. She's quite a severe-looking woman, her light brown hair cut short in an austere, asymmetrical style, and she's folding her arms on top of a stereotypically unfashionable lawyer's black jacket, but I sense instantly that she must be lovely if she's Ian's marital choice.

Immediately I click on his email link and type 'Dear Ian. Remember me? This is Annie Towcester, your friend from primary school. I've been looking online for a solicitor and your name popped up. Would it be OK if I came to see you? I'd love to catch up and maybe you could help me with my query. Congratulations by the way on your degrees – you've made up for my lack of education! Best wishes, Annie x'

A minute later, after I've stood up and thrown my plastic cup into the waste bin, my phone beeps. That was quick! Yet it's not Ian, it's a text from Gareth asking me to go to Alexandro's restaurant on Friday night with him. I don't know it; I didn't exactly eat out in restaurants when I was a teenager, but he says he's heard good things about it from Mo. I bite the bullet. With Priti not around I'd rather spend a Friday night eating pizza with Gareth than watching my mother snooze on the sofa in front of *Coronation Street*. I text him straight back saying I'll see him there at 7.30.

Right as I walk out of the café to go back to the ward the mobile beeps again. This time it's Priti.

Any news? I've traced someone I think is Mike. Will email you the link. Mwah x

I must buy more credit for my phone because, what with all the online searching I've been doing, I've virtually used up all I had. I hope that I hear about the healthcare assistant bank job soon or I'll need to go to an agency and see if I can get any cleaning or call centre work that will fit around Mother's appointments. Mind you, if I don't buy any credit, I won't be able to hear about the job application result at all.

Back on the ward, my mother is still dozing. She looks incredibly fragile and shrivelled. Her hands are clasped together as if in prayer and her mouth is slightly open at the right-hand side with a drop of spittle oozing from it. I gently close her mouth without waking her to give her some dignity. Una notices and shoots me an approving smile. She comes over to talk in whispers so as not to disturb her sleeping patient.

'She's doing well. You being home is helping her. She's gained two pounds in weight – you're cooking for her, aren't you? Before you came home I suspect she skipped meals when she wasn't hungry.'

'If I cook something she feels obliged to try to eat at least a little of it. Hey, how did your date with your boyfriend go?' Una flushes a little then gives a wicked smile. '*Very* well, if you know what I mean,' she tells me. I don't push her for more details, just nod and reciprocate with an understanding smirk.

'I met a man on Saturday. He's texted asking me to go to dinner with him.'

'Ooh get you!' she laughs, flashing a perfect set of white teeth. 'You've only been in town a week and the lads come flocking!'

'Ah – we'll see.'

'Do tell me how it goes. I'm a romantic at heart,' she replies before adding: 'Got to dash. Call me if your mum needs anything.'

A couple of hours later we're back home and Mother is in bed resting. I take the time to check my email and there it is, the message Priti said she'd send me. Slumped on the sofa, I open it quickly. It contains two links to web pages. I open the first, which goes to a news story about a Mike Braithwaite, who'd be the same age as Gemma if she was still alive. The story is about him organising a charity concert in South Yorkshire to raise funds for a three-year-old girl suffering from a rare blood disorder in order for her to travel to the US for pioneering treatment. His face is easily recognisable as the curly-haired boy in Gemma's photo. Indeed, the years have been kind to him, for, despite a few crinkles around his eyes and a spot of grey around the temples, he hardly looks much older.

The second link leads to his business website, Mike Braithwaite Accountancy Services. Scrolling down the page I spot another photo of him, this time wearing a shirt and tie, smiling at the camera to reassure clients that he's kosher. Right at the bottom of the page there's a contact telephone number. On a whim I dial it without thinking first about what to say.

A receptionist answers. Looking at the clock on the wall I see it's 5.15 p.m. – not quite early enough for the office to close. 'Good afternoon, Mike Braithwaite Accountancy Services, Nazreen speaking, how may I help?'

I fiddle with my cuticles as I do when I'm nervous. 'Hello,

I'd like to speak to Mr Braithwaite please, is he available?'

'Whom may I say is calling?'

'It's Annie Towcester. He doesn't know me.'

'Hold on please, I'll put you through.' There's a pause then a click on the line.

'Mike Braithwaite speaking.' His voice has an affable, yet professional tone.

'Oh, hello, Mr Braithwaite, my name is Annie Towcester. I believe you knew my sister Gemma from school?'

There's another pause. 'Gemma Towcester? Yes, we were in the same class. Are you looking for an accountant?'

'Me, no. I'm looking into her disappearance and because you were friends with her I wonder if you wouldn't mind talking to me about her, please?'

'School was a long time ago. What is it you want to know?' His tone is more brusque now, verging on accusatory.

'What she was like, if anything unusual happened before she disappeared, that sort of thing.'

He replies straight away. 'I'm sorry, I can't help you. Gemma and I weren't that close. I don't know anything.'

'But I just want to find out more about her, I was only five when she went missing. What was she like as a person? What was her relationship with Toby Smith?'

'As I said before, Miss Towcester, I'm sorry I can't help you. I'm a very busy man, so unless you want an accountant please don't call again.' He hangs straight up. I'm blindsided by his reaction. Gareth had told me that Gemma and Mike were as thick as thieves and in the photograph upstairs they are sitting next to each other on a bench and certainly appear friendly, enjoying a joke together.

I look down. There's a large droplet of blood emanating from the nail bed of my left thumb. I suck it better but another ruby red one immediately takes its place.

Thursday 4th May 1989. 8.10 p.m.

Diana had only been back to sleep a few minutes when the shout ripped her from her dream about flying above the rooftops towards the clouds, higher and higher until the town below was barely a speck of dust on the horizon. The first call she ignored, but when it was repeated she dragged herself out of bed, slid her fluffy mules on her feet, put on her towelling dressing gown over her tired frame, and walked to the top of the landing. She tapped her chipped nails on the bannister and suddenly wished she was in a permanent sleep that Frank's demands couldn't wake her up from. Deep breaths. Slowly in and out like the doctor said.

'What?' she shrieked.

'Di, love, can you come down please? I'm really sorry but Gemma can't take Annie to school today and I have to be at work on time. Can you walk her?'

Diana sighed, feeling the little energy she had seep out of her body with her breath. Her heart began to beat faster at the thought of having to go outside.

'Are you sure you or Gemma can't take her? It doesn't matter if she's a bit late for school, does it?'

'She's got exams soon Diana. She's revising with a friend before school.' Did Diana hear an exasperated edge in her husband's voice?

'Right, I'll get dressed then, shall I?' It came out sounding martyrish but wasn't meant that way, more as an instruction to herself on what she had to do. Diana was sadly aware of how little she did for her daughters, how the mother she thought she'd be before pregnancy was so far removed from today's reality. She would walk Annie to school, force herself to leave the house and nod and smile when the other mothers spoke to her. She knew what they were thinking, that she was a mad mother. A bad mother. She would bear it until tablet time when she could truly be herself wrapped up in her own little cocoon.

Annie's bedroom door was slightly ajar and from inside there came a mangled up yet endearing rendition of 'The Wheels on the Bus'.

'Annie, stop singing and get dressed. I'm taking you to school.'

Diana barged into the bedroom, her robe coming undone at the tie revealing her slightly-scratched knees.

Annie was sitting on the floor wheeling a toy bus on the carpet. 'School bus stop! Children get off!' she said, not registering her mother's presence. Was it deliberate? Diana thought so, exasperatedly, but then took some more deep breaths and the voice in her head told her to try harder.

She bent down on her knees to lower herself to her daughter's height. 'Annie, dear, you've got to get dressed. It's nearly time to go to school.'

Annie looked up at her mother with big, wide eyes. 'You're taking me?'

'Yes.'

'But Daddy or Gemma always take me.'

'Well today I'm taking you.'

Diana tried to lay a soothing hand on her daughter's shoulder to guide her up but Annie flinched.

'I haven't done anything bad!' she wailed. Diana winced at the knowledge that her daughter thought that physical interaction with her mother was a punishment, not a show of love. Yet love, in her brain fogged and permanently exhausted state, was what she found so difficult to express.

'I didn't say you had, Annie. Now come on, I'll take you in the bathroom to brush your teeth and wash your face then I'll find your school uniform.' Diana opened a few drawers in the dresser.

'Where do you keep your underwear?'

Annie stood up and went over to the bottom of the wardrobe where there was a cardboard box full of clean socks and pants.

'Right, off with your nightie and put some clean socks and underwear on please.'

Footsteps stomped up the stairs and Gemma's bedroom door slammed shut.

The noise. Diana couldn't stand it. The sound throbbed in her head. She walked to Gemma's bedroom door and opened it. 'Gemma, do you have to be so loud? Are you incapable of climbing the stairs without imitating a herd of elephants?'

In her room, Gemma was rifling through books on the floor. When on her knees, her skirt rode up so short that Diana could see the bottom of her knickers.

'And for goodness sake, put a longer skirt on. People will think you are a prostitute.'

Gemma exploded. She turned to her mother with

violence in her eyes – latent energy just waiting for a release.

'Shut up, you useless cow! Look at you, still in your dressing gown at this time of the morning! Moaning on because once, just once, you have to take your daughter, your own daughter, not mine, to school. Don't you dare lecture me!'

Slap.

It happened before Diana had thought about doing it – an almost mechanical response: a lever turns, the hand raises, the palm flattens out and then quickly collides with Gemma's cheek.

The two women faced each other in horror.

'Don't touch me,' screamed Gemma. 'Don't come near me. I hate you. I never want to see you again.'

~ 12 ~

The next few days pass quite slowly, my new routine embedding itself in: cleaning, cooking, helping Mother, going for a brisk walk every day and sharing texts with Priti about what we've found out. Ian got back to me the day after I emailed him. He sounded really pleased to hear from me and said that, whilst he was 'up against it' this week with meetings (I laughed at how he has embraced corporate speak) he will be free late afternoon on Monday. We arrange a time for me to meet him at his office.

Mike's reaction still bewilders me. Why was he so defensive? Does he have something to hide? Or is he, as he said, a busy man who can't spare the time to talk about the past? Somehow I don't think so. Priti immediately puts him down as a prime suspect, coming up with lots of lurid theories about his guilt. Did he kill Gemma during a lovers' tiff? Was he a drug dealer and Gemma planned to grass him up to the police? Does he know who murdered Gemma but is too frightened to say so? Was he in league with Toby Smith? Or perhaps he'd helped Gemma disappear and she was still alive somewhere?

I am about to go in to town to research recruitment agencies when the phone rings. I'm hesitant to answer it because 'caller unknown' appears on the screen, but after a few rings I pick up in case it's important. I'm glad I do because it's the HR department at the hospital trust offering me an interview next Monday – someone else had dropped out and then they received my application. I'll have time to attend before my meeting with Ian. I thankfully confirm that I'll attend and hang up with a smile. I want this job. It has surprised me that going with Mother to her chemo appointments, even though it hasn't been for that long, has piqued my interest in nursing. It would be great to get a job that leads to a qualification, even a career, and smash the minimum-wage ceiling I've been stuck under.

What will I wear to the interview though? My clothes are out of date and I don't own any smart clobber. I didn't need any for my previous jobs and it's never been my style to dress up. I think about going to a charity shop but they're hit and miss and these days they aren't the bargain they used to be. Besides, I don't have any spare cash to buy anything – I bought more mobile phone credit with my ever-stretched overdraft – and I'm certainly not going begging to my mother. I doubt she's got much to spare herself anyway; treatment and car parking are free on the NHS but cancer still costs a lot of money due to things like loss of earnings and extra heating bills. Did she used to have a job? It occurs to me I don't even know that.

I heat up the leftovers of a chicken casserole I'd batch cooked two days before. Whilst we're having dinner, or rather I'm wolfing it down and mother's picking at it like a sparrow, I fill the silence by telling her about the interview.

'Well done, Annie, I'm proud of you.' She looks genuinely pleased.

Proud of me? That's a phrase I've never heard before.

'Nothing's guaranteed. I'll have to wait and see.'

'You only applied a few days ago. They must be impressed by you.'

'Or they're desperate,' I joke.

'Don't be silly. They'd be lucky to have you.'

Really? Does she think that or is she rolling out a stock platitude?

'Someone else pulled out. I'm not sure what to wear. I ought to dress up smart, I think.'

'Yes you should. I read an article in a magazine last week that said women should dress for where they want to be and not where they are.'

'So I should rent a nurse's uniform from a fancy dress shop?' This makes us both laugh.

'No, you should dress as if you are the head of the company.'

'I don't own any suits,' I reply. 'I've never needed any in my previous jobs.'

Mother places her knife and fork neatly together on her half-full plate to signal that she has finished eating.

'What did you do before?'

'Call centre work, that sort of thing. I was a receptionist once and also did a few stints as a barmaid.' I hesitate. 'Did you have a job, before the cancer came, I mean?'

Mother sighs and sits back in her chair. 'I did casual work on a market stall selling fabrics. I had to give it up when I fell ill.'

'Weren't you entitled to sick pay?'

'No, my boss couldn't afford it. She paid me shift by shift.'

I wonder whether she means cash in hand, nudge nudge, wink wink, don't tell the taxman.

'That's a shame. Did you enjoy it?'

'Yes, very much. We often got new rolls of material in. I liked talking to customers about what they were making. It's fashionable again to sew your own clothes and curtains.'

Perish the thought. Why sew it yourself when you can buy it cheaply from a chain store? That's a thought I politely keep to myself.

There's silence, only punctuated by the scrape of moving chair legs, whilst I clear the table and replace the used plates with fruit and yoghurts for pudding.

'Not for me, thank you, Annie.'

'You've got to eat something. Try a yoghurt. For me.' I realise I'm treating her like a five-year-old.

She chooses a raspberry one and peels off the lid then places it carefully on the table. No licking yoghurt lids in this house. Strange how although mother rarely used to eat with us I still picked up all her culinary foibles.

Mother eats a few teaspoons-worth and then pipes up with, 'Why don't you see if there's something in my wardrobe that will fit you? Before I lost weight I was about your size. I can use my sewing machine to make any alterations you need.'

I baulk at the thought of wearing some outdated flowery number with shoulder pads that smells of mothballs. Then I realise that before I returned I hadn't seen my mother for years and I don't know what she wore during that time before slacks and old jumpers became her sickness uniform. I've got nothing to lose and can always decline the offer if there's nothing suitable. At the very least I'll get to have a chuckle at fashion that time forgot.

After I've done the washing up – mother offers but I decline as she looks as if she'd collapse if she tried to stand up at the sink for too long – we go upstairs to her bedroom. It has been decorated since I was a teenager. Gone are the chintz curtains, matching duvet cover and old wallpaper, they have been replaced by plain walls painted a pale blue, stripy curtains that tone in with the paint colour and pure white pillow cases and a duvet cover. I hardly ever came in this room when I was a child for Mother was usually resting and not to be disturbed. On the left bedside table there's a framed photograph of my father placed on top of a couple of paperbacks, and on top of the right one there's a small lamp, a pill box and an old school photograph of me.

Me, not Gemma.

I'm about twelve and am on the cusp of turning from a child into a young woman. My short ginger hair contrasts starkly with the blue of my school uniform and I'm smiling at the camera. If the viewer didn't know any better they'd think I was a happy young girl.

I perch on the side of the bed whilst mother opens her wardrobe. She has taken over the side where my Father's clothes, albeit few of them, used to hang. Most of the garments are covered in the type of plastic bag that a dry cleaner returns your item in. I brace myself for something hideous and am amazed that what emerges from the covers aren't actually that bad. Some are shop bought, some home-sewn but all are what fashion magazines would describe as 'classic' styles – not the sort of thing I would usually wear but suitable for the smart, bland look that my interview requires.

With Mother's encouragement, I try on quite a few pieces, looking in the wardrobe's internal full-length mirror to see what I look like and doing a catwalk-style twirl. Mother has more clothes than I imagined but then again she was brought up with the culture of never throwing anything away in case it could come in useful in the future. I don't bother with the dresses and skirts as I really wouldn't feel comfortable in my skin wearing them, so I stick to trousers and jackets.

Eventually, Mother and I whittle it down to a pair of tailored wool black trousers with a side zip. The leg length is slightly too long but straight away she disappears into the spare/my bedroom for her sewing kit and pins them up perfectly. I pair the trousers with a red silky-collared blouse and tuck it in at the waist. On top of that I wear a black single-breasted jacket. It comes with shoulder pads – I knew it! – that rock the 1980s look but are ridiculous on me. I have broader shoulders than my mother. She cuts out the shoulder pads with embroidery scissors, sticks a few pins in to alter the shape and voila, even though I say so myself, I actually look quite good. Mother beams at her little project and says she'll try and sew them up properly tonight.

The next task is to work out what to wear on my feet. We share the same shoe size. All I own are trainers, knee high winter boots and a couple of pairs of ballet pumps. Mother's day-to-day shoes are lined up in the hall downstairs but she tells me to look in the bottom of her wardrobe where she keeps her boxes of best shoes.

She's looking even more tired now and unable to bend

down on her knees to sort through them herself, so I sit on the floor and have a rummage through the cardboard boxes. There are ten in total. I reject the three pairs of high heels, aka ankle breakers, as I've never worn them before and don't wish to start now. I prefer to be able to walk freely and not totter on a stiletto heel. I also reject the three pairs of boots as too practical and unstylish to wear with the trouser suit.

Next are a pair of black kitten heels. They're not my taste but, trying them on, they are a comfortable fit and I can just about walk in them. They add a feminine touch to the outfit. The adjacent box contains a pair of espadrilles and the one after that some white, strappy sandals.

If the shoes in the final box are unsuitable then the kitten heels it is de facto. I'll practice walking in them in the house to wear them in before the interview.

The last box is heavier than the others. Walking boots, perhaps? Yet when did my mother ever go on a ramble? I take the lid off and discover that it doesn't contain shoes at all but what looks like a jumble of notebooks and letters.

'Put that back,' says Mother abruptly, pushing herself up from the edge of the bed where she was sitting to near standing position. 'They're private.'

I'm taken aback by her sudden change in mood. Of course, telling me not to look in the box piques my curiosity and encourages me to want to do so even more.

I put the lid back on but not before seeing the name Gemma stand out on one of the letters. 'What is in there?'

'I told you, it's private.'

I feel a surge of anger rise from the pit of my stomach.

'Don't you think that if there's something in there about

this family I have a right to know?' I fold my arms in a defensive position.

Her mouth opens wide like a goldfish's before saying, 'Once again, that box is private. My business. Now take off the clothes and I'll go in your room and sew the alterations. Go downstairs please.'

What am I, six years old?

I presume she tells me to go downstairs to stop me snooping when she's out of the room sewing. This time I decide not to pick an argument and sit on my anger until I can push it down firmly and lock it away. I change and put the shoeboxes back in the wardrobe where I found them on top of the 'private' box.

Downstairs I switch on the television. It's a wildlife documentary, but I barely watch it or listen to it. What's in the box? I vow to sneak in and find out in a couple of days' time when Mother is out at Aunty Lena's and has hopefully forgotten about our exchange of words. I'm fed up of secrets, there have been too many in my life. What is it that Mother is keeping from me? What will those letters tell me about Gemma?

On the television the roar of a female lion grabs my attention. She is killing her cubs, pouncing on them and tearing at their throats until they bleed profusely and stop struggling. The pictures are accompanied by a voiceover that remarks: 'Lionesses killing their cubs isn't that uncommon. Some mothers just aren't good at being mothers.'

~ 13 ~

Days pass and the chance to go into Mother's room to look in the box eludes me. Apart from for a GP appointment, which I accompany her to, Mother does not leave the house. Her bedroom door remains firmly closed. I make a mental note to speak to Aunty Lena alone when we go there on Sunday for dinner and encourage her to ask Mother to go out with her somewhere. Anywhere will do, just as long as I can get the house to myself. I won't invite Priti to come too as two of us snooping will make the whole situation more obvious.

Friday comes and it's the day for my evening date with Gareth. The day passes by in my usual routine and I leave a stew in the microwave for Mother to heat up and eat when I'm out. I then luxuriate in a hot bath and think about my date, Monday's interview and meeting with Ian.

I'm towelling myself down and applying body moisturiser in my bedroom when my mobile rings. I look at the screen. It's Shaun. This time I decide to answer; I'll have to speak to him sometime. I can't avoid him forever. There may be post at his house or something else practical to sort out.

I realise that there no longer is a churning sensation in my stomach when I think of him, nor am I scared I'll break down on the phone: cry, shout, or anything else that would make him believe he still has power over me. I take a deep breath, smile, then press the green button.

'Hello.'

'Annie? Finally I've got hold of you. It's Shaun.'

'Yes I know, your number came up on my phone.' My voice has an unnatural, happy, pleasant lilt, devoid of my usual edge but not quite of my trademark sarcasm.

'Are you OK? Have you got somewhere to live?'

'Yes, thank you.' He doesn't need to know the details. He's forfeited the right.

'Where are you? Are you still in Leeds?'

'No.' Again I'm playing my cards close to my flattish chest.

'Look, I was angry. I shouldn't have kicked you out. I thought I'd see you again but you left when I was at work. I'm sorry...'

There's a pause where he breaks off with a sigh and I say nothing.

He speaks again. 'I was so angry with you that you'd not trusted me. You made the decision to have an abortion all by yourself without even talking to me. It was my baby too. You didn't give me the chance to support you... I was furious. I'm still furious. But I shouldn't have told you to leave. Did you think I'd stop you getting rid of the baby?'

Right at this point my good intentions fly out of the window. Good cop takes a tea break and bad cop returns firmly to the fore.

'Angry? You're angry, are you? Enough to run straight into some blonde slapper's arms?'

'What?'

'You were seen down the pub. The abortion was just an excuse wasn't it to get rid of me and move on to the next woman you already had lined up. Stop playing the victim card, Shaun.'

'It's you who is waving the victim card, Annie. Twisting things so you come out of all this with a halo. You always did play the "poor me" act.'

His Irish accent is harder to decipher now as it always is when he is vexed.

'I haven't moved on to someone else. I met up with Soph, my ex, one night at the pub if that's what you're referring to. Mark was there, I guess he ran and told Priti. Yes, I fecking flirted. I was angry with you. We had a laugh, a hug, but that was it. So don't accuse me of something I haven't done.'

'Oh.' That truly blew the wind out of my accusation.

'The world is not against you, Annie. Why do you think you're so badly done to all the time? *You* made the decision to have the abortion without talking to me about it, without trusting me to support you. Couples are supposed to talk to each other, but no, you just went out on your own and completely ignored my existence.'

'I couldn't be a mum, I just couldn't be. I don't know how to play happy families. That was my decision, mine alone.'

'Come on, Annie, surely you can at least see why I'm angry.' His voice is lowering now. He pauses then carries on.

'Honestly, I didn't call for an argument. I just want to know how you are, if you're alright.'

'I'm doing OK, thanks.'

'Does it, does it still hurt? Was it painful?'

'It wasn't pleasant but I'm fine now. Look, I've got to go. Is there post or anything for me at yours I need to collect?'

'Just a bit. I've kept it for you.'

'I'll ask Priti to pick it up.'

'Is that all you've got to say? Asking about your post? Jesus. I'll put it by for Priti. You take care of yourself, Annie. I'm sorry things ended this way but they'd been going downhill before you did what you did.'

He obviously doesn't want me back. No romantic hearts and flowers endings here. No midnight dashes or declarations of undying love. This is Yorkshire, after all.

'Bye Shaun.'

Just before I disconnect the call I add: 'I'm sorry too.'

I hang up then curl into a ball and cry, cursing the world and swearing these will be the last tears I'll shed over him, the foetus, the loss of two years together, me wrongly thinking he'd moved straight on to another woman.

Afterwards, when my tears are all used up and I manage to compose myself, I plaster extra foundation on my face to cover the red eyes and blotches. I consider cancelling my date with Gareth but Priti's drunken words, that to get over a man you have to get under another, haunt me. I'm not going to sleep with him but a spot of flirting will be good for my ego.

I'd misjudged Shaun. Hard as it was, I had to admit to myself I did deserve some blame. I realise he was right when he said I'd not trusted him enough to tell him I was pregnant. I hadn't. My focus had been on me only. Perhaps if I had really loved Shaun then I would have discussed it with him first.

I tell myself I won't make the same mistake with Gareth,

or whoever my next boyfriend will be. Even if I'm taking the contraceptive pill I'll insist on using condoms to make double sure.

I pull on my best skinny jeans and, taking a leaf out of Priti's book, a brightly-coloured tunic. With a dash of lipstick I'm ready to go.

Downstairs, Mother is reading a book on the sofa whilst the television chatters away in the background. How can she concentrate with both competing for her attention? She looks up to see me when I walk into the lounge and smiles. 'You look lovely. I hope you have a good time tonight.'

'I will do. Have you got everything you need? There's a stew in the microwave.'

'Thank you. I'll be fine. Take care of yourself coming home. Don't walk back – make sure you get a taxi. Be safe.' She struggles to her feet using her narrow arm and vein-lined hand to push herself up from the sofa and picks up her handbag that's lying beside it. Out of her purse she gives me £20. I hesitate in taking it but then realise I haven't got the cash myself to pay for a cab home. Despite my usual going Dutch principles I'm banking on Gareth paying for me tonight. I don't want the embarrassment of my credit card being declined. I had considered driving but parking would cost a lot anyway and on a first date I could really do with a drink.

I thank her, and she appears pleased that I've accepted the money. 'I promise I'll get a taxi home. You'll probably be in bed by the time I get back. See you tomorrow.'

With that I pick up my denim jacket and leave the house, shutting the front door with a firm thump. Fortunately, I don't have to pass Reg's house to walk to the bus stop as it's in the opposite direction.

The bus arrives late but it's not too busy: most workers have made it home by now and the party-goers have yet to travel into town. I get on and sit next to a careworn-looking older woman with three plastic bags full of shopping at her feet. Some teenagers at the back of the bus are laughing and making fun of each other, causing the lady next to me to press herself closer to the window to distance herself from their bawdy chatter.

Twenty slow minutes later, after five stops, it's finally time for me to get off. I ring the bell and dash to the door. As soon as I do, the woman puts her plastic bags on the seat I've just vacated as to form a physical barrier between her and the teenagers.

I checked the way before I came out and it's only a short walk to Alexandro's. I'm enjoying the slight nip in the air and looking at the turning shades of brown on the trees' leaves, the oaks having been planted decades ago to bring a smidgen of the countryside into this urban area.

It's getting busier now and harder to keep my fast walking pace going. The volume of people moving at different speeds makes going quickly more difficult. In particular, in front of me there's a blonde woman wearing a yellow rain mac taking up most of the width of the pavement. She's pushing a buggy and pulling along another child, who looks about seven, on her right side. Impatience at her blocking my way and then déjà vu hit me. She looks familiar. There's something about her. A car beeps its horn and she looks behind her to see where the noise is coming from. When doing so, her blonde, streaked locks brush against her chin. Her hair is cut in a neat bob. What is it about her hair that's prompting me to try and remember something? After an oncoming car has gone past I step onto the road to overtake her and catch a glimpse of her heavily-made up face. The answer pings into my head and I gasp as it does. Thankfully she doesn't see as I'm now in front of her and am regaining my usual pace.

She looks like Olivia, the girl with the plaits from school. Suddenly I can't wait to get away. Recognising her has unnerved me and is an unwanted link to my past. To her I'm still the bully who pulled a clump of her hair out. She doesn't know the new me and I intend to keep it that way.

At the speed I'm walking it doesn't take me long to reach Alexandro's. It's on a street corner and has a huge glass window beckoning passing customers to go in. By the door there's a crate full of vegetables on display and I wonder whether they are real or plastic. Plastic, I assume – in this neighbourhood at night anything fresh would soon be nicked.

Through the window I can see Gareth sitting at a table for two at the side of the restaurant. He has swapped his previous jeans and long-sleeved T-shirt combo for brown chinos and a white shirt that's unbuttoned at the collar. He's made an effort. In front of the him on the table are a bottle of Italian beer and a large glass of white. For me, I hope.

He looks up as I approach and grins in my direction, standing up and waving at the seat opposite him to tell me to sit down. I kiss him on the cheek awkwardly, then sit down, placing my jacket on the back of the seat and my handbag under the table. I'm pleased to see him again.

There's a small sheen of sweat on his forehead. I think

he's nervous. Funnily enough that makes me feel a bit nervous too. I force myself to put this evening's phone call with Shaun out of my mind and concentrate on the here, now and the man who is raising his bottle in my direction.

'Cheers!' I say, clinking my wine glass against his bottle. I take a quick sip. It's dry yet citrusy and very palatable. Gareth certainly hadn't chosen the cheapest on the wine list.

'It's good to see you again. Thank you for coming.' he says with a slight falter to his voice. He really is nervous. Perhaps he hasn't dated much since his divorce.

'Pleasure. Looks like you've made a good choice of restaurant. Lovely wine by the way.' We make some small talk about how our days were – of course I didn't tell him about the conversation with Shaun – though I do tell him about the healthcare assistant bank interview on Monday. He responds with a tale about the shenanigans in the store today, when a security guard chased a shoplifter around the aisles, and congratulates me on my good news.

'It's just an entry-level job but it could lead on to something better. They provide training. If I don't get it then I'll need to find something else quickly.'

'We're recruiting soon for extra seasonal staff over the festive period. I could put a word in if you want me to.'

'Thanks, that's good to know. We'll see how it goes.'

The waiter comes over with the menus and hovers whilst we decide what to eat. Gareth opts for a starter so I do too, followed by a pizza. My first choice would have been spaghetti carbonara but on a first date I didn't want to be sucking up spaghetti and dripping sauce down my chin like a toddler.

We exchange more small talk and I find myself relaxing, probably helped by the glass of wine I've drunk. He tells me he plays football at the weekends and enjoys cooking Indian food. He was the chef in the house when he was married and since they split he was determined not to slip into a lazy habit of reaching for microwavable ready meals for one. 'I might sell them but God knows I wouldn't eat that slop,' he jokes.

Starter over and another round of drinks ordered I move the conversation on to our discussion at the pub. 'Thanks for telling me about Toby Smith. I rang the police to tell them but they said I need a solicitor's request in writing for them to investigate further.'

'Are you going to do it?' he asks, balancing a dripping piece of lasagne on his fork.

'Yes. I've got an appointment on Monday, actually, after my interview. It's quite a coincidence. I did an internet search for solicitors and found that a guy I was friends with at school has his own practice not far away.'

Was it a trick of the light or did I see a slight glower on his face when I mentioned another man?

'He set it up with his wife a few years back,' I add.

The glower disappears.

'Great. If I can help with anything just ask. I'm sorry I can't remember anything more about Gemma.'

'That's OK. I did track down the Mike fella you mentioned, though. He's an accountant now and couldn't wait to get me off the phone when I mentioned my sister. Very odd.'

Gareth furrowed his brow. 'That's weird. I had the impression they were good friends.'

'He denied it. Said he hardly knew her.'

'Perhaps I was wrong.'

'Or perhaps he's lying,' I counteract.

We carry on eating in amiable silence. When we've both finished he pipes up, 'So Annie Towcester, are you good at making breakfast?'

That surprises me. Is he hinting or expecting payment in kind for the meal? He hadn't struck me as that sort of bloke.

Not sure how to take his comment, I laugh. 'I've got to get back tonight to check on my mother. Do you remember I told you she's being treated for cancer?'

Gareth looks embarrassed. 'Oh God, yes, of course. I'm sorry to hear about your mother. I wasn't suggesting, I mean it would be lovely to spend the night with you, but I wasn't implying, it's a bit soon, I was trying to make a joke about your surname. Toaster.'

It all becomes clear. 'Ah, right.' I flash him a cheeky smile. 'I'll believe you. Thousands wouldn't. It's Towcester by the way.' I pronounce the syllable tow as in ow with a double-you followed by sester. 'Nothing to do with kitchen appliances.'

He chuckles and raises both his palms in front of me. 'You've caught me out. My dreadful sense of humour.'

'I've heard much worse before. And had people breaking into the song "Tomorrow" when they hear my first name. Please don't inflict that on me.'

We both laugh.

The evening carries on with dessert and another round of drinks. As the cliché goes, the time really does pass quickly. I'm enjoying myself immensely and can't remember the last time I had this good a first date. The longer I spend in his company, the more attractive I find him.

The restaurant turns its lights up as a reminder to customers that it's near closing time. Gareth offers to pay and I mumble something about reciprocating when I've got a job. He says he'll hold me to it as he'd love to see me again, but doesn't want to wait until I'm gainfully employed.

He walks me to the taxi rank and kisses me briefly on the lips before I get in a cab, leaving me wanting more. I wave until the taxi drives out of sight of him.

Back at the house, I let myself in what I think is quietly after drinking a bottle of wine. Mother is asleep upstairs. With my flush of post-date adrenaline, I'm so very tempted to sneak into her room and see what's in the box in the wardrobe whilst she's asleep. What stops me is knowing that if she wakes up and catches me I may never get another chance.

I climb into the single bed and, for the first time in a long, long time, go to sleep feeling something akin to happiness.

~ 14 ~

At Aunty Lena's on Sunday I don't get a chance to speak to her alone. As soon as mother and I arrive for food, she ushers us into the warm kitchen and there we stay until the delicious roast chicken meal has been eaten, coffee served and drunk and it's time to leave. Lena doesn't pick up on any of my hints to take a walk in the garden and I can't even follow her when she goes to the loo because Den won't stop asking genial questions about my date (which my gossipy mother let slip) and my interview tomorrow. When will I have the house to myself?

I ask Aunty Lena when she and Mother have another girls' night planned. Mother then invites Lena around to our house to watch a DVD, saying that as the nights are getting colder she doesn't much like going outside unless she has to. I wonder whether the real reason is that she doesn't want to give me a chance to snoop?

That evening, Mother and I sit in front of a period drama on the television, a Victorian story I vaguely remember from the school English lessons I actually turned up to, then when the news comes on I make my excuses for an early night. I want to make sure I feel fresh and alert tomorrow for my interview.

After going to the bathroom I can still hear the television on downstairs. I check my watch and there are still ten minutes of the news bulletin left to go: or maybe seven if Mother skips the sport at the end. Feeling emboldened, I take my chance and creep into her bedroom without turning the light on, gingerly open the wardrobe doors and crouch down to open the infamous shoebox.

Except it's not there.

Only nine shoeboxes are stacked up at the bottom of the wardrobe. I look through them as quickly as possible and all they contain is footwear. The box with the notebooks and letters has gone.

There's not enough time for me to check the rest of the wardrobe and chest of drawers. I close mother's bedroom door with about two minutes to spare before I hear her switching the television off and padding slowly up the stairs.

Where has she put the box and what is in it that she doesn't want me to see?

That night it takes me a long time to get to sleep because my brain won't shut out all the thoughts boxing each other in my head. I have a classic anxiety dream where I climb a stepladder to reach the box but fall from the top; Gemma is at the bottom but, instead of trying to catch me, she turns her back and walks away. I wake up gasping for air just before I hit the ground.

Poor slumber means I oversleep and am in a grump for most of the morning. My mood does not improve after I've put on my interview outfit – the kitten heels remind me of the missing shoebox – and when I see myself in the mirror wearing the black suit I think it will be obvious to the interviewers that I'm an imposter. Even the bus journey to the hospital takes longer than it should due to roadworks.

To my surprise, despite my low spirits, the interview actually isn't too bad. Although I haven't had any care work experience, I talk about looking after my cancer-stricken mother, leaving out the fact it has barely been for over a week, and give lots of examples of working with customers. Thanks to an hour's free internet access at the library on Saturday, I'd done my research and dropped in some details about the NHS trust and current political issues affecting healthcare in general.

The panel, a friendly-enough trio comprising an HR manager, the manager of the healthcare assistant bank and a Ward Sister from orthopaedics, say they'll let me know in the next day or so. I treat myself afterwards to a chocolate bar from the vending machine to raise my energy levels before catching two more buses to Wilson & Zedda.

Their office is located in a small but smart building on the ground floor of an office block that contains four different businesses. I head to Wilson & Zedda's coolly-designed reception, decorated in different shades of grey that contrast with the dark green of a huge yucca plant in the corner, and tell the receptionist that I have an appointment to see Ian Zedda.

She leads me to the second door on the right and ushers me in where I find Ian sitting in an electric wheelchair behind the desk.

'Annie! Come here, bend down and give me a kiss. I won't tell my wife,' he jests. I'm aware his speech is slightly slurred, something I'd forgotten, as when I was a child I had become completely used to it.

I do as he asks and kiss him warmly on the cheek, also giving him a friendly squeeze on the shoulder. He beckons me to take a seat on the other side of the desk.

'How lovely to see you again after all these years!' he enthuses. 'I often wondered where life took you. What have you been doing?'

I cross my legs. 'Nothing exciting. I lived in Leeds for fourteen years but came back recently because my mother's got cancer.'

'Your mother?' He raises his eyebrows. He obviously remembers my fraught relationship with her.

'Yes. Kidney cancer.'

'I'm sorry to hear that, but am glad it's brought you back.' Good old Ian.

'And you? I know you're a solicitor and you're married – congratulations – anything else to report?'

Ian shakes his head. 'No kids, yet, just work, work, work. It's early days but the business is doing well and takes up most of our time. It's our baby. I have a wonderful wife.'

'Is it difficult living and working together?' I question.

'Not really, we enjoy it. Most of the time we hardly see each other during the day anyway because we have our own clients. In the evening it's great being able to talk about work with someone who understands it all.'

'Well, your office is certainly impressive.'

'Glad you think so, it cost enough to deck out. We wanted to look the part. How can I help you solicitor-wise?'

Pulling my chair a little closer to his desk, I explain about Gemma, Toby Smith and my phone call with DI Glass. Ian listens intently and prompts me for a few more details.

'I'm so sorry that your sister is still missing. With my solicitor hat on I have to advise you that after such a long time it's very, very unlikely Gemma will be found alive.'

I look down at my kitten heels. 'I know. But if Toby Smith had anything to do with her disappearance I want to find out.'

'I understand. I'll certainly write a letter, free of charge for an old friend. I'll write it tomorrow. I'll need your address please and the date Gemma went missing.'

I tell him and he speaks the details into a Dictaphone.

Work talk finished, he says, 'You know, I did look once on Facebook but couldn't find you. I assumed you'd got married and changed your surname.'

I waggle the bare fingers of my left hand in front of him. 'No husband, no name change. I've never bothered with social media. I like a bit of anonymity.' I specifically never registered with Twitter or Facebook and the like because I don't want to be found. Once, around the twentieth anniversary of Gemma going missing, a journalist tracked me down who wanted to rake up the past for some maudlin piece about how the family was coping. I gave him short shrift and sent him on his way but the experience worried me and made me more convinced than ever not to leave a digital footprint. He'd apparently found me because my name was listed on the website of the company I was then working for, they were big on trying to appear as if their staff were your new best friends and not trying to fleece you out of your spare cash to buy an insurance product you don't need. I swiftly resigned, moved on to another firm and changed my personal email address to my first name and four numbers.

Towcester is a recognisable surname. With hindsight, I should have changed it by deed poll, but I'm too broke at the moment to do so.

'Jen and I are having a party at home on Saturday night to celebrate her birthday. Do come along, bring a plus one if you'd like to. I've told Jen lots about you and she wants to meet you. It'll be fun.'

'I'd like that.' I wonder whether to invite Gareth along. It'd be a cheap way for me to reciprocate his hospitality last Friday night. Since then we've exchanged numerous flirtatious texts and I'm due to meet him for a drink tomorrow evening.

'Great. I'll email you the address. Come anytime from 7.30 p.m. You don't need to bring bottle – we'll get plenty of wine and beer in.'

With that we say our goodbyes. I leave his office much lighter and spritelier than I did when I left the house that morning. Fingers crossed that his letter will do the trick and the police will agree to question Toby Smith in prison.

I decide against calling Mike Braithwaite again because it's doubtful he will have done a 180-degree turnaround and agree to help. Instead I think again of the photo on the pinboard and Gemma's room and have an idea. The girl in the group snap, the one with the long black skirt and frizzy perm, who is she? Would there be any 1989 class lists online or some other way of tracking her down? Maybe Gareth will recognise her? On the bus home I call Priti and rope her in to help me find out. She's more than willing.

Perhaps finding this girl could be the key.

~ 15 ~

I'm late for my drink with Gareth on Tuesday because Mother has a bout of vomiting and I want to make sure she's OK before I leave the house. Aunty Lena agrees to come round and sit with her whilst I go out, insisting that I shouldn't cancel my date.

I hadn't even thought about doing so but I wasn't going to confess that to Lena. Instead, I thank her for mother-sitting and, as soon as she has set foot in the house, dash off to the pub where Gareth and I are due to meet.

I expected a busy, booming bar aimed at young professional workers to con them out of their wages after a stressful day by charging exorbitant amounts for the latest fashionable concoctions. What I find instead is a quaint, old-fashioned pub with a roaring fire and gastro-menu.

This time we kiss on the lips for a few seconds when we meet and I run my palm down his back, feeling the taut muscles under his shirt. He has already ordered and once again there's a large, chilled glass of white wine waiting for me.

It's much less awkward than the beginning of last Friday's date. Firstly, he asks me all about how the interview went. I did text him yesterday filling him in on the bare bones but today he wants a full breakdown. As part of his supermarket manager job he often interviews potential employees. After I give him a blow-by-blow account of what was said he comes to the conclusion that I've done well and that if they'd decided I was wrong for the job they wouldn't have kept me talking for a full forty-five minutes.

'They haven't called today, though,' I say. I must have checked my mobile phone a thousand times between the hours of 9 a.m. and 5.30 p.m.

'Didn't they say it would be a couple of days?'

'They said "in the next day or so".'

'So maybe "so" day will be Wednesday.' Gareth takes my hand and entwines his fingers between mine. I catch his eye and smile, enjoying the pressure of his fingers on mine and the casual intimacy.

'I wondered if you'd like to go to a party with me on Saturday? The old friend I told you about, Ian, the solicitor, invited me to his wife's birthday do. Do you fancy it?'

'I fancy it and you,' he replies, goofing around.

I raise my eyebrows in what I hope is a flirtatious manner rather than a gargoyle impression. 'Good. Friday night it is then.'

'I've got a store meeting on Friday afternoon but it shouldn't run over. There's an unwritten rule that, unless there's an emergency, Friday nights are sacred if you're not rostered on. I'll pick you up.'

'Thanks.' That'll save me the bus fare.

'Did Ian agree to write the letter to the police?'

I pick up my drink with my left hand, not wanting to pull away from Gareth's grasp in my right. 'He did. He texted me this afternoon actually and said he'd written it today. Here's hoping it does the job.'

'Are you going to call DI Glass to tell him?'

'In a couple of days. I want to leave enough time for the letter to arrive first. Oh, I've just remembered.' This time I do pull my hand away from his and instantly miss the warmth of his fingers. I use both hands to dig around inside my handbag and pull out a colour photocopy I made at the library on Saturday. It's the photograph of Gemma, Mike, Toby and the mystery girl. I show Gareth the piece of paper. 'This is a copy of the photograph I found in Gemma's room.'

'She's still got a room?'

I roll my eyes. 'Don't ask. Long story. I've worked out the two boys are Mike and Toby. Do you know who the girl is?'

Gareth picks the paper up and holds it nearer to his eyes to get a closer look. He takes his time scrutinising it. 'Well, you're right, Toby is the blonde boy and Mike is the one looking at Gemma. The girl? I'm not sure. She looks familiar but I can't quite place her.'

'Do you know if there was a leaver's yearbook or there's anywhere I might be able to find a class list?'

'She might not be in their class,' Gareth replies. 'She could be a friend from outside school.'

My heart sinks. I hadn't considered that.

'But see the bench they're sitting on and the huge tree behind it? That's the woods behind the playing fields. Did you go to the same secondary school as Gemma and me?'

'Yes but by the time I got there the school had relocated to a new purpose-built site. Wasn't the old one built in Victorian times? It had asbestos so the council knocked it down and built a housing estate on the land.'

'They did, I'd forgotten I'm a bit older than you.'

I grin. 'Best not start comparing children's TV programme memories. We'll have no shared cultural references.'

'Hey, I'm not so old as to have watched Muffin the Mule,' he says in mock high dudgeon.

'Not even Bill and Ben, the Flowerpot Men?' That's one my father told me about from his childhood.

'Cheeky. That's definitely the park behind our old school. The bench was a popular hang-out after hours when there was nothing else better to do. If she's there it's odds on the girl in the photo went to the same school.'

Gareth goes to the bar and comes back with another round of drinks. His face looks animated as he tells me excitedly, 'I've had an idea. On social media there's a closed, invitation only group for people who went to our school. It was set up to organise a reunion. I only signed up for the group for my year but I can see if I can get access to the one for Gemma's. The girl in the photo may have joined it.'

'Great idea!' I say and, without thinking it through first, throw my arms around him, knocking his elbow and causing him to spill some of the beer he's holding in his hand. It drips on to his black, shiny shoe. 'You owe me a beer,' he says with a happy smirk.

'I think you're earned one,' I reply.

The evening rushes by in a way time at work never does and I have to leave relatively early to go home and relieve Aunty Lena. Gareth takes me home in a taxi – giving us time for a smooch in the back – before carrying on in it to go home himself, even though my house is out of his way. The taxi drops me off a couple of houses too early because someone has parked a huge great van outside Mother's house, meaning that if the taxi stopped there it would be blocking the road.

We share a long kiss goodbye and Gareth promises to call soon to firm up the plans for Friday. I'm too busy thinking of him to realise that I have to walk past Reg's house. I shiver but not because of the evening chill. The light is on in the upstairs bedroom illuminating the torso and head and shoulders of Reg staring down at me. He opens the window and calls out, 'Annie!'

I ignore him and rush to the front door. In a kerfuffle I drop my keys and bang on the door whilst I fall to my knees and try and find them in the dark. I've only just picked them up when Aunty Lena answers the door. 'Annie, what's wrong?'

Pushing my way inside I usher her in, slam the door shut – with no thought that Mother is probably asleep – walk through to the lounge, shutting the connecting door firmly as well, and collapse on the coach.

'What is it dear? What's happened?' Lena wrinkles her nose with concern and reaches out to me.

I lower my voice, finally remembering my mother upstairs. 'It's Reg. He keeps watching me when I go past his house. He was upstairs by his bedroom window and shouted down at me. He frightened me, he really gives me the creeps.'

'Oh thank goodness that's all it is,' says Lena, sitting down next to me on the sofa and pulling me into a hug.

'What do you mean that's all it is?' I reply incredulously. 'His is not normal behaviour. You don't call out at night to a woman on her own.'

Lena gasps. 'You didn't walk home alone did you at this time of night?' The clock on the mantelpiece says it's 10.45.

'No, Gareth dropped me off in a taxi but there's a van right outside the house so it parked a few doors down.' I'm still cross about her reaction.

Lena lets me go, takes my hand and looks me in the eye.

'Reg is a drunk. Someone ought to do something about it but his wife and son don't want anything to do with him. He's got a reputation for being a nuisance when he's had too many, which is probably most of the time. He's harmless enough, though. Try not to let him get to you. Ignore him and walk on.'

'Why are you being so easy on him?'

She chooses her words carefully. 'Sorry, Annie, I thought you were going to say that your date had hurt you. God forbid. I suppose I'm used to Reg being the local weirdo. I remember who he used to be when he was married and his son was young – he was such a fun, lively, gentle man. If he bothers you again let me know and I'll go and talk to him.'

'I will do.' Still a bit disgruntled, I change the subject. 'Is Mother asleep?'

'Yes. I managed to get her to drink some water and she kept it down. It might be worth you ringing the doctor's surgery tomorrow to mention what's happened. It may be a reaction to the drugs she's on.'

'OK. You go home now, Lena. Thanks for coming.'

She puts her coat on, kisses me goodbye and leaves the house to walk the very short distance to her own.

I wonder if Reg watches *her* walk down the street.

When I go upstairs to go to bed myself I look outside

and see a glow in the road to the right that's coming from his bedroom window.

In the safety of my own room, I relax and feel a bit of a twit for how I've reacted. Aunty Lena has a good point: Reg is a sad old harmless alcoholic who probably just wants someone to talk to. Everyone else on the street has given up on him. He must see me as a face who remembers the old him, before he turned into a walking can of Special Brew. I shouldn't be scared of him, I should pity him, maybe even try to encourage him to join an alcohol support group if he hasn't already. Perhaps I can pick up some leaflets for Reg from the hospital next time I'm there. If I want to work with lots of different kinds of people with various illnesses I'm going to have to toughen up a bit.

My mind drifts back to the couple of acquaintances I had in the Leeds social group who spectacularly fell by the wayside. Who knows? There but for the grace of God go I.

~ 16 ~

I'm in the middle of eating my breakfast when I get the call from the hospital offering me the job. It's a zero-hours contract that the HR manager explains will entail me filling in for permanent staff's annual and sick leave. At the moment that suits me fine because it means I can turn down any shifts that clash with taking Mother to the hospital. There will be training sessions on the job that will lead to my earning a vocational qualification in health and social care. The hospital runs day-long induction sessions once a month, she says, and the next one is in two days' time. Would I mind attending that? Once new employees have completed their induction they can be called on anytime to work.

Will I attend? Will I ever. Mother doesn't have any doctor's appointments that day. They'll pay me for the induction – finally I'll be earning some cash again. I don't want to have to wait until next month's induction day to start work.

The woman asks me to bring along my passport, P45 and bank details to the induction day to speed things up. I'll be given my staff uniform then. She hangs up and I do a little victory dance round the kitchen, with toast hanging out of my mouth and a cup of coffee in one hand.

Two days later, after I've taken Mother to see her GP to discuss her sickness episode, the good news keeps on coming. DI Glass calls me to tell me that Ian's solicitor's letter has arrived. After speaking to me originally, DI Glass explained the situation to his DCI, giving her a heads up. The Chief Commissioner immediately passed the solicitor's letter on to her when it arrived and, whether it be for PR purposes or because she thinks it's a genuine new lead, gave her permission for DI Glass to interview Toby Smith in prison.

Gareth texts me back a big thumbs-up sign and Priti is ecstatic when I call her with the news. She's much easier to get hold of in the day than Gareth is what with his high-up management job. 'That's fantastic!' she gushes. 'That man is going down – again!' I don't point out that maybe Smith had nothing whatsoever to do with Gemma's disappearance because I don't want to break the good mood.

When I was a young child I was good at hiding in shadows, pressing my back against the wall with hot breaths held in so as not to make a noise. It was this way that I picked up on pieces of information the adults didn't tell me, them thinking that I was too young and stupid to make sense of snatched words, secret visitors and the heavy atmosphere in the house that pressed down on all of us unbearably. I'd be told to go upstairs/outside to play or be given a packet of sweets as if brightly-coloured sugar could cure all the ills in the world. Here, have a lemon sherbet and go away, this is adult time, not for your ears. I'd suck the sweet so as to savour the taste as long as possible and secrete myself somewhere, being careful to wait until the sherbet tickled my tongue and not give in to temptation to crunch its saccharine surroundings, and listen in, hugging my knees to fold myself up as small as I could to go unnoticed.

Sometimes the adults thought they were talking quietly but their voices would become louder, more animated, and from where I was hiding, behind the sofa, on the stairs or wedged in between the staircase alcove and the telephone table, I could make out snippets, my ears keened to pick out words I could recognise. Now and then different people, the police lady, the neighbour from down the road, or the tall man with thick black glasses whom I didn't recognise when he came in the house, said the same things even though they contradicted themselves, such as, 'It's the not knowing that's worst,' and, 'No news is good news'. I'd sit there in my hidey-hole until I got cramp or needed a wee, at which point I had to show myself. When I did, nobody seemed to care where I'd been. The return of my presence would barely raise an eyebrow and I'd soon be swatted aside like an annoying black fly to leave the room and the adults to it.

One day in the holidays when Father was out, summer was at its peak and Mother had one of her visitors, I crept out of the house with a Kit Kat and can of Coke stolen from the fridge. There was a four-pack in there for Gemma and Father said I was too young to drink it: if I did my teeth would turn black and fall out. Our garden is long and narrow with a gate at the bottom leading on to the snicket that runs along the back of all the houses on our side of the street. The patch of back garden nearest to the kitchen window was laid out as a lawn, on top of which stood the mucky white rotary washing line, and by each fence next to the grass was a flower border, now looking unruly with weeds fighting the faded flowers that needed deadheading for precedence. Behind that were Father's bountiful vegetable patches, laced with potatoes, carrots and runner beans, and further back still his greenhouse containing numerous red-fruited tomato plants.

I let myself in to the greenhouse, bathed in the reflected sun and picked some of the small, bright red tomatoes, feeling the pressure of their skin resisting my teeth as I bit in and released their delectable juiciness. Father usually picked them as soon as they were ripe but now the green stems were hunched over with their abundance of fruit and their leaves, deprived of water, were turning crepey and brown. I picked as many as I could, counting each one as I went, and shut them inside the greenhouse in a pile.

Behind the greenhouse there's an apple tree whose boughs hang over a shady patch of concreted path next to the back fence. I knew from watching my father go down the garden from my bedroom window that whoever stands behind the tree can't be seen from the house. To shelter from the sun I sat there, hearing footsteps and voices in the back alley and drinking my fizzy pop for what seemed like hours. The chocolate soon melted when I unwrapped it from its silver foil in my palm. I licked it off hungrily for my tummy was complaining about, apart from the tomatoes, not having had any other food since a bowl of Frosties at breakfast.

Someone would notice I'd gone and come and find me for tea, surely?

Eventually I must have dozed off, for when I was awoken by an apple dropping off the tree and missing my head by a few centimetres the bright daylight was gone, replaced by a languid dusk. The sun fading low on the horizon had let in a nippy breeze that fluttered amongst the leaves above my head. I didn't have a cardigan with me. In the musty shade under the tree I felt chilly and alone. It must have been well past my bedtime and I began to cry, feeling scared and wanting the comfort of my bed and the soft teddy bear hiding within it. It wasn't yet too dark for me to find my way back to the house so I ran into the back door and threw it open only to be greeted by silence. On the clock in the kitchen the big hand was at twelve and the little hand pointed to nine. No lights were on, I couldn't quite reach the switch anyway, but I knew my home well enough to be able to run upstairs in the shadows.

On the landing, Mother's bedroom door was open far enough for me to peer in. She was sprawled on top of her bed, fully clothed in a yellow summer dress, snoring quietly.

She hadn't even noticed *I* was missing.

Half-sobbing and half-snivelling, I put myself to bed on an empty stomach, still wearing my white patent leather buckled sandals that chafed against the back of my heel. I only realised I had forgotten to take them off when I woke in the morning and saw a smear of grass and soil across the tangled bed sheet.

When Aunty Lena came the next day to take me to the park she helped me change clothes, stripped my bed with a look but not a word, and bundled the laundry into the washing machine. Father had gone to work – later I overheard Mother shouting something at him about a pub and beer – and Mother was still locked away in her room.

In the park, Aunty Lena bought me a Mr Whippy ice cream from the van parked by the entrance. Whilst I bit into the chocolate flake and licked the creamy drips from the side of the cone she explained that Mother was very sad at the moment. The police came to tell her yesterday that the sighting of Gemma in London a member of the public had told them about turned out not to be her, and that I needed to be a big girl for my mummy who loved me very much.

I was five.

So many sightings, so many leads that led to nothing, so many members of the public who thought they were being helpful but just raised and then dashed hope. Should I have raked it all up again? Was I right to have got involved, breaking my decades-old policy of staying well clear?

At the back of my mind also is the dark thought – if the police do find proof that Gemma was murdered, apart from my having closure from solving the mystery, would I really care?

Thursday 4th May 1989. 8.50 a.m.

Diana and Annie hovered by the school gates where other mothers kissed their children, told them to eat all their school dinners and chatted with each other about the minutiae of parenthood.

Diana deliberately stood apart from them. Although she'd made a specific point to remember to wear a jacket and make Annie put on her light summer coat, Diana looked down with horror to see that protruding from her feet were the fluffy bedroom slippers she'd put on this morning when she got out of bed. The other mothers were looking, gossiping, too polite to say something to her face but not too polite to bad mouth her to each other. Diana could see them whispering. Laughing. She's the mad mother, the bad mother, the one who hardly ever brings her child to school and when she does doesn't get dressed properly. She could feel her anxiety levels rising, clutching hold of her, pushing near to her limit. She cracked her knuckles to centre herself, bring her back to the present moment, and clutched her handbag close. Her pills were in there. She was safe: it doesn't matter if she has to take more than the doctor had told her to, the pills would block out the world and give her a slow-motion kind of peace. A few minutes more, then she would be back home.

A voice interrupted her ritual. 'Diane, long time no see. How are you?' Diana froze. She thought the brown-haired, stocky woman talking to her and who got her name wrong was the parent of a boy in the same class as Annie. They'd come across each other in the maternity ward after giving birth within a day of each other.

'Hello!' she replied, rather too brightly, her voice an octave too high, her eyes shiny and glassy.

'Can I go in now?' Annie asked. She was standing a foot away. Diana was conscious that Annie wasn't holding her hand like most of the other little girls did with their mums. She'd tried to take Annie's hand when they had left the house but Annie had swiftly pulled it away as if her mother was too hot to touch. Was it possible to scald your own daughter with your presence? She'd certainly done enough scolding of her over the years.

'It's time to go in, nice to see the kids keen to get to school, isn't it? My Johnnie went through a phase of crying when it was time to walk here.' That's because you're a good mother, thought Diana. Your son doesn't want to leave you. My daughters can't wait to get away.

Diana forced a smile on her face. She curled the edges of her lips unnaturally. 'Yes, it's good they like school. Go in, Annie, don't keep your teacher waiting. I have to get back home.' Annie bolted towards the playground without looking behind her. Diana broke eye contact with Johnnie's mother and scurried off back down the road, head down, adamant to avoid the whispers, the looks and the judgements she felt sure were raining down on her. She counted every step it took to take her back to her house. Three hundred and forty-five.

In the safety of her home, behind the locked front door,

the curtains closed, she began to feel a little soothed, aided somewhat by the little white pill she washed down with a glass of milk. Diana sat down on the sofa. She shut her eyes and timed her breaths to coincide with the ticking of the carriage clock on the mantelpiece. Tick, breathe in, tock, tick, breathe out, tock. Her heart began to beat less erratically but her mind was still in deep distress.

She had hit her child, her darling eldest daughter, and didn't know if she would, should or could be forgiven. Her youngest had flinched under her touch. How could she repair this, be the mother she wanted to be and that the girls deserved? A headache began to rear up behind her temples. Her pain was physical. Elaine was due to pick Annie up from school this afternoon as per usual. The thought occurred to Diana that she could ring Elaine and say she'll go instead. Show Annie she cares. Ask about her day and maybe stop off at the ice cream café on the way home, but, but… Diana felt so tired. The simple act of moving her limbs seemed to forsake her. Within moments she was asleep, her cheek pressed against the piping of the sofa cushion causing a red dented line to appear.

~ 17 ~

DI Glass calls to say that he has arranged with the prison to interview Toby Smith on Friday morning. It's an informal interview, he stresses, and Smith is under no obligation to co-operate.

If he knows anything and has a smidgeon of decency then he will tell DI Glass, I hope, but then speedily acknowledge that convicted attempted murderers aren't usually renowned for their public spiritedness.

My job induction focuses my mind on other things for a day. It's an eight-hour whirlwind of tea, biscuits, forms to fill in, presentations from staff, a whistle-stop tour of the hospital and videos about basic hygiene and health and safety. The others attending are a mixed bunch of university leavers, career changers and two mums (plus a dad) who are returning to work now their children are school age. There's so much information to take in that we confide in each other we'll never remember it all; but by the end of the day there's a great sense of camaraderie amongst us, other than the man in his twenties who didn't return after the lunch break, and I'm looking forward to starting the job for real. Even the polyester uniform isn't too bad.

Looking forward to going to work is pretty much a first

for me. Usually I have to haul my carcass out of bed and bribe myself with wine and chocolate later on to make it to the call centre on time. Every work day brought the Monday morning blues.

I'm so knackered from the day's full concentration that I pick up a couple of pizzas on the way home instead of cooking. In the kitchen I load all the slices onto one plate then carry them through to the lounge, along with a couple of sheets of kitchen roll for napkins and two side plates, where Mother is reading a magazine. Whilst we are eating she asks me lots of questions about the day and seems genuinely pleased at my enthusiasm. She asks me how long I'm planning to stay and I realise that it's not something I've thought through, what with not knowing how long her cancer treatment will take or how well she will recover. If she does that is. It strikes me that I've found it much easier to treat her as a sick adult in need of help rather than my mother, firmly delineating the past from the present.

I still have nowhere else to go but living here hasn't been as bad as I'd imagined. Then I remember the missing box, the secrets she is keeping from me and once again I feel like an angry, frustrated teenager. I tell Mother I don't know how long I'll be here but that I'll pay her rent when I'm earning if that's what she wants. At that she looks hurt and I almost feel guilty for saying it.

I reach for the television controller that's perched on the sofa arm by my side and press the on button, shutting off the possibility of any further conversation.

Whilst Mother watches a game show, my thoughts turn to Gareth, our date at the party tomorrow, and whether he has had luck with his social media hunt for the frizzy-haired girl on the photo. Priti texted to say that as yet she hadn't found anything out about her. It occurs to me that the girl may have moved away or even be dead herself.

As promised, Gareth picks me up on Saturday evening in his fancy grey company car and greets me with a lingering kiss. I'm wearing my skinny faux leather black trousers and a long silky-grey top. It's a tried-and-tested outfit that always gives me confidence, something I feel I need after spending the morning wondering how DI Glass's interview with Smith went. Seeing Gareth again makes me wish I were free to go home with him tonight instead of having to get back to check on Mother. No way will I invite him back to my single bed that's only a few flimsy walls away from Mother's room. For me, knowing my mother can hear everything we get up to is the ultimate passion killer.

Gareth draws me into his arms and I sink in quickly, breathing in the comforting smell of his warm, spicy aftershave. I'm hesitant to pull away but I bolt apart when, over his shoulder, I see Reg staring down at us from his upstairs window. When he spots that I've noticed him he waves, stony-faced. There's still something about him that gives me the creeps, but then I think of Aunty Lena's words and remind myself he's a sad, lonely alcoholic. Even still, I usher Gareth into the car to start our journey to Ian and Jen's house.

They live about thirty minutes' drive away in a suburb that estate agents would describe as 'established' and 'sought after by professionals'. There's a lot more greenery than where I live and the roads, lanes and cul-de-sacs are home to pre-Second World War built detached and semi-detached houses with the occasional bungalow thrown into the mix. It's a prosperous area with, I imagine, a price tag to match. Instead of kebab, charity and mobile phone shops, the parade we drive past hosts a delicatessen, artisan café and modern chain of hairdressers.

After taking a wrong turn, we eventually find Ian and Jen's house and park where we can – the drive is already chock-a-block. Theirs is a double-fronted, brick-built bungalow with a concrete ramp leading up to the front door. Coloured lights hang from the fading tree in the front garden as a nod to the occasion; there's also a Happy Birthday banner above the front door.

Clutching the present I've bought for Jen in one hand (I rustled up enough cash to buy her from a charity shop a mug that has 'Trust me – I'm a lawyer!' emblazoned in black lettering on the side) I knock on the door with the other. An older man with a bushy beard and flushed cheeks answers and welcomes us in. He introduces himself as a colleague of the pair then turns back to talk to the group he is with.

We walk along the entrance hall, which is papered with old-fashioned chintz-wallpaper and covered with a few scenic paintings. I clock that having spent so much launching their firm, Ian and Jen must have not had the time or money to do up their house. On our left is a door to the bustling living room where about fifteen people are chatting above an unidentifiable pop soundtrack. Gareth and I go past that and walk through the door at the end of the hallway that leads to a dated, but functional kitchen. There's Ian next to a dinner table laden with snacks and booze, pouring drinks for a young couple.

'Hello you!' I say, pleased to see him again and, I must admit, relishing the nosey opportunity to see him in his own environment. Watching property programmes on TV and fantasising about which I'd choose is a favourite of mine, even though I don't have a hope in hell of affording to buy a property on my own.

'Annie!' he gleefully replies. I bend down to kiss him, Gareth shakes him by the hand and Ian introduces us to the other couple in the kitchen, another pair of lawyers, then thrusts a glass of red wine each into our hands.

It's a happy, convivial atmosphere and soon I forget that I don't know anybody else there. Instead, I enjoy mine and Gareth's first social night out as a couple. When I introduced him to Ian I said, 'and this is Gareth,' to which he smirked. Next time Gareth takes the lead and introduces me as his date, Annie. Later he enquires whether I'd minded but I didn't at all, indeed I was glad we had got one potentially awkward stumbling block out of the way. It's only later that I think of Shaun and wonder whether I've moved on too quickly.

Ian wheels through to the lounge so we can meet Jen. In her civvy clothes she looks much softer and more approachable than in the photograph on the firm's website. She's evidently already a few glasses of wine down and hugs me as if I were an old friend. I think I'll like her very much. Gareth works the room and I catch up a little with Ian and what his life's like now. Someone turns the music up, blasts out a compilation of nineties Britpop tunes, and three people start to dance, kicking off their shoes and jumping to the rhythm of their childhood.

It's later, after Jen has invited me into the back garden to accompany her whilst she has a drunken smoke, that the topic of this morning's interview with Toby Smith comes up. She tells me that when Ian told her about the letter he'd written she'd done some digging into the case.

I'm feeling somewhat light-headed myself as I'm on my fourth top up of wine. We're standing in the light of the kitchen window. The rest of the garden is barely illuminated by the crescent moon far up ahead; I hear an animal scuffling in the undergrowth somewhere nearby.

Not having met Jen before, I don't know whether alcohol has loosened her tongue or she's usually this ebullient. 'I've seen a lot of shits in my career,' she confides, 'but Toby Smith really is one of the shittiest. One of my friends was on the prosecution team. Smith tried to use every trick in the book to wheedle his way out of the charge, even claiming it was his wife's fault that he hit her. His barrister nit-picked at every legal technicality. Thank God it didn't work. You'd be surprised at the number of times it does and the bastards walk free.'

She takes her last drag then stubs the butt out underfoot, picks it up and buries it in the mint herb planter on the floor next to us. 'Hiding the evidence,' she winks. 'If Ian asks why I smell of smoke I'll tell him it's because I've been around other people who were smoking. Want a mint?' She pulls a packet out from her handbag.

I shake my head to decline.

Jen sucks on the mint with applied fervour, then adds, 'Smith's campaigning for an appeal, you know. Says he's got an expert who can prove he was a victim of psychological abuse and went into some sort of dissociative state that caused him to beat his wife half to death. His brother sold his house to pay the legal fees. Would have been better off disowning him if you ask me.'

'Is he likely to be granted an appeal?'

'I'd usually say not likely but you never know what the brother has up his sleeve. I've heard a rumour that a group that campaigns for male domestic violence victims is considering supporting him. It's laughable. Smith knew damn well what he was doing. His wife never had a chance to defend herself.'

'Do you think he could have something to do with my sister's disappearance?' I ask, interested in her professional opinion. Instinctively I wrap my arms around my chest to keep warm and take another gulp of vino.

'It's possible. Don't get your hopes up, though. Without a body it's very difficult to prove a murder. It's awful that you've spent all these years not knowing what happened to her. It must have really fucked you up. Oops, sorry, I'm not saying that you are fucked up, rather that no one would blame you if you were.'

At that she links my arm and leads me back inside. 'Come on, let's have a top up. We must get together again sometime. Ian's said lots of lovely things about you. He had a hard time with bullies growing up. I'm glad he had you in his gang. Gareth's well fit. You bagged a good one there.'

The night draws in further and people begin to leave, calling taxis and hugging old and new friends goodbye. Gareth stuck to one glass of wine and is the soberest of the lot. We bid our leave and promise to see Ian and Jen very soon. In the car on the way home, as the traffic lights flash past in a soporific fashion, I remember to ask Gareth if he was able to find out any more about the frizzy-haired girl on social media.

'I got access to the Facebook group,' he replies, 'but I'm not sure if she's there. A few women don't have a photo of themselves on their profile. Without a name it's impossible to know if she's in the group or not.'

I'm too tired and too tipsy now to think further. When Gareth drops me off at the house, Reg's bedroom light is off and the curtains closed. I feel silly for even checking and letting him bother me earlier on. Right now I'm longing to keep mine and Gareth's date going until the morning. I apologise to him that I can't invite him up.

'That's OK, I've got to get back to my wife and three kids,' he jokes. I punch his arm in mock horror.

'I hope I'll have a get out of jail free for the night card soon,' I tell him. 'I'll see if my aunt will stay over one night. That's if you don't mind me coming over to yours.'

'Perfect. I'll even change the duvet cover for you.' With that, I go inside and put myself to bed. Thoughts of Gareth and fantasising about what could lie ahead for us push Gemma, Toby Smith, Reg, Mike and the frizzy-haired woman far into the wilderness of that night's dreams.

~ 18 ~

It's Monday morning and I'm rushing round the house putting together a bag of essential things for the chemo session today when there's a loud bang on the door. Mother is in the bathroom putting on some make-up – I've noticed that whilst she doesn't usually wear make-up at home, she takes care to ensure she looks her best for her hospital treatment – and shouts downstairs to me to ask me to answer it.

It's Aunty Lena. She hasn't put her jacket on in the rain and the drizzle has turned her hair frizzy. A blob of water drips from the end of her nose: she wipes it away with a hand that's holding a newspaper. I can tell there's something amiss.

'Where's your mother?' she asks conspiratorially.

'Upstairs in the bathroom. Why?'

Lena comes in the house and leads me through to the kitchen, shutting the doors behind her. From here it's very unlikely that we can be overheard upstairs. I've never seen Lena so vexed before.

She throws the paper on to the table. It's the local rag. I hadn't realised it is still in print, assuming that it would have died a death years ago thanks to the internet. The paper is open at page five. My eyes are drawn straight away to two pictures accompanying the text: the first the mugshot of

Toby Smith I've seen before in reports about his conviction, and the second is Gemma. It's a school photograph of hers taken a couple of months after she started the fifth form. The original stands on the top of the bookcase in the lounge. My sister is smiling angelically, appearing very much the innocent, studious, attractive white girl that the press loves far more than a missing, surly teenage black boy in care.

Seeing the pixelated image of her sends my heart beating faster. A cold clammy film of sweat sheens my forehead. The article headlines reads: 'Attempted murderer's brother claims police harassment'.

'Read it,' says Lena. 'You didn't tell me love that the police have interviewed Toby Smith, I thought you'd only written a letter. Does your mother know?'

I shake my head. She doesn't. I planned to only tell her if something came of it. Despite Ian's suggested threat of going to the media, I didn't expect they'd pick up on the story. I certainly didn't speak to the newspaper and DI Glass, once he'd been given the go-ahead by his superiors to re-interview Smith, had advised me to keep it an internal matter for now. So who spoke to the newspaper?

The partisan article soon tells me.

It seems that after DI Glass interviewed Smith in prison, Smith called his brother Robert who, enraged, went straight to the local paper. In the article he claims that Toby Smith was a victim of a miscarriage of justice two years ago due to the judge prohibiting evidence of Jasmine's emotional abuse of him to be submitted at his trial, and that the police's interview of him in respect to Gemma constitutes harassment and is a blatant attempt to smear his name and scupper his chances of a retrial. 'My brother was never a suspect. He was a good friend of Gemma's, who was a troubled girl, and didn't have anything to do with her going missing. There is no evidence to suggest he did. The police are desperately throwing mud at an easy target and trying to make it stick to cover up that they have failed, for more than twenty years, to find her.' My heart sinks even further when I read another line where Robert Smith says that police are also to blame for placating and giving false hope to the relative of Gemma's who asked for the case to be reopened. There's only Mother and I left, and with her cancer treatment, she's in no fit state to co-ordinate a Justice for Gemma campaign. It won't take anyone long to pin the blame on me if they believe this rot.

I sit down at the kitchen table and cradle my throbbing head in my hands. Robert Smith has twisted the story to suit his own purposes, shoving Gemma back into the shadows instead of at the forefront where she should be. The word 'troubled' insinuates she may have brought whatever happened to her onto herself. It's a cheap shot to libel the dead. What kind of journalist would write that? There isn't a byline, only the words 'staff writer'. There's also no contradiction of Smith's point of view, just a cursory mention that Toby Smith is in prison for the attempted murder of his wife. There's a short line saying the police do not comment on ongoing investigations and one about the paper having tried but failed to contact Gemma's family for a quote. I think back to the two calls from an unknown number I didn't answer on Saturday. Could they have been from a journalist? I hadn't looked to see if the caller left a message. Part of this is my fault. If I'd have known that the paper was going to publish the piece I might have been able to do something about it.

'We'll tell her together,' says Lena, who is busying herself by boiling the kettle and lifting down three mugs from the top cupboard. The hinge creaks ominously as she shuts it.

'I've got to take her to chemo in quarter of an hour.'

'We have to explain to her what's happened. The paper will be on sale in the hospital. She might see it or someone might recognise her name and ask her about it. It has to come from us.'

'You're right.' My temples are pulsating even more now and I can hear the echo of my heart pumping my blood. Whoosh, whoosh... I grasp the edge of the table so tightly that a red weal appears in my palm.

'We've got to pray the story doesn't set her back,' says Lena as she goes about the ritual of putting the tea bags in the mugs and pouring in the water. Tea first, milk last.

'I'll go and find her.'

Upstairs I hover until I hear the loo flush and the click of the bathroom door handle. When Mother comes out I ask her to come downstairs. Immediately she picks up on the mood in the house, whether it be from my body language or the serious tone of my voice, and shoots me a look of concern.

The many seconds it takes her to walk downstairs, left foot down a step followed by right foot, holding tightly on to the handrail with her right hand so as not to fall, tick past in tempo with my burgeoning headache. When she can't see me I glance at my watch and calculate how much time there is before we have to leave for the hospital. More seconds go by leaving us less time for explanations. I have absolutely no idea how she will react.

'Elaine's here in the kitchen,' I say. 'There's something we want to talk to you about.'

'What is it?' Mother starts to pick up a little speed once she's downstairs and walking to the kitchen. Aunty Lena's sitting at the table with the three steaming mugs on top of it. The newspaper is nowhere to be seen.

'Sit down, Mother.' She does so obediently. 'Has the hospital rung? Is there a problem?'

'No love, it's nothing to do with that.' Lena gently pushes Mother's mug towards her and then squeezes her fragile hand.

'Then what is it? You're both looking very serious.'

Lena gives me the nod as if to say, 'you made this bed, now you can explain why'.

I clear my throat. I could do with a couple of paracetamol. Outside it has started to rain harder – water whips loudly against the smudged window, showing no mercy. Aunty Lena is still holding mother's hand as tightly as she can, bolting her to the table.

'There's an article in the local newspaper today about Gemma.'

Mother gasps. Lena and I catch each other's eyes. I go on.

'When I came back here I found out that a boy in her class she was friends with, Toby Smith, was sent to prison two years ago for the attempted murder of his wife. I called the police to tell them in case they hadn't put two and two together; to me it seems a bit too much of a coincidence and I thought it was worth them interviewing him in prison to

149

find out whether he had anything to do with Gemma going missing.'

Mother is staring at me. I think she's trying to take it all in. 'And did he? What did the police say?'

'Nothing yet. My contact, DI Glass who was in the force when Gemma disappeared, said it would take a few days after he'd interviewed Smith in prison for he and his colleagues to decide whether there was any new relevant evidence. They might have to re-check alibis and things like that.'

'When will you know? And why is it in the paper?'

'I'll call DI Glass later today. Smith's brother went straight to the paper to complain the police were harassing his brother. He's got the gall to suggest that it's Toby Smith who is the victim here.'

'Can I have a glass of water please?' I jump to my feet to fetch one. Mother gulps it down, perhaps to settle her queasiness. She doesn't say anything else. I'm not sure what I'm expecting. Histrionics? A weeping fit? Fainting? Anger at me for sticking my nose in?

'We've got to leave for the hospital. I'm sorry about all this happening now,' I say.

Lena, who still has hold of Mother's hand, helps her to her feet then fetches her coat. I turn to leave the room to get the chemo goody bag to take with us.

Mother's words stop me in my tracks.

'Thank you, Annie. Thank you for standing up for your sister. I don't want to read the article, I've read far too many of them over the years, but please do tell me if the police find out anything more.'

I wasn't expecting that.

She looks so weary, hardly capable of making it to the car. 'I will. I'll be back in a second.'

As I walk into the hall I hear the click and thump sound of post being delivered. Lying on the doormat is a letter addressed to me but instead of being handwritten or typed the vowels and consonants have been rather comically cut out from a newspaper. I get a paper cut on my forefinger as I open the letter and a few drops of blood drop on to the letter enclosed. This too is made up of newspaper print. The words make me feel sick.

It says: 'Back off and go home'.

There's no one outside, not even a dog walker, when I open the front door to see who posted it through the letterbox. The rain is keeping people inside. In the distance I hear an engine running. Could the person who delivered the letter have gotten away by car? Or is he or she hiding somewhere along the street? Is this Robert Smith's doing, whether he delivered it himself or delegated his dirty work? I don't have time to run down the road to see if there's anyone there.

Sickness turns to defiance. I'm not going to back off and I don't have another home to go to anyway. Whoever wrote the letter doesn't know me well enough to realise that. I hastily put it back in the envelope and then stuff it in the chemo bag under a magazine just before Mother, aided by Aunty Lena, walks through into the hall. No one other than DI Glass needs to know about this.

'Let's go,' I say, plastering a cheery smile on my face. I open the umbrella in the house to escort Mother outside.

It's only when we're both in the car that I remember that it's bad luck.

~ 19 ~

At the hospital, when Mother is mid-treatment, I make my excuses and once again head to the WRVS café. There's a table free in the corner where, amongst the hustle and bustle, I won't be overheard. Clasping my fingers around the obligatory polystyrene coffee cup I call DI Glass and confide in him about this morning's threatening letter. He's seen the morning newspaper and is fuming. Nor does he have positive news from this interview with Toby Smith. It's a difficult conversation that leaves me feeling no better. Neither he nor the caffeine stop my headache pounding.

'We didn't get much information out of Smith,' he tells me, 'other than he claims Gemma's disappearance had nothing to do with him. We'll of course double check his alibi, but with the passage of time memories fade, CCTV is lost, if it was ever there in the first place, and it becomes trickier to corroborate evidence.'

'Do you believe him?'

'He's a slippery character and definitely has a history of violence but it's our job to rely on facts and as yet there are no witnesses or other information to prove he's lying. But if he was involved with Gemma's disappearance there's no incentive for him to tell us. A confession that leads to a successful conviction would significantly lengthen his prison term and his lawyer is still trying to appeal Smith's original attempted murder sentence.'

'Is that it then?' I've finished the coffee and am picking apart the cup, crushing it into little white polystyrene balls that roll across the table.

'No, as I said we have his alibi to check out. But I won't lie to you, Annie. Without any further leads there's nothing else for us to go on.'

I move my handbag from the aisle so a young mum can park her pushchair adjacent to the next table. She is pulling smiley faces at her giggling bundle.

'What about the photo I told you about of Gemma and three friends in the park? I still don't know who the girl with her is. Can you track her down and see if she knows something? Did I tell you I called Mike Braithwaite, the other boy in the picture, and he wouldn't talk to me? Can you try? You're the police, he'd have to answer your questions.'

'Not necessarily, particularly if he's not under caution or arrest, but yes, it's another avenue to investigate. As for the photo, why don't I pop round and take a copy? I can look through the case files from the time and see if we can identify her.'

'I'll post it to you,' I say hurriedly. 'Mother is having cancer treatment and isn't very strong. She doesn't want to get involved unless there are any concrete leads. I'd like to keep the police away from the house if possible so as not to upset her.' Father's dying words flashback to me in my head: 'Look after her when I'm gone'. He's got what he wanted. I'm in too deep now to walk away from it all.

'It's quicker for me to meet you in person to see the photo and take the letter you received. It may have fingerprints on it and we need to keep it as evidence. The police take harassment very seriously.'

'Who do you think might have sent it?' I ask.

'I can't say without having forensics look at it. Smith's brother or another of his family or friends, however, could be in the frame. That newspaper article this morning was a low trick. Our press team will decide whether to make an official complaint to the Editor.'

'I'll try and drop them off at the station later. I'm in hospital at the moment for Mother's chemotherapy. She usually goes to bed at home afterwards and I should be able to leave her for half an hour.'

'Try not to contaminate the letter. Wear gloves and put it in a plastic bag such as a freezer bag. We'll need to take your fingerprints as well to rule them out.'

'I will do.' Priti would love all this skulduggery. I must call her later.

I walk back to oncology having bought water, chocolate bars for energy, two cheap women's magazines that assume all the fairer sex are interested in is reality TV and bikini bodies, and another polystyrene cup three quarters full of brown liquid that I suspect contravenes the Trading Standards definition of tea.

As well as Mother, three other people are hooked up to IVs, one of which, an older woman whom I recognise from a previous visit, has newly arrived. A brightly-coloured crochet granny square blanket envelops her slender frame; her head is covered 1940s-style with a floral headscarf tied at the front in a knot. I nod at her and she smiles at me then turns back to the book she is reading: a fat tome with enough pages to keep her going through more than one chemo session. Mel isn't there.

The other two patients, or 'service users' I now know from my induction is the correct term, have nodded off, their heads leaning to one side of their bodies resting in the top wing of the chair. Next to one is a tired-looking gentleman of late middle age, holding what I assume is his wife's hand whilst trying to complete a newspaper crossword in his lap with his other.

A few empty chairs away is my mother, where I left her, seated under a mass-produced watercolour of a bowl of fruit that is secured to the wall as if it were as precious as the 'Mona Lisa' in the Louvre. Her knees are covered with the lavender fleecy blanket from the sofa at home that I'd packed earlier in the chemo goody bag.

The powerful medication enters her veins via the intravenous port secured in her left lower arm by white tape. I wonder whether it causes pain or discomfort – Mother's eyes are half-closed. I'm not squeamish looking at needles or injections but don't like to have them myself.

I sit on the black plastic chair next to her. 'I'm back,' I say. 'I've got magazines and drinks – do you want the water or the tea?'

She turns to me drowsily. 'Whichever you don't want, dear.'

'OK, half each then. Tell me if you want something passing. How is it?'

'Same as last time.'

'Not much fun then?'

'Not pleasant but bearable if it's what it takes to keep me alive.'

'Well, yes.' What else can I say to that? Nothing.

The clock on the wall ticks the seconds away. Una walks briskly around the ward to check the IVs. I haven't had a chance to chat to her today or tell her the good news about my induction. I hope she'll have a quick break before I leave.

To pass the time and distract my thoughts from my pounding head and the unfruitful conversation with DI Glass, I read a magazine story about a daytime TV presenter having a social media row with another daytime TV presenter about looking fat on screen. That's another ten minutes of my life I've wasted.

Mother hasn't moved in her chair. I break the silence. 'I forgot to tell you, the other day at the café I got talking to a woman who is having treatment for breast cancer. She was buying some lunch for her young son. Apparently if you have breast cancer there's a special centre in the hospital you can go to that has free coffee, not from a vending machine but proper filter stuff. And there's a big bowl of complimentary fruit. I bet it's nicer than this room. The woman told me it runs yoga and meditation classes as well. She's going to a session there on Friday where they show you how to put make-up on and can try on different wigs.' Mother doesn't need a wig as she still has some hair. She had it cut pixie short to disguise the thin patches.

'Really?' Mother opens her eyes.

'Yes. How come breast cancer patients get that and kidney ones don't? That's discrimination.' I'm gabbling, I realise, filling in the silence.

'Yoga? Can you imagine me doing the lotus position?'

I look at Mother's face and see a twinkle in her eye, which prompts an involuntary snort to escape from my mouth. 'Ommm,' I reply, shutting my eyes and holding my thumb and forefingers together in a circle to mimic a meditation pose.

Mother laughs weakly, then coughs and adds, 'Make-up? Do I want to look like I'm going to a tarts and vicars party?' She seems to have forgotten the neutral-coloured lipstick and blusher she put on this morning.

'Mother!' I'm stunned – she said the word tart! That's on the level of the F word coming from her. 'You could get a curly perm wig, like your hair was in the old 1980s photos…'

'Stop it, Annie.' She's still laughing and wincing at the same time due to the physical pain the act of laughing inflicts on her feeble body. 'That hairstyle was fashionable then. Top of the range home perm – Elaine used to do it for me.'

'It showed,' I jest.

'I have two words for you, Annie Towcester. Pink. Hair. Fourteen you were when you did it. Pink, I tell you.'

'Hmm – it seemed like a good idea at the time.' I was surprised that she remembered my pink hair dye foray. She was right, it was dreadful, but I'd never have admitted it at the time. My terribly-bleached fuchsia hair split off when I brushed it. Mother barely said a word when she saw. Father, however, rang up Aunty Lena straight away and she turned up the next day with a packet of brown home hair dye and a pair of rubber gloves.

A tired-looking middle-aged woman pushing a trolley offers Mother a drink that looks no better than those from the vending machine downstairs. She's dressed in the same uniform I was given at my induction. Maybe I'll be doing her job soon. I've yet to receive a call about when my first shift will be.

One of the sleeping patients awakes with a cry of pain. I catch Mother's eye. 'Seriously, does it hurt? I can ask Una to give you something extra if it does.'

'I'm fine, thank you.' Is she really OK or is she being a martyr?

Another pause before Mother says, 'This isn't the worst thing that's ever happened to me, Annie. Cancer is horrible and I wish I hadn't got it, but it's not the worst.'

I think of the conversation at the kitchen table this morning and the framed picture in the lounge of Gemma on her final birthday, blowing out her cake candles. We're back to her again.

'Is the worst not knowing what happened to Gemma? What was in the shoebox in your wardrobe?' There, I've said it. Mother's physically attached to a drip. She can't run away and avoid the question I've been longing to ask.

Mother looks down at her lap. She exhales a breath of defeat. 'The shoebox. Its contents *are* private but I suppose I ought to tell you since you saw it. Your father and I kept too many secrets from you when you were a child. We thought we were protecting you, but…'

She pauses before continuing. I find I'm holding my breath in anticipation. 'You know I spent a long time in bed when you were a child and I took pills. Too many. I've had clinical depression for a long time, both before Gemma… before she… and afterwards. After you left I saw a psychologist regularly for years. She encouraged me to keep a diary of my thoughts and feelings in a notebook, to write them down and acknowledge them rather than pretend they weren't there. I wrote letters too, to Gemma. I know I wasn't a good mother to either of you. The letters, well, I wrote down everything I would say to her if she were here. The things I didn't say when she was. They're in the shoebox.'

'All that sleeping, locking yourself away in your room, you were clinically depressed all that time? I knew you weren't well but when you spent all that time in your bedroom I thought you just didn't want to be with Father and me. Could the doctors not help?' I ask whilst I have the golden opportunity.

'Not then. Nowadays what with the pills and the GP support I can manage it, I know when it's coming and I know what to do.' She picks up the women's magazine on the side table and flicks the pages. 'If you believe magazines like this it seems that everybody today is depressed. It's a fashionable thing to be now. It wasn't then. It's the worst thing you can imagine, the bottomless pit of despair and you don't know why, there's no reason…'

I sit up straight and press on. 'And Gemma's death made it worse, did it? I barely remember you before then.'

Mother wraps her hands around her lap blanket, fidgeting. She lowers her tone. 'We don't know she is dead, Annie. The depression started long before Gemma went. People didn't talk about it in those days. I was so ashamed, I think your father was too.'

'When then, when did it start? How?' I place my hand on top of her left one to acknowledge this isn't an easy subject for her to discuss, even though my mind is full of confusion.

No one ever told me when I was a child that Mother was depressed. Not well, yes, but never why. Was it that she just couldn't help being the mother she was, rather than that she chose to be withdrawn and never there for me?

'When I gave birth to Gemma. I'd had an easy pregnancy, barely any morning sickness. I bloomed. I loved being pregnant. I felt so beautiful, as if by becoming a mother I had a purpose.' The corners of her lips turn upwards in remembrance.

'We'd wanted to start a family young. Gemma's birth was easy compared to some of the stories I heard from other women. A six-hour labour, no stitches. But when they passed her to me, when I looked at her…' Mother clutches her mouth with her free hand. 'When I looked at her I felt nothing. I'd expected to fall instantly in love but there was none there. The nurses kept telling me to try and feed her, to hold her, but I was so tired and only wanted them to look after her so I could sleep and not hear her crying. Just take her away, I said, let me rest. When we took her home I tried so hard, your father did all he could to help, Gemma smiled for him, but for me, she just cried and messed her nappy. I pretended to others that I was a besotted mother then felt dreadful that I wasn't. I lied through my teeth.'

I clutch her hand a little harder.

'Then one day, when Gemma was about three months old, I was hanging washing out in the garden. Back in those days it was normal to leave the baby outside in the pram to get fresh air. But she just wouldn't stop crying. I tried everything, a bottle, picking her up, walking her round, everything, but she wouldn't settle. Then I put her back in the pram and thought how easy it would be to cover her face with the blanket and make her be quiet. I was so shocked to have those thoughts, I walked straight out of the back gate, leaving the pram in the garden, and kept walking.'

'Oh my God, what happened?' This is the longest conversation about the past I think I've ever had with my mother. Did I ever know her at all?

'Karen next door heard Gemma crying. She couldn't find me so she pushed the pram to your father's garage to get help. He knew something wasn't right, that I wasn't right, but didn't want the authorities involved. He asked Karen to babysit Gemma at her house whilst he tried to find me.'

'And where were you?'

'It's hazy. I was at the park, he said he found me staring down at the lake. I told him I'd gone to feed the ducks, but I hadn't. I was thinking how long it would take to die if I waded into the water, whether it would be pain-free and over quickly. If I was dead I couldn't harm my baby. But there were lots of people around and I didn't have the guts to do it. And then he came and took me home.'

I really don't know what to say. She had wanted, if only for a moment, to kill Gemma? Is this the chemo drugs talking? Or is her recollection of events true?

'The next day your father took me to the doctor's. The medication – back then it was as bad as what it was supposed to cure. Post-natal depression, what the doctor said I had, was shameful. I had to live with the knowledge and regret of what I nearly did. The pills blocked it out, but they blocked everything else out as well. What do they call them these days, those monsters on television? Zombies? I felt like a zombie,

161

so tired, every emotion sucked out, and such shame at being a failure as a mother. It took over a year before I loved my daughter, before I could truly feel a bond and when I did, oh how I loved her and how I hated myself for the way I'd been, all that time I'd lost. But she wasn't an easy child, you know, the rows, the arguments… Gemma was clever, cleverer than me, and she knew how to play on it.'

She pauses and takes a few deep breaths to regain her strength.

'And then years later you came along. This cancer, it has really got me thinking. I'm so sorry, Annie. You were a surprise. When I found out I was pregnant with you I was terrified. What if it was all going to happen again? What if I couldn't love you? But when you were born I felt it straight away. Motherly love. I'd do anything to protect you. Your beautiful face, the little tufts of ginger hair on top of your head. This time, I thought, this time it would be different. I'd be everything to you that I hadn't been to Gemma at the start.'

This is all so much to take in. Have I been wrong all my life? Mother did want me, she did love me? My heart clenches and doesn't know whether to beat or bleed.

'Then a month later it started again. The bleakness, the inability to get out of bed, the hatred of myself and other mothers who laughed and smiled with their children whereas I felt incapable of even going outside the house. I told your father, he took me to the doctor's again. More pills, more hospital visits, your father ran the house when he was back from work. He never said it but he made sure I was rarely alone with you as a baby, made sure that I never had the chance to leave you in your pram and walk away. There was Gemma, Elaine, his parents when they were alive, always someone around to do things, so I stopped trying. I wasn't a good mother to you, Annie. But I did love you, I didn't tell you, but I did. I thought you were better off without me.'

Bloody hell.

'When Gemma disappeared that day I knew it was my fault. My punishment for the time when I'd thought about killing her myself, for the way I'd behaved. My fault, my guilt, if I'd been a better mother I would have kept her safe, but I hadn't. I did something terrible, unforgiveable. She didn't want to come home because of me. Or maybe someone took her because I hadn't been there to protect her. Either way, my fault.'

'No,' I say, 'you don't know that, like you said earlier we don't know what happened to her. It wasn't your fault.'

Tears are running down her face now, pent up tears I've never seen her cry before. 'A tissue?' I offer.

'I've failed you too, Annie. I pushed you out and you didn't come back for fourteen years. I'm so sorry.' I realise I've been grasping her hand so hard, pressing her finger bones so tightly together that her wedding ring has left a red indentation on my palm. I take a deep breath in to calm myself and with its release feel a weight lift from my mind, from my past, and from my future.

Una walks over to take routine observations. From the look on her face I can tell she's noticed the tears. 'Is everything alright?' In this ward she must come across a lot of emotion and see the whole gamut of human experience.

'We're fine,' I smile and thank her.

'Your mum's doing well, five more minutes then we'll take her off the IV.'

'Thanks. Oh by the way I got the HCA bank job. I had my induction and am waiting for the phone to ring for my first shift,' I tell her.

'Well done you!' she smiles. 'We'll make a nurse of you yet. I've got a brochure in the office for that access to healthcare college course I told you about that you need to take to get a place on a nursing degree.'

'Are you on commission?' I ask, lightening the mood. People like me don't do a degree. Mother is dabbing at her tears with a tissue.

'Getting extra money out of the NHS? Fat chance.' Una checks Mother's IV. 'I suppose I'm quite evangelical about nursing. There aren't enough – we need as many trainees as we can get. Who knows? Maybe you'll get a shift on this ward.'

'It'd be nice working with you.'

'And you. Give it another five minutes and Mrs Towcester will be ready to come off the drip. I'll bring the brochure over to you in a bit.' She takes her leave and bustles over to another service user.

Before the moment passes I grasp the mettle once again and ask my mother, 'Why leave Gemma's bedroom as it is? Why the presents?'

Mother stuffs the tissue up the sleeve of her cardigan on the arm that isn't hooked up to the IV.

'I suppose it must seem a little eccentric.' She smiles wanly.

'Well, that's one word for it. I'm not sure it's healthy to have them there and keep her room as it was.'

Mother nods then pauses before speaking, taking her time over her next words. 'I know. But in my head if Gemma's room isn't there, then she can't come back to it. There was still hope when I bought the first present, still the possibility that she'd run away but might come home. It was a ritual. I didn't want to stop doing it, to jinx her, to forget her.'

I steel myself. 'She's not coming back Mother,' I say with a hint of tenderness, as if I were talking to a small child. 'It has been too long. Gemma's not coming home.'

'Yes, I realise that now. But for a long, long time I didn't want to.'

And with this the conversation ends. Someone switches on the TV, jolting the room with the theme tune of an afternoon soap opera. Across the ward the husband is discussing with his wife what he will cook for tea. A well turned-out middle-aged couple arrives to take home the younger woman with the book. Only the older woman with short, cropped white hair sleeps through the noise.

Una returns. 'Here's the brochure, Annie. Just give us a few minutes now to sort Mum out and disconnect her from the IV then you're free to take her home.'

'Thanks Una. When will we know if the treatment is doing its job?'

'Well that's something to ask the consultant at your mum's next appointment, I think she's due one soon. There will be another scan and blood tests to monitor the tumour. Meanwhile, as usual, make sure your mum drinks lots of water over the next forty-eight hours and watch out for her feeling nauseous as a side effect of the chemo. She needs to rest and take it easy. You need some rest too. It's not easy being a carer, particularly when you're about to start a new job. She's doing a grand job, though, isn't she Mrs Towcester? How are you feeling? Let's get that IV out. You've done brilliantly as always.' Una has the nursing patter down to a tee.

With the brochure stuffed in my bag to think about another time, I smile at Mother and walk out of the ward, taking my cue to visit the loo and freshen up before the drive home. This time Mother feels too weak to walk all the way to the car park so I borrow a wheelchair that swallows my mother's small frame whole and push her through the automatic doors, out of the building and into a slight rain shower. So as not to get either of us wet I push the chair to the car as fast as I can without jolting her.

After I've helped her into the front seat and returned the wheelchair to the hospital entrance, once again running the gauntlet of the rain, Mother speaks up. 'I wonder if you can spare a few hours tomorrow, Annie? I think it's time to start clearing out Gemma's room and perhaps you'd like to help? The charity shop will be glad of some of the things and perhaps the presents can go to the Salvation Army.'

I briefly cover Mother's hand with mine. 'Yes,' I say, 'I think I can find a window in my hectic work schedule. I'll go to the supermarket first thing and buy some bin bags.' She smiles.

With that I turn the windscreen wipers on and drive off back home into the setting sun of an English evening.

~ 20 ~

True to form, Mother goes to bed when we arrive home, taking what feels like an eternity to propel herself up the stairs, and I tell her I have to nip out for half an hour or so to run an errand. In an old jiffy bag, I enclose a photocopy of the photo of Gemma and her friends along with this morning's letter in a plastic bag as instructed, seal it and address it to the police. DI Glass isn't at the station when I arrive but one of his colleagues comes to greet me, and takes the evidence and my fingerprints. I'm back home, despite the rush hour traffic, within the hour.

I take the portable radio from the kitchen and a jug of squash to Mother's room, only to hear retching noises from the bathroom that she unsuccessfully tries to drown out with the running of tap water. I lift my fist to knock gently on the door but stop as it reaches a centimetre away: if she wants me she will ask. I personally wouldn't want anyone to see me throwing up. Instead I say loudly, 'I've put the radio and squash in your room, Mother. Give us a shout if you want anything else.' A heartbeat, then two, then three, followed by a 'thank you'.

I wonder if it's the chemo that's making her sick or if it's also the case that she's purging herself of years of regret and remorse, ridding her wracked body of the tension and stress released by her confession? I'm still discombobulated (that's a word I remember learning at school, loving the shape of my lips as I broke the word down into syllables to learn for a spelling test) by what she'd told me, and the anger I held at her for making me think that I couldn't be a mother because I had never learned what a good one should do. Yet, deep down, was she an easy excuse? I hadn't understood as a child what she was going through mentally and as an adult it had never occurred to me to try. I chose to abort Shaun's baby. It was nothing to do with Mother. I hadn't seen her for fourteen years. I'm an adult and this was my decision alone. If I'd really wanted the baby, wouldn't I have kept it, fought for it, loved it even though it was only just a collection of cells multiplying inside me? Does that make me depressed too, like her? Is it genetic? I know instinctively I don't want to be a mother, not yet anyway, and that's about me, not her or Shaun. Intellectually, I may feel a pang of 'what if?' but emotionally, instinctively I know I made the right decision, one supported by the doctor and counsellor at the clinic. Somehow I know it's going to be alright, I'm going to be OK. But is Mother?

At least I didn't leave my baby in a pram in the back garden and walk off! If someone else had told me Mother did that I'd have been certain they were lying. Baby abandonment and attempted suicide in Greville Road. Who'd have thought it, imagine how the tongues would have wagged if they'd have known and had something better to gossip about other than a neighbour's caravan permanently parked outside another person's house.

168

All those years I thought she was a bad mother and used a vague illness as an excuse, but if I believe what she says, it wasn't that she didn't want to spend time with me or give me attention; it was that she was zonked up to the eyeballs on not-so-happy pills. How I wish she'd told me this much, much earlier.

She'd thought about killing Gemma! Gemma had been a difficult child! Did Gemma know? Did she ever find out what Mother had done, and if so, what must she have thought and felt? Was that why she walked out – if indeed that's what she did? I'd always assumed her life, up until the day it froze in time, was golden. Charmed. Had Gemma in fact felt neglected and unloved? Perhaps she did, despite my father's protestations, want to run away. Could she have done it? Was it practically possible to walk out of the front door and step into a new life, with no money, no passport, no ID, just the clothes on your back and a school bag? For the first time in my life I think, however improbably, it could, for a while at least, until her youth and circumstances led someone to prey on her and end her life. Now I understand why Mother had held the running away theory so close when others thought it was obvious that something fatal had tragically happened to Gemma. Mother thought she'd pushed her away, that Gemma had fled from her, that there was no murderous stranger lurking in the bushes and it was all her fault.

I decide to keep this information private and not tell Priti, Gareth or DI Glass. It's not relevant to the investigation and I want to hold precious the first time Mother has confided in me. When I speak to Priti and Gareth on the phone before I go to bed I tell them about the newspaper article – Gareth has already seen it but Priti, living in Leeds, has not – and my conversation with DI Glass. I don't mention the threatening letter because that's something best to discuss face to face rather than on the phone.

Late the next morning, Mother, who has changed out of her fleecy pyjamas in to what I presume is her gardening and DIY outfit, a pair of worn-looking black trousers and a paint-flecked jumper, surprises me by declaring it's time to sort out Gemma's room. She's babbling slightly, skirting round the issue with ideas about colour schemes and potential future uses.

'Your room is rather small, I started using it as my sewing room when I enrolled on the evening class. This room is bigger, perhaps you'd like it? You could decorate it how you want to. Lemon might be nice, but it doesn't have to be, you choose, Annie.'

There's no way in hell I'm sleeping in Gemma's shrine, even if it's emptied out and the walls are painted yellow. The heavy atmosphere would still be there, clinging on to the plaster and bricks it insinuated itself into long ago.

We're standing at the threshold of the room. Mother takes the pottery 'Gemma' sign off the door. I wonder how long I will be staying in this house and how long it will be until Mother gets the all clear – or the opposite. I realise that I hope it won't be the opposite.

'I'm fine where I am in the spare room. I'm not sure how long I'll be here for.' For obvious reasons I don't state why. Mother makes a quip about maybe I'll move in with a fella. It's far, far too soon for me to contemplate that again, however much more cheaply I could live as opposed to renting my own flat.

'Or a pale green?' Mother goes on. 'Perhaps I can pick

up a paint chart? Get a book on colour schemes out of the library?'

She's clearly set on the idea of redecorating the room so I encourage her wholeheartedly. I'm not the only one who needs to move on. 'Yes, good idea. The sun hits this room at the end of the day, not in the morning. There must be a colour that's best suited to that.'

We're still standing at the threshold. I look at Mother and she looks back at me with a slight look of panic in her eyes.

I take the lead and go to the window, flinging it and the curtains wide open to let the morning light in, sensing it's now or never.

'Right, let's get started, shall we?' I say. 'I've got black bin bags for rubbish, white ones for things fit for a charity shop and anything else you want to keep goes in this cardboard box.' I've deliberately only brought up a small box. The idea is to throw things out, not just move them to a different place. To start I kneel down besides the pile of wrapped presents.

'Shall we open these and decide if they're fit to give to a charity shop?' When I tear a corner of the garish red paper emblazoned with silver bells I see Mother flinch, then take a deep breath.

'Yes, dear. Good idea.'

She perches on the side of the bed and I realise that she physically can't get down on the floor.

'I'll open them then pass them to you to decide. And next perhaps make a start on the clothes?'

'I didn't wash what's hanging up in the wardrobe. I hope moths haven't got to them.' They're destined straight for the black bin bags.

I pass her the first present. When the wrapping is torn off it is revealed as a 1990 *Smash Hits* pop annual. I remember Father mentioning that Gemma regularly bought the magazine and pulled out the song lyric pages. 'Charity shop or rubbish?'

'Oh, well I don't know…'

'That's OK,' I say. 'No rush, we can put that to one side. We've got all the time in the world.'

Once all the presents are unwrapped and the paper stuffed into a bin bag we begin to clear the more personal items hidden away in a chest of drawers and the wardrobe. I'd have to have the hide of a rhino not to be touched by seeing the detritus of a life sadly now dated and faintly musty smelling. We throw the clothes and underwear straight out. In one of the drawers there's a jewellery box with a few cheap trinkets in that Gemma probably bought from the market. There are also necklaces with plastic beads and thin bangles the same colour. The jewellery that hasn't turned grey with age goes in the charity shop pile.

'Do you know if Gemma kept a diary?' I ask.

'I think the police found one when they searched the room along with some letters and notebooks,' she replies. 'I don't think they held any useful information.'

'Was it in one of the dressing table drawers? Where is it now?'

'I assume they've still got it as evidence. Why?'

That'll be why I found the drawers empty in the dressing table. 'I'd just like to know more about her, that's all. What she was like, who her friends were, that sort of thing.' I point to the photograph on the pinboard we've yet to clear out. It's the photograph of Gemma in the park with her three friends that I took photocopies of.

'Do you know who the girl is on the right? The one with the curly hair and long black skirt?' I unpin the photo from the board so I can pass it to Mother. She slides her tortoiseshell glasses from her head to her nose so she can look more closely at it.

'She does look a little familiar. I didn't know many of Gemma's friends, though. She rarely brought them home. Occasionally one of them would ring the doorbell to call for her.'

I press her further. 'What about the other two? The boy with the blonde hair on the left is Toby Smith.' I hold my breath in case the mention of his name unsettles her.

'Yes, I think I remember him. A boy wearing eyeliner isn't right. I wondered whether he was, you know…' Mother raises her eyebrows and tips her head to the side to make her point, as if saying the word would burn her lips.

'Gay? Would it matter if he was?'

That shuts her up for a few seconds.

'No, of course not,' she mumbles.

'Well, he isn't. He's straight, unfortunately for his wife, whom he attempted to murder.'

Mother hastily changes the subject. 'The other boy, the one with the dark, curly hair, now I do remember him. Mark, is it?'

'Mike,' I correct her. 'Mike Braithwaite.'

She squints and peers even more closely at the photo. 'Ah, Mike, that's it. He often walked to school and back with Gemma and they were in the orchestra together. I thought he was rather sweet on her but Gemma never talked to me about boyfriends. He called round for her quite a few times at the weekends. She said they studied together. A polite boy, he was.'

I deliberately choose not to tell her about my recent abrupt phone call with Mike. 'Can you remember anything else about him? What made you think he fancied Gemma?' By now I've sat down on the bed bedside Mother to look at the photograph as well.

Mother thinks back. 'Erm, it was the way he looked at her – like a puppy dog. He seemed eager to see Gemma and disappointed if she wasn't in or said she didn't want to go out. I'm not so old that I can't remember what a man who finds me attractive looks like.'

'Bully for you!' I jest whilst finding the idea of someone other than my father fancying my mum rather improbable.

We carry on clearing out until the last thing left is the pinboard resting on top of the dressing table. Mother asks me to unpin the photos and put them in the cardboard box. There's very little else in there. I fold the corners of the top flaps to keep them shut. The box is dwarfed by the bags destined for the charity shop and rubbish tip. With everything out the room looks bare, faded and dirty. I think that if I have time I can make a start on whitewashing the walls and painting the skirting boards. Perhaps Gareth will help, or maybe it's too soon to ask as we've only been out a few times. Mother has decided she wants rid of all the furniture too. I can take the bags to the tip and charity shop in my car, although it'll take a few trips, but will need the help of someone with a van to dispose of the wardrobe, bed, chest of drawers, chair and dressing table.

Mother yawns and decides to go for a lie down. I've been so busy bagging things up I hadn't heard my phone ring. The phone's screen says I've missed a call. It's the hospital offering me my first shift that evening to cover for sickness absence. I phone them back and enthusiastically accept. I'll prepare Mother's dinner before I leave and she should be alright getting to bed on her own. She can call Aunty Lena if there are any problems.

My phone then informs me there's another message for me to listen to. It's DI Glass. 'Annie?' he says. 'Please call me back. I think I know who your girl in the photo is.'

Thursday 4th May 1989. 11.30 a.m.

When Diana climbed into the flower-scented bubbles, some escaped over the side of the tub, wetting the bathmat and leaving a foamy patch on the peach bathroom carpet. She'd woken only a few minutes earlier and still felt groggy; she was unbalanced on her feet walking up the stairs to the bathroom and found it hard to piece together her thoughts and remember what she had to do for the rest of the day.

She bent her knees and pushed her bottom nearer to the taps, enabling her to recline into the water until her knees stuck out and her face and hair were totally submerged under the bubbles.

How easy it would be to stay down there and never come up. Good mothers didn't do that. Good mothers didn't think about leaving their children without their parent. Good mothers didn't have a bath in the daytime when they should be cooking, cleaning, working and getting ready for the children to arrive home from school. Good mothers didn't slap their children or be shunned by them.

Her heart started to pound in need of oxygen. She waited as long as she physically could, dancing with the possibility of death, until involuntarily she sat straight up and gulped a lung full of air, followed by a coughing fit. Above the water she soon felt chilly. She turned on the hot tap but it ran cold for the hot water in the tank was all used up. She'd have to switch the immersion on to heat up more, but that would involve climbing out and by the time she got back the rest of the bath water would have cooled down too much anyway.

Stay or go? Even that was too hard a decision to make. Her thoughts slowed to the pace of an arthritic tortoise as she stared at the tap, mesmerised by the rhythmic sound of the drip from the end. Diana didn't know for how long she sat there, her skin puckering up and developing goosebumps whilst she shivered with her arms wrapped round her pointed-up knees.

The doorbell rang. It shook her back to the present, back to the memory of her eldest shouting that she hated her. Diana got out of the bath and slipped on the iron surface. She reached out to grab on to the wash basin to block her fall but whilst doing so banged her knee on the bath. That'd cause another bruise. The bell rang again. She wrapped her fluffy dressing gown around her and crept into her bedroom where the curtains were still shut. Peeking out of a small gap in them to the front garden below she saw a postman with a parcel in his hand. She couldn't answer the door, especially not to him. He delivered to the whole street and the neighbouring ones. He'll have picked up on the gossip about her, the shut curtains in the daytime and the criticism from other housewives. That woman at 22 Greville Road, she's mad she is, you don't want to go there. She neglects her children.

Diana took a sharp step to the right, away from the curtain gap and turned her back to the window. Her breaths were quick and shallow. Just wait. Be patient. He'll go soon. The doorbell did not ring again. She heard the letterbox bang

– he must have put a missed delivery form through the door. She could relax now. What was it she had to do? That's it, get dressed.

She rubbed herself dry with the dressing gown then slipped it off her shoulders and let it drop down onto the flowery carpet. The back of the wardrobe door had a full-length mirror on it. Diana opened it and looked at herself naked, seeing the existing bruises where she'd fallen or knocked herself, her slim waist and the light protruding of her ribs giving away the fact that she regularly skipped meals through lack of appetite or will to physically go downstairs and participate in the act of cooking. Hurriedly, she shut the wardrobe door, disgusted at the sight of herself, and reached for the underwear and dress she had cast off earlier. She had to face the day, although all she wanted was to reach for the pills again and for her mind to go blank for as long as possible.

~ 21 ~

I call DI Glass back right away. He says that he's combed through the old case files and found a photograph of pupils in Gemma's year with their names written on the back. The frizzy-haired girl is on there. Her name is Fiona Glenton, although, he reminds me, she could have changed her surname since then. DI Glass mentions that his DCI has put him on the case of a pensioner who was attacked by an intruder in her own home yesterday. I get the feeling that he's now too busy to chase up Fiona Glenton.

Immediately I call Gareth only to hear his voicemail message. I tell him about my shift tonight and the discovery of the girl in the photo's name. I also text Priti – I'm too busy getting things sorted for my first shift to have a long chat – with the news about Fiona Glenton. Perhaps Fiona knows something or maybe she's as in the dark as the rest of us. Whichever it is, I want to know. She might be able to shed a light on Gemma's relationship with Mike and Toby.

I'm so busy working my shift that by the time it's over I'm exhausted with tired limbs and aching feet from being on my feet all the time. Now I understand why nurses wear sensible shoes. Even though it did involve some bedpan sluicing, I enjoyed every minute of it and am keen to return.

The staff nurse who supervised me on the ward gave me good feedback for my first shift.

It's still dark when I return home in the morning on the early bus. The streetlights are on and about every second house is showing some signs of activity, whether it be open curtains or a yellow glow shining through a window. Some leaves have fallen overnight. I kick them out of the way as I walk down the street. To my relief, Reg's house is still battened down for the night and there's nothing on the mat by the letterbox in Mother's house. The house is quiet – she must still be asleep. I leave some bread out by the toaster for her, place the butter, jam, a plate and knife on the kitchen table then head straight upstairs to crash out.

I awake about midday to a knock on the door and Mother bringing a flask full of tea. 'Sorry, I couldn't carry a mug up the stairs without spilling your tea, so I brought up a flask and an empty mug in a bag instead,' she explains. After placing the bag on the bedside table, she opens the curtains, letting the daylight stream in. My eyes take a while to adjust. I wipe some sleepy dust away from the corners and sit up, yawning the morning in.

'Thanks.'

'A pleasure. I've been dying to hear how your shift went,' Mother says. She seems unusually perky today. It might be a sign that the treatment is working. There's some colour back in her cheeks and she seems less lethargic. She's even wearing lipstick.

'Really well. I loved it, except I didn't realise how physically tiring being on the go all the time can be. I'm used to sitting at a desk at work and making phone calls.' I twist the top off the flask, pour some of the steaming brown liquid into the mug, then take a welcome sip.

'I'm glad. Do you want to go to the library later on and look at decorating books?'

'Yes, if you'd like to.'

'Good. I'll leave you to it and let you get up and get dressed. Your phone is flashing by the way.'

As she leaves, I pick up my phone that's sitting beside the flask on the bedside table. The screen says that I have a text message. My first thought is that it's Aunty Lena telling me there's been another story about Toby Smith in the newspaper. Thankfully it isn't. The message is from Priti.

Got her! See the link on Fiona Glenton, now Fiona King! Hope the shift was amazing. Call me! Mwah x

I click on the link in the message and it brings up a web page from a luxury hotel. The page is PR blurb about the wedding services they offer and includes a case study of the ceremony and meal for the big day of one Tom King and Fiona Glenton. In it the new Mr and Mrs King gush about how the hotel staff catered to their every need and made their special day perfect (I hope they got paid for saying that). There's a stereotypical picture of them on the day posing, gazing lovingly into each other's eyes in the hotel's grounds. She's wearing white not black, heels instead of DMs, her hair is in a stylish up do scattered with pearls and the Dalmatians have long gone, but it I can tell that Fiona King née Glenton is the girl in Gemma's photo.

I know I won't be able to speak to Gareth until after

his work tonight. He's behind on his OU coursework and is spending a few evenings catching up. I miss him. It's a disconcerting feeling – it's unlike me to get close to someone so quickly, particularly after everything went spectacularly wrong with Shaun. Or am I over-analysing?

At the library, Mother chooses three interior design books and asks to stop off at the local DIY store on the way home to pick up a paint colour chart. She's really serious about the Gemma's room renovation prospect. Before heading home, we visit a café for a slice of cake each to celebrate my new job and I get a call offering me some more shifts at the hospital. I gladly accept the ones I can that fit around Mother's treatment.

Finally, at home after dinner, in the privacy of my room, I have a chance to call Gareth. He sounds pleased to hear from me, although I suspect that may be partly due to the fact that my call has given him a good excuse for a break from the intricacies of tort law. I remember him picking Ian's brains about it at the party and me finding the talk so boring that I left them to it. When I tell Gareth that I now have a name for the girl in the photo, Fiona King, he logs on to his Facebook account whilst I'm on the line to see if he can find her in the closed group for people who attended his school.

I can hear him tapping the keys on his laptop down the line and swearing when the screen freezes. Eventually, after rebooting, he enters the closed group and tells me he's looking through the names.

'There she is – Fiona King!' he says excitedly.

'She's there, are there any personal details about her? Anything we can use to track her down?' I say, wishing I had a computer of my own. My pay-as-you-go smartphone really doesn't cut the mustard. The temptation is killing me.

'There's lots of stuff on her profile page about holidays and training for a fun run…'

'Anything else?' I'm now pacing around the room.

'A night out at a restaurant and pictures of her drinking cocktails with friends.'

I curb the urge to tell him to look properly. 'Nothing about where she lives or works?'

'No, nothing, hang on, wait a minute. She's tagged in a picture of a work fundraising day.'

'Where is it? Where does she work?'

'I'm not sure, they're all wearing fancy dress. The picture must have been taken last Christmas. I think Fiona is dressed as an elf.'

I hold the line very impatiently.

'It's a car dealership! There's a sign I can make out at the back of the photo. Cars for You. I'll search for it online. Give me a second… nearly there… got it. Cars for You used car dealership and service centre. It's not that far away.'

'Is her name on the website? Does she still work there?' I ask, hoping Fiona hasn't moved jobs in the last nine months.

'We're in luck. She's still there. The website lists her as the PA to the MD.'

I let out a celebratory whoop. Gareth laughs down the line. Now I have to think of the best way to approach her. After Mike's reaction when I rang him, I think that face to face with Fiona may be the best option. Gareth suggests he can drive me to the car dealership in a few days' time when he can leave work early and I'm not on shift. He thinks that him taking me would be safer than my being alone in case there's a problem, that he'll wait in his car for me whilst I talk to her and then the two of us can make an evening of it afterwards. We agree on a time for him to pick me up. I don't tell him but I wonder whether I can persuade Aunty Lena to invite Mother to stay at hers that night. I'll make sure I'm wearing my best underwear, best meaning one of the few pairs of knickers I own that haven't got holes in or have gone grey in the wash.

I go downstairs thinking that I'll pop over and see Aunty Lena now and also watch the TV quiz with Den that I'd promised to when the phone rings again. The number is withheld but feeling that it might be important I answer.

'Annie?' the woman's voice said. I recognise the slight accent but can't quite place it.

'Yes? Who is this?'

'It's Una from the hospital. I hope you don't mind me calling you in the evening. Mrs Towcester has put your number down as her next of kin contact on her patient form.'

'Is everything OK? Mother is here watching TV.'

'I wanted to tell you rather than your mother herself. It's distressing news I'm afraid and I thought it would be best coming from you. Her friend Mel passed away this afternoon.'

'I thought she'd not been at the chemo sessions for a while, I assumed she'd finished her treatment.'

'No, she took a turn for the worse, was admitted a couple of nights ago and died today. I'm so sorry.'

I sit down on the stairs, flummoxed. 'What do I say, how do I break it to her?'

'Tell her the truth and that Mel was well looked after in hospital and didn't suffer. If your mother has any more questions I'd be happy to answer them when she's next at the hospital for her chemo.'

I briefly consider accidentally forgetting to pass on the news, instead walking out of the door over to Aunty Lena's and following that up with a trip to the pub. Or I could get in the car, drive away and never come back. How do nurses and doctors deal with death every day? Yet if I put it off I know it will only get harder to say something. I tuck my hair behind my ears, clear my throat, steel myself then walk into the lounge to break the sad news.

There are tears, tissues and lots of hot, sweet tea that I brew to feel like I'm doing something useful. The cynical side of me thinks that Mother only knew Mel for a month or so, it's not like she was family or her best friend or anything. I'm aware, however, of the unmentioned subtext.

If Mel can die so suddenly, then so can Mother.

~ 22 ~

I leave Mother napping after telling her the bad news. She cries for her friend and the emotional energy she uses up with her tears wears her out. Neither of us broach the possibility of the same thing happening to her. It's like the rogue fly I shoo out of the window before closing it firmly shut.

Round at Aunty Lena's, the daft television quiz Den is addicted to gives me the welcome opportunity to switch most of my brain off and only concentrate on American states beginning with the letter 'D'. Aunty Lena is out shopping and Den seems delighted to have different company. The house smells the same as it always did back in the day, a warming vanilla scent, which must be the air freshener or cleaning products Aunty Lena uses but to me smells like a cocoon of safety. Den is sitting in his favourite faded, flowery chair with his legs resting on a footstool and together we spend a pleasant half hour shouting out our answers at the TV.

When one team have won that episode's trophy and are told to come back tomorrow to try and retain their title, Den asks, 'How's your mum doing? Have they strung that Toby Smith fella up yet and put his head on a spike outside Leeds Town Hall?' He's only half joking.

'No, that sort of thing went out of fashion about 500 years ago, Den.'

'Well then it's about time it came back in fashion for this lot. Lots of things have come around again. Like vinyl and gin.'

I smile. 'I doubt hanging, drawing and quartering will join them. Anyway, there's no evidence to suggest Toby had anything to do with Gemma going missing and if he was guilty it wouldn't be in his favour to admit to it. Not whilst he's trying to get off an attempted murder charge. I think his solicitor would tell him that it's not a good idea to confess to another one.'

I go and boil the kettle and bring another two cups of coffee into the lounge. There's something I've been wondering whether to ask Den and decide whilst I've got the opportunity to give it a go. I take a deep breath.

'Den, Mother told me she had a difficult time, mentally you know, when Gemma and I were born. Did you know that? I knew she was ill but never realised that severe depression was why she was the way she was – never there, always sleeping.'

Why am I nervous about his answer? Could Mother not have told me the truth in hospital? Surely she couldn't have made all that up?

'Aye, she did have it bad, Annie,' he replied, before taking another slurp of his drink. 'The word depression was never said but we all knew she wasn't well in the head. It just wasn't the sort of thing you wanted people to know back then. Your dad wanted to keep it in the family. Didn't want any gossiping. Thought that he as the head of the family should be able to look after his wife himself.'

That made sense. I remember Father as a rather quiet, private man.

'But she did go to the doctor?'

'Yes, but all he gave her was pills. More and more of the things and it seemed the more she took the less she did, around the house, you two kiddies… your mum's a lovely woman but back then it was hard on your dad trying to keep his job, look after Diana and you two girls as well.'

I hadn't thought about it being hard on Father. All I'd thought about was it being hard on myself.

Den carries on. He's on a roll. 'You know, sometimes I thought our Elaine got too involved, that if she backed off a bit then your mum would have to do more things with you. But I don't think your dad totally trusted your mum to come up trumps. That's why he paid Elaine to pick you up from school and such like.'

I think back to all the times I went over to Aunty Lena's house, all those days she waited for me at the school gates or took me out to the park on a Saturday when my father had to work an extra shift. I never knew she was paid to do it. I'd thought she did it because she wanted to. Because she cared about me. Perhaps the only one who really did.

Den must have seen my face crumple. 'Don't get me wrong, Annie, she loved doing it. Elaine's always had a soft spot for you, we both have. You were, I mean are, always welcome here. I'm just saying that looking back, with hindsight you know, perhaps your dad could have persuaded your mum to do more with you rather than organising it so she didn't have to do anything.'

Such a sadness overwhelms me and I swallow it down, as

far deep into my guts as I can push it. Aunty Lena had been the one constant in my life, but she was paid to be it. She didn't do it out of pseudo-motherly love. Was it just for cold, hard cash? I try hard not to catch Den's eyes. The clock on the wall clicks ten times.

'I've said the wrong thing, haven't I? I'm sorry, Annie. I'm always putting my size tens in it, you ask our Elaine. You know we were both thrilled when you came back.'

It crosses my mind whether Aunty Lena suggested I come back to Mother just because she didn't want to have to nurse her herself. Surely not? Den's voice breaks me away from that thought. He's talking about his sweet tin and pulls it out from under his chair, waving a peace offering at me.

I take a toffee and we sit in silence for a minute, sucking. Den finishes first and then says, 'You and Diana, well you're like family to us.' He pats me on the arm.

'Did you never want children yourself? If you don't mind me asking, I mean.'

He smiles. 'Hell no. We both like children but neither of us wanted one of our own. We make a good twosome. It's lovely to see little ones but then it's great to give them back too. It's like the rhyme my old mum used to say, "How wonderful it is to see our dear relations come to tea, but better still it is to know that when they've had their tea they'll go".' Den laughs at his own joke as my illusions shatter around me. Sure, Aunty Lena cared about me and she still does but she wasn't a second mother. She never wanted to be one. I only have one mother, however inadequate she was.

I have to like it or lump it.

~ 23 ~

A few days later, Gareth is right on time as usual, picking me up to drive to the Cars for You showroom. It's in one of those out-of-town retail parks that look the same wherever you are in the country. By the time we arrive it's 4.30 p.m., surely too early for Fiona to have left for the day.

The showroom isn't busy when I walk in. A man with a goatee beard and shiny suit pounces on me sensing a sale but his jollity soon dissipates when I explain I'm not here to buy a car, rather that I'm looking for Fiona King. He sends me over to the reception desk where a bored-looking middle-aged lady says it's Fiona's day off. Would I like to leave a message?

I feel very deflated at the wasted visit and stupid for not having thought to call first to check she was working today. Priti would have thought of that. I leave my mobile number with the receptionist and ask her to give it to Fiona and tell her that I'm Gemma's sister.

'Oh well, the night is still young…' says Gareth as I explain what happened. The annoyance in not getting to see Fiona has put a dampener on my mood but Gareth throws his arm around my shoulders and pulls me towards him. 'You'll get the chance to talk to Fiona soon. Now, how about we forget about her and enjoy the rest of the evening?'

I'd squared it with Aunty Lena for her to keep an eye on Mother for a night. I'd felt like a naughty teenager when I'd said I wanted to stay over at a 'friend's house'.

Traffic is busy as we drive back to Gareth's place where he has prepared a three-course dinner complete with candles and soft jazz in the background. Secretly when he is in the loo I check his kitchen bin for telltale leftover packaging – despite him saying in the pub that he sells them but wouldn't eat them, does the proposed feast consist of ready meals from his supermarket?

No, it's all his handiwork: smoked salmon for starters followed by a roast chicken dinner and then strawberries and cream, washed down with a bottle of white wine. I'd imagined that he'd live in a stark, minimalist fashion with a leather sofa, huge TV and lots of gadgets, but in reality his house is a cosy Victorian terrace with a galley kitchen and small dining room. The walls are all painted in light but warm colours; there's not a scuffed carpet or piece of tatty wallpaper to be seen. His study books are arranged tidily in the lounge on a table next to his laptop. It's a far cry from Shaun's place that seemed to be a living entity in itself, constantly breeding beer cans and pizza boxes when I was ensconced as a resident.

Gareth had explained that when he and his wife divorced they sold their marital home and he bought this house. He must be earning lots of money to afford it, I think. The prospect of me being able to buy a similar house on my own is such a pipe dream it's laughable. As is the idea of me having a boyfriend who was rich enough to do so.

He ushers me briefly out of the dining room with a glass of wine in my hand so he can bring the food in and then lead me back to my seat. Alone in the lounge for a minute, I take a quick swig of the Pinot Grigio and then look at the three photographs clustered together on a bookshelf. The nosey part of me would love to see what his ex looks like. There are no photos of a woman, however, who could possibly be her. One is of an elderly couple smiling in what looks like a restaurant. His parents, perhaps? The next is of a woman who bears a resemblance to Gareth. It's one of those modern posed photos where the sitters wear bright clothes against a white background. The woman is jumping in the air, arms pointing to the ceiling; next to her is a man around her age and in front of them two young boys who look like twins. I wonder if Gareth will introduce me to them sometime.

The third photograph is much older, what appears to be a framed holiday snap. I pick it up to peer closer. Four people are standing in front of a mountain with the background sun casting a vague shadow over their features. It's a family scene. The elderly couple from the other photo are in the middle looking much younger and less world-worn. The man has his arm around a girl on his right who must have been, what sixteen or seventeen? It's the woman from the jumping photo. She must be Gareth's sister. His mother, I presume, has her arm around a gawky adolescent version of Gareth wearing shorts and walking boots. I smile involuntarily. I remember what it was like to be at that in-between age, no longer a child but not yet an adult.

Gareth calls me to the table and I hastily put the frame back in its position. There isn't even any dust on the shelf. I bet he has a cleaner. For a moment I can see myself living here, having my own key to the door, coming back after a busy shift to a home-cooked dinner and a man eager to see me. But that's all it is – just a fantasy. I quickly recall what the day to day reality was like living with Shaun and it punctures my daydream bubble.

We're halfway through the main course when Gareth remarks on the overnight bag I brought with me. 'So your mum's staying with your aunty tonight?' There's a mischievous glint in his eye.

I smile back in a way I hope is flirtatious and not cross-eyed. 'Elaine's not my real aunty but she's as good as. Yes, Mother's staying there tonight. I think they're having a soap marathon on TV. Early night for me then back to her house?'

He mimics a crestfallen face. 'I was rather hoping I might get lucky…'

'Oh! A roast chicken dinner and you think I'm anybody's!' I reply in mock horror.

'Not just anybody's, I hope. Mine.'

'We'll have to see how good the pudding is first.'

'Coming right up in a minute, the finest strawberries the supermarket has to offer. No cheap frills ones for you. I'll even take them out of the plastic tub and put them in a bowl,' he teases.

'You know how to romance a woman, don't you. Proper spoon and not a plastic one?'

'Of course! I'm a Yorkshireman, not a heathen!'

I laugh. 'I wondered if you'd like to go out for a meal with Ian and Jen sometime?' I've finished my main course now and put the knife and fork down together on the plate. 'Only if you want to, of course…' I hope that suggesting what my mother would call a 'double date' doesn't scare him off.

'Yes, I'd like that. Has Ian said any more about Gemma's case? What is the police's next step?' He starts gathering the empty plates together. 'Hold that thought, I'll be back in a minute with the strawberries.'

So the conversation has turned back to Gemma when I was vaguely hoping that I might get a feel as to whether Gareth sees me as a fun fling or if he's hoping for us to have some sort of a future beyond the next week. Still, the whole premise of the evening had been about talking to Fiona to see if she could tell me more about Gemma and her relationships with Toby and Mike. I can't really complain.

Gareth comes back in carrying, waiter-style, two bowls of strawberries and a pot of cream. They look delicious. 'You were going to tell me about the police. Any news?'

'Nothing you don't know already.' I look down at the table, as I remember I haven't yet told him about the threatening letter. I'd hesitated as I don't want him to worry, or for Mother to know unless she has to. 'DI Glass, or one of his officers anyway, is checking alibis and reviewing the case file, I think. There must be something there to work on, some line of enquiry that they didn't follow through at the time.'

Gareth is pouring cream onto his strawberries, the runny white liquid glugging into his bowl. 'What about DNA? Those techniques weren't around in the late 1980s.'

I finish my mouthful. 'No, there's nothing to test. No body, no clothing or blood.' I think for a second then add, 'I doubt there's any way they could find out Gemma's DNA profile. Her GP records will have her blood type and her dentist her dental records but there isn't any hair, bone or blood or anything they could test for her DNA.'

'Nothing still on Toby Smith?'

'No, not as far as I know.'

He glowers for a second then eats another spoonful of strawberries. There's red juice on his upper lip but I'm not bold enough to lean over and kiss it off. Instead I take the opportunity to change the subject.

'I saw your photos in the lounge. You were a cute teenager. Is that your family you're with in the picture?'

'The one in front of Ben Nevis? Yes, that's my parents, my sister and me. The place looked a bit bare when I moved in so I put a few photos in frames.'

'Where do they live?'

'They moved to Filey when they retired. They're near the sea and like walking their two dogs on the beach every day.'

'And your sister?'

'She lives in Bradford with her family.' He starts to tell me funny stories about his two nephews and how they believed he was Father Christmas when he dressed up last Christmas Eve to surprise them. We finish the strawberries and drain the last of the wine bottle, amiably chatting and me enjoying finding out about his normal family and happy childhood when the most dramatic thing that happened to him was that he and his friend were expelled from the Scouts after his sister dared them to take a bottle of beer, nicked from their dad, to camp. It's a far cry from how I grew up.

I'm so busy laughing that I nearly forget the thought that pops into my head. Gareth taking me into his arms and kissing me instantly dismisses it again from my consciousness, only for me to concentrate on his body, the smell of him and the pleasure two bodies can make together in the darkness of a bedroom.

It's only later, much, much later as he spoons me under the duvet that the thought comes into my head again: *I could get used to this*.

Gareth drives me home early in the morning before the start of his shift. It's just getting light as I walk up to the front door, turn my key and go inside, giving me time for a shower before Mother arrives back from Aunty Lena's. I don't want to have to introduce Gareth to Mother and risk her inviting him round for tea yet. It's far too soon for me to inflict her on him.

When I swing the door shut I notice two letters protruding from the letterbox and pull them out of its jaws. One is marked private and confidential and is addressed to Mother in a hospital-branded envelope. Hopefully it's her appointment with the oncologist. I stand it on the shelf in the hall so Mother will see it when she gets back.

At first glance, I presume the other letter, a folded sheet of A4 paper inside a blank envelope, is a flyer put through the door from a local business, the kind that offers plumbing or roofing work. I nearly put it straight in the recycling bin but something about it that's faintly familiar stops me. There are shadows on the reverse of the white paper and its surface is slightly puckered. I open it up and my hand starts to shake when I read the text that someone has cut out of a newspaper and stuck on the sheet.

Not again.

When I ring DI Glass and get hold of him at the start of his shift I read the words to him in a panic: 'Keep out or it could be you next.'

~ 24 ~

At DI Glass's behest I once again take the letter into the police station for analysis, telling Mother that I'm going out to do some shopping. I'm not out of the house for too long but worry that in my absence another letter might be delivered by hand and not through the Royal Mail. Did whoever wrote it know Mother was out of the house when he or she put it through the letterbox or was it just a coincidence? DI Glass says they can look at installing a panic button in our home but thinks that may be presumptuous at the moment because the letters haven't contained a specific threat.

Writing 'it could be you next' to the sister of a missing girl feels specific enough to me.

He organises for a police car to drive past our house intermittently for reassurance. I find the locks on the back and front doors far more reassuring. One letter could be someone fooling around. With two they mean business.

Re-interviewing significant people who made statements back in 1989 is taking time, mostly due to tracking down their whereabouts. DI Glass assures me he'll speak to Robert Smith again regarding the threats. At the moment, he tells me unofficially, Smith is the most likely suspect but there is no proof. It could be anyone pushing poison through our front door: it might be someone I've never met, someone I would never suspect or even someone close to me. I mention Mike again to DI Glass and how keen he was to get rid of me when I phoned him. Mike, as he was Gemma's on and off boyfriend, is on the police's list of persons of interest to re-interview. Could he have sent the letters? He would have known the address because Mother is in the same house he visited to see Gemma when they were teenagers. But how would he know I'm living here now?

Suspicion, mistrust, fear: these are all the emotions the letters engender in me. I find myself looking out of the front window periodically to check if there's a police car monitoring our house. I'm anxious, on edge, not sure whether, when I do spot a marked car, it gives me comfort or worries me more that DI Glass thinks the threats could be serious. As soon as the sun starts to set on the horizon, I shut the curtains to block out life beyond these four walls.

The one thing I don't do is tell Mother. I ought to, I know, in case another letter arrives and the threat escalates. Yet her oncologist appointment is next week when she will find out whether the chemo is doing its job. What with that and Mel's death still fresh, I feel Mother has enough to deal with right now. Every day when I'm not working, I make sure I regularly check to see if anything has been posted through the letterbox. A general unease continues to hang over me, remaining by my side wherever I am, whispering danger softly into my ear. I consider talking to Aunty Lena about the situation but then worry that if I do so the most likely outcome is one more person will be dragged into the letter writer's net.

What with working as many shifts at the hospital as possible, looking after Mother and constantly being in fight-or-flight mode on the edge of my nerves, I'm dog tired. Sleep comes with difficulty and it's fractured and dissatisfying. Although I'd love to see Priti, I turn down a weekend visit in order to stay in the house in case there's a problem. I don't even get much of a chance to meet up with Gareth and the plan to arrange a meal with Ian and Jen goes on the back burner. I can't bear the strain of meeting the three of them face to face and having to keep quiet about the letters.

It's when I'm thinking about the meal that the thought strikes me that the best person to confide in would be Ian alone. He'll be able to advise me as well as keeping what I tell him confidential. I decide to ring him rather than make an appointment at his office, that way I don't have to leave Mother on her own in the house. I choose a moment when she's having a daytime nap and make the call.

Ian is concerned when I update him on the situation. I can tell he's slipping into solicitor mode to reassure me.

'The police are following the correct procedures but you must let them know if there's something, anything that strikes you as odd,' he says. 'It doesn't matter if you think it's trivial or could be irrelevant – tell them.'

'Odd like what?' I ask, thinking that shoving two anonymous threatening letters through someone's door is rather more than odd.

'Someone hanging around your house. A car parked suspiciously. Anyone knocking on your door wanting to sell something. If anyone, like an electricity meter reader, wants to gain entry into the house take their details and call the company to confirm their identity before you let them in.'

'You think the letter sender might try to get into the house? Do you think he or she really means us harm?'

'Annie, it's probably a sad crank who gets a kick out of scaring other people and wouldn't dare see you face-to-face. You must be careful, though, and err on the side of caution. Keep a diary of what happens and how it is affecting you. That will be very useful if the case goes to trial.'

'Trial?'

'Yes, if the police catch whoever is doing it. Under the Malicious Communications Act of 1998 it's an offence to send a threatening letter to another person. If the letters cause the recipient to fear violence the sender can be sentenced to up to five years in prison.'

'I hope the police catch them. DI Glass says Robert Smith is a person of interest but there's no proof. They've questioned him and he's denied it.'

'If there isn't any forensic proof or eyewitnesses who saw him post the letter then he would deny it.' Of course he will, if he thinks he can get away with it.

It sounds like Ian takes a swig of a drink and then he goes on, 'As a solicitor, I can advise you on the law, but as your friend, I'm worried about you. Are you sure you don't want to tell anyone else about this? You deserve some support…'

'I don't want Mother to worry unnecessarily. If I tell anyone else they'll probably overreact and it'll get back to her anyway. I don't want to give the bastard the satisfaction of doing more harm.'

'I see where you're coming from, but remember, Annie, you're not on your own. Jen and I have got a spare room and a sofa bed in the study. If for any reason you don't want to stay in your house bring your mother and stay with us. Please.'

'I don't want to put you out…'

Ian interrupts me. 'And I don't want you to stay in your house if you don't feel safe there. Promise me you'll think about it.'

'OK.' I know I should think about it, but I don't want to imagine a scenario where I think it's unsafe for Mother and I to remain in the house. I'd certainly have to tell her what's going on if I announced we're moving to Ian and Jen's for a while.

When I end the call with a fake positive note that I'll be fine, I see on the screen that the voicemail message is flashing. I press the button to listen to it.

'Hello,' says a woman's voice coming from the earpiece. 'It's Fiona King, you left a message for me at work. I remember your sister well. When do you want to meet up?'

~ 25 ~

Fiona is friendly enough when I ring her back but she explains that she can't talk for long because she's at work. We make an arrangement to meet in a café after my night shift, which gives Fiona enough time to meet me before she starts work herself. Whilst I'm dying to ask her questions now, I respect her wishes and keep the call brief. At least she sounds like she'll be a lot more forthcoming than Mike was.

Finding a date when we are both free to meet up was difficult, therefore I have to wait over a week before I can see her. Until then, I feel that I'm in limbo, waiting to see if anything else comes through the letterbox.

A few days later it's Mother's appointment with the oncologist to see how the chemotherapy is working. Mother is matter of fact about it as I drive her to the hospital, saying that she can't change her test results, whatever they are, so there's no point worrying about it. 'What will be will be, Annie,' she says, 'what will be will be.' She might be convincing herself but not me.

As we're slightly late for the appointment, having been stuck in roadworks on the way there, I borrow a wheelchair from reception to push Mother to the clinic quickly. There I check her in and take a seat amongst all the other people waiting to hear their fate. The feet of the plastic chair make a scraping sound on the floor as I drag it beside Mother's wheelchair. In the background a television is on and there are magazines on a side table but Mother, like some of the other attendees, is lost in her own thoughts.

To my surprise, we don't have to wait very long. The nurse calls us in on the dot of our appointment. I smile at Mother and push her into the consulting room. 'What will be will be,' she says again.

The consultant is Mr Sharpe, an amiable-looking red-faced man who is probably in his fifties. He shakes our hands politely then starts to go over Mother's test results. Some terms I recognise from the chemo clinic but others go over my head. I'm about to interrupt when I remember it's Mother's appointment and not mine. Her face has drained of colour in anticipation and there's a faint sheen of sweat on her forehead. My mind loses track and for a few seconds I find myself concentrating on the whirring of the fan above and the flickering of the florescent strip light on the ceiling.

I'm jolted back to the here and now by Mother squeezing my hand. In panic I look to her shocked face, and then over to Mr Sharpe. He's smiling whilst he's talking.

'All in all,' he's saying, 'I'm pleased with your results. The chemotherapy is doing its job and has shrunk your tumour by the amount I wanted.'

'What does that mean?' asks Mother, still clinging onto my hand.

'Don't look so worried,' he replies in a jocular tone. 'It's good news. Your cancer is behaving itself and we can stop the chemo for now. We'll still be keeping an eye on you at regular check-ups. It's important that you understand that the cancer hasn't gone, but we've got it under control and if the tumour does start growing again we can consider further surgery and/or chemotherapy. In your case it's the best result we could have hoped for.'

'So she's not going to die?' I ask, forgetting my resolution not to butt in. I've let the elephant loose in the room.

'Not now, no. Hopefully she has many more happy years ahead of her. I can't give you a guarantee, of course, no one can, but I can see no medical reason at the moment why you shouldn't be around for a long time yet, Mrs Towcester.'

'Thank you, thank you, doctor,' replies Mother with tears in her eyes. She adds her other hand to the one already squeezing mine and I clutch back.

'We're so grateful for everything you've done, Mr Sharpe,' I add. 'No more hospital visits for a while then?'

'My secretary will send you a check-up appointment in the post. Until then, enjoy yourselves. You have something to celebrate tonight.'

As I push Mother back to the car, I ask her what she'd like to do later on to mark the occasion. 'How about cake? Pizza? Why don't we see if Aunty Lena wants to come over to hear the good news?'

Mother takes a deep breath in and exhales slowly, relishing the fresh air. 'I can breathe easily now,' she says. 'I can't believe I don't have to have chemotherapy again. I was prepared for the worst.'

'I know.'

The fading sunlight glows orange on the horizon to welcome us back into the world.

'Chocolate cake, do you want some wine too, Annie? Pizza, yes, that's a good idea. There's the last part of the drama Elaine and I have been watching on the television tonight too. Will you ring her up please and invite her round to join us? Don't tell her the news on the phone, I'd like to tell her myself face to face.'

'Doesn't she know you were seeing the consultant today?'

'No, I kept it quiet in case Mr Sharpe had bad news. I didn't want her ringing me up and asking me, it would make me feel more nervous.'

'Fair enough. I'll phone her when we get in.'

Reg's house is quiet when I park outside it – yet again someone's van is parked in front of our house – and the only paper that has been put through the front door is an Indian takeaway menu.

For an evening, I relax and enjoy the pleasure on Mother's face when she tells Aunty Lena the good news and bask in the relief that permeates the room. Gemma, aged sixteen, smiles along with us from the confines of her photo frame.

After much pizza has been consumed, most of a bottle of wine drunk between Aunty Lena and I (Mother sticks to lemonade) and the credits have rolled on the television drama, it's time for the party to end. Mother raises a toast to Mel's memory and we all think about what might have been. 'So, Annie, now your mum's recovering, what are *you* going to do?' asks Aunty Lena when she's putting on her coat to leave.

It's a question that startles me, particularly when I realise I know the answer without having to take stock.

'I think I'm going to stick around for a while.'

Thursday 4th May 1989. 1.30 p.m.

The doorbell rang again. This time it couldn't be the postman because they stopped lunchtime rounds years ago. Diana waited for it to stop but when it didn't she slowly walked out of the kitchen to the front door, still hoping whoever it was would go away.

Through the frosted glass she could see it was Reg. 'Diana, I can see you're in there, open the door please, love,' he implored. 'I need to talk to you.'

Reluctantly she opened the door. It was a long time since he'd last called and a very long time since that time she'd let him in in the quiet of the mid-afternoon, Frank not expected back home from work for hours.

'I'm busy, I haven't got long,' she said, knowing full well that the whole street knew she was never busy. She never did anything.

'A quick cuppa?' he asked. Diana sighed – as long as it was quick – and let him go through to the kitchen where she scraped off a bit of the print off the kettle whilst it was boiling. The pain in her fingertips forced her to stay in reality.

She filled the teapot and put it and two mugs down on the table.

'What do you want, Reg?'

He smiled up at her, the corners of his thin moustache pointing upwards with the movement. 'You're so beautiful, you know,' he stated and reached out to push a stray lock of hair behind her left ear.

'Stop that.' Diana pushed his hand away.

'You liked it once.'

'Once. Just once. A long time ago, Reg. All in the past. We agreed not to talk about it again.'

Reg inched his hand as near to Diana's as he dared. 'But wasn't it a wonderful once? It was years ago, I know, but I can't stop thinking about you, Diana. About us, what we could be. You know I can't. I tried to make it work again with Karen, I really did, but I've decided. I made my mind up today. I'm going to leave her.'

Diana held her hot drink with both hands in front of her like a weapon. 'And why are you telling me?'

'I'll get a flat. We could give it a try you and me, see what we're like together. You could even come and live with me if you want. I'll get a two-bedroom place so there's room for your girls to stay. We could be happy.'

'I am happy. With my husband.'

'Oh, come on, Diana, stop kidding yourself. You're not happy. You haven't been for years. All Frank does is drug you up. What kind of life is that? He doesn't love you. I do. I'd take care of you, make you laugh, treat you like a Queen, give you the life you deserve.'

'I don't deserve anything.'

'Of course you do!'

Diana put the mug down. Reg inched his finger so close to hers that they nearly touched.

'I'm so tired, Reg. I can't cope with this again. I need a tablet and a lie down. Stop upsetting me. Please.' She began to shake. He spotted her weakness and took her hand.

'Frank doesn't give you what you need, doesn't see you for the beautiful woman you are. He grinds you down, Diana. What you need is love, not those pills the doctor keeps giving you. When we are together we can both be happy.'

'No. You're kidding yourself. What happened between us was a one-off, Reg.' Diana's head was thumping. She was finding it hard to breathe and tried to take deeper, longer breaths in through the nose and out through the mouth. That's what the doctor had said to do. In and slowly out.

'I'm telling Karen tonight, then I can come over and see you. Think about it, Diana. Please. A fresh start for both of us.'

For a tiny moment she saw a chink of hope open up in her dark sky. She imagined a flat far away from Greville Road with peace, quiet, no noise or interruptions. No postman knocking at the door or other women judging her.

What she didn't picture was Reg there too.

'No, Reg, no.' The breathing exercises gave her a little bit of confidence. 'I made a mistake before but I'm not going to make another one. I hope things work out for you but it won't be with me. I've told you that before. Please go now.'

His crestfallen eyes looked like a puppy dog's after being denied its supper.

She led him to the front door where he said, 'I'll still come round tonight. If you change your mind I'll let you know where I'll be.'

'I won't change my mind. Goodbye, Reg.' Diana shut the door behind him and bolted it. The pain in her head increased. She went back up to her bedroom. Another couple of pills shouldn't do any harm and would keep her calm until tonight when the children get back. She swallowed a couple with water and lay down. Oblivion would come for a few precious hours.

If only there had never been a once in the first place.

~26~

I'd arranged to meet Fiona in a café near the hospital a little while after my night shift, giving me a chance to have breakfast in the canteen and get changed. Although I'm not quite as weary as I was after my first couple of shifts, I'm still exhausted, hot and slightly woozy when I dash in a couple of minutes late. I recognise Fiona immediately from the website photo – she's sitting expectantly at a table facing the door waiting for me.

I put my hand out to shake hers. 'Hi, Fiona? Thanks so much for coming.'

Fiona smiles back and I can tell by her demeanour that she's going to be a lot more forthcoming than Mike was.

We make some small talk about weather, the traffic and whether an espresso is better than a mocha before I get down to the nitty gritty. I tell her that I'm trying to find out more about my sister and that I traced her from the group photograph, then pull out a colour photocopy of it from my bag.

She grins in recognition. 'I remember this! It was taken after school one day. We'd all gone home, got changed, had dinner, then met up again in the woods. We used to do that quite often. In those days there was no internet or Netflix – nothing to do at home.'

'So four of you, I mean you, Gemma, Toby and Mike, hung out a lot together?'

'Yes, we had other friends but the main group was the four of us. Gemma was lovely, a great friend. I still miss her. We were close.'

'Can I ask if she was in a relationship with Toby or Mike?'

'We were just teenagers, all mates together. Gemma and Mike were sort of seeing each other but it was on and off, they were mainly friends who kissed now and then and played at being boyfriend and girlfriend. He took it more seriously than her, I think, but she enjoyed the flirting, as you do when you're that age.'

I smile in recognition, remembering the extent I went to at sixteen to get the boys' attention.

'And Toby? What about him?'

'Well...' Fiona, who has been so chatty up to now, suddenly clams up. 'You know he went to prison?' she asks me.

'Yes I do. That made me want to know if he could have been involved in Gemma going missing. What was his relationship with Gemma? Did he fancy her? Do you know if he was ever violent to her in any way?'

Fiona goes quiet for a moment. I can tell she's hesitant to tell me something. Instead of prompting her I wait for her to answer me. She rips open a sugar packet and pours it into her empty cup, watching the crystals collect at the bottom.

'There was an incident. I promised Gemma at the time I wouldn't say anything.'

I sense with excitement that she's about to tell me something more important than teenage gossip. Thankfully, her proclaimed reticence to tell me doesn't last very long.

'I suppose it doesn't matter if I say anything now. Gemma's not here for me to betray her confidence. There was a party one night at the house of a girl in our class. Her parents were out and some older kids brought beer and vodka. Gemma wasn't used to booze and got quite drunk. Very drunk really. Mike told her to not have any more and she argued with him, saying he couldn't tell her what to do. He left in a huff. Then Toby made a play for her and they disappeared into a bedroom. I was jealous, God knows that man makes my skin crawl now that I know what he did to his wife, but back then I quite liked him and wanted to know why he'd gone off with Gemma and not me. After a few minutes I banged on the door, then Gemma came out half-undressed and said she was going to leave. Toby ran after us to the front door but he didn't follow us after that. She was sick in the bushes on the way home; like I said, she wasn't used to drinking. She said that Toby had wanted to have sex and they got halfway there but then she changed her mind. He was trying to persuade her to carry on when I banged on the door.'

'Was she OK? What happened next?'

'She had a huge hangover at school the next day but otherwise she was fine, relieved that she hadn't actually had sex with Toby. It made her realise that she was more interested in Mike than she thought. Gemma didn't tell him what had happened. A week later, though, the day that she went missing, someone told Mike about Gemma and Toby being locked in a room and said that she'd slept with him. At lunchtime outside on the picnic benches Mike called her a slag and tried to hit Toby but Toby was too quick for him.

Mike stormed off into the woods and Gemma followed him. I never found out what they said, we had different lessons in the afternoon. I usually walked home with Gemma after school but she left before me and I went with Toby instead. He was cut up about what happened.'

'So you're his alibi?'

'Yes, the police contacted me recently to confirm I was with him for an hour after school before he went home. His mum said that Toby didn't leave the house until the next morning.'

'You say Mike tried to hit Toby, was Toby violent back?'

'No, he blocked him, held on to Mike's wrist when he tried to punch him until he calmed down. I never saw Toby be violent. We lost touch a few years after school and I was shocked when I heard he'd gone to prison for attempted murder. I'd never have thought it. It makes me think that anyone is capable of anything.'

At this I shudder, thinking of the two threatening letters. It could be anyone who sent them.

'Do you think Toby could have harmed Gemma?'

'No, as I said, he was with me after school that day until he went home. He said he'd been drunk too at the party and he felt bad for trying to persuade Gemma to do something she didn't want to do.'

'Did you tell the police this?'

'No.' Fiona takes another long sip of her coffee. 'Gemma had asked me to keep what happened at the party a secret. She was a virgin. She didn't want anyone calling her a slag. I thought she'd run off for a bit to clear her head and didn't think it was relevant. Toby and Mike would never have hurt her. Like I said, we were all good friends back then.'

I look again at the photo of the four of them in the woods.

'By the way,' I say, my curiosity piqued, 'out of interest, can you remember who took this photo? Was it another person in your group of friends?'

Fiona rubbed her nose as if to think more clearly. 'No, it was usually just the four of us. That photo, it was probably this boy who kept following Gemma around for a while who took it. She put up with him for a bit, they were in the orchestra together. He'd come to the woods with his camera and take photos then give them to her a few days later.'

'Who was he?'

'He was younger than us, seemed harmless at first but then kept on following us, giving Gemma presents, love notes and things, although she asked him to stop. In the end I think Toby said to him that if he turned up again he'd have him to deal with him. Mike was a bit too cowardly to do that sort of thing.'

This could be a lead. I lean towards her.

'Do you remember his name?'

'Um, it began with G I think. Gary, Gareth?'

It feels in my chest that my heart stops beating for a moment. I taste the acrid thickness of adrenaline in my throat.

'Are you alright?' Fiona asks.

I go to my phone and scroll through the pictures saved on there. There's one of Gareth I took at Ian's party. Do I really want to know? Before I give myself time to cop out I pass the phone over to her.

'Is that him? That is Gareth Mitchell.'

Fiona picks up the phone and swipes the screen to home in on the man's face. 'Yes, I think so. Obviously he's a lot older but so are we all! That's Gareth.'

I go cold and then flush back straight to hot.

'Do you know him them?' Fiona asks.

'You could say that,' I reply.

She pulls her chair closer to the table conspiratorially.

'Look, I haven't got any proof of this, but at the time I suspected that it was Gareth who told Mike about Gemma and Toby at the party. He's the only person I could think of who would have anything to gain from trying to split them up, although I haven't a clue how he found out himself. Toby was embarrassed about his behaviour – and probably about Gemma turning him down – and wanted to keep it quiet. Mike never said to me who told him. After Gemma went missing our group sort of fell apart. We did our exams then I left to go to secretarial college. Toby went to work at a plumbers' and Mike stayed on to do A Levels.'

I feel so angry. I've been duped. A fool. That night we met at the pub, Gareth only wanted to get to know me because he wanted to know more about Gemma. He'd been in love with her and used me for information. Was he thinking of her when he slept with me? Did he imagine her face when kissing my lips? I swallow the vomit that's rising in my throat and gulp down the rest of my coffee.

'Thanks, Fiona, you've been really helpful,' I say.

'Are you sure you're OK? Your face has gone red, if you don't mind me saying.'

'I do feel a little bit ill. It was a long shift at the hospital. I'd better go. Please give me a call if you think of anything else.'

We say our goodbyes and I half-run to my car, adamant about where my next stop will be. Then an even worse thought hit me. If Gareth stalked Gemma, could he have killed her?

~27~

I manage to drive into the last space available on the suburban high street, swerving into it about three seconds before an annoyed four by four driver could. Tough luck, there's no time for me to waste. I'm hot, shivery and furious.

This time I'm not going to give Mike the chance to hang up on me. His office is above a hairdresser and I run up the stairs two at a time. Each foot stamp on the staircase fuels my determination to make him tell the truth. I'll sit here all day if I have to.

Behind a non-descript brown door with a 'Mike Braithwaite Accountancy Services' sign on there's a dingy reception area staffed by an older lady. She smiles when I walk in but her expression changes to one of disconcertion when I refuse her offer to sit on the adjacent stained brown armchair. I tell her I urgently need to speak to Mike and without waiting for her to reply, take my chances and walk to one of the two doors – apart from the entrance – in the room, breezing through when I find it's unlocked.

I'm in luck. Instead of walking into the loo or cleaning cupboard, I'm in Mike's office. He looks up over his computer monitor at me when he hears the noise of the door and the receptionist flapping about, pointlessly telling me Mike is busy and can't see me without an appointment.

Ignoring her, I look Mike straight in the eye and say, 'I'm Gemma Towcester's sister, Annie. You need to talk to me, I know what happened on the day she went missing.'

His pale face morphs into an even whiter shade. He dismisses the receptionist with a line about being able to see me and gestures at the seat opposite his desk. I'm not sitting down and letting him take the authority here.

'I won't take up much of your time if you tell me the truth,' I say. 'Please, for Gemma's sake.'

To my surprise, in contrast to his belligerence during our previous phone call, his attitude changes to that of a wounded man. He rubs his chin where the stubble would have been at half past seven this morning, casts his eyes down then asks, 'What do you want to know?'

'On the day she went missing you rowed with Gemma and didn't tell the police. You thought she'd slept with Toby at a party.'

Mike won't catch my eye. 'Yes.'

'Why didn't you tell the police?' I'm standing right by him with my palms flat on his desk.

'It was private, between the two of us. At first I thought Gemma must be with Fiona, or she'd gone off with Toby, but after a few days when I knew that wasn't true I thought she'd run away because of what I'd said. I didn't want people to find out or my mum and dad to know. I was ashamed. OK? Is that enough for you? Who told you?'

'Your old friend, Fiona. She also told me that Gemma and Toby had kept their drunken snog at the party quiet but that, on the day she went missing, someone told you they'd had sex at the party. Who told you?'

'Why is this relevant now?' he whines.

'Because she's my sister and I deserve to know everything I can about what happened that day. Did you hurt her?'

There's a pause. Oh God, was it Mike? Did this supposedly mild-mannered boy kill Gemma because he thought she'd had sex with his best friend? I wipe the sweat off my forehead with the back of my hand and am glad that behind the desk he can't see my knees wobbling.

He speaks softly. 'I pushed her, that's all, nothing more.'

'Where?' I shout.

'I pushed her by her shoulders and she fell over.'

'What! No, I mean where were you?'

'We argued during the lunch break and I stormed off into the woods behind the school. She followed me and kept saying that she only kissed Toby and it meant nothing.'

'Then?'

'Then I called her a slag again and pushed her. She fell backwards. I waited until she got up and I knew she wasn't hurt then ran back to school. That was the last time I spoke to her. I've regretted it ever since.'

Vile, cowardly man. I jump to my sister's defence. 'She didn't sleep with Toby.'

'Really? He said she didn't but then of course he would. Ever since I heard that Toby was convicted of attempted murder I've wondered if he'd tried to rape her. That bastard. I'm so sorry. I should have said something at the time.'

At that he starts to cry, little yelps he tries to bite down on and unsuccessfully contain. What a pathetic figure. My eye catches a photograph on his desk of him in a family portrait with a woman of around the same age and two boys whom I'd guess are about fifteen and twelve. I wonder if his wife knows how spineless he is? I hope she's a decent person or their children stand no chance in life.

'Who told you, Mike? Who told you about the party?'

'This boy who had a crush on Gemma, he kept hanging around us for a while. He said I had a right to know what my girlfriend had been up to. His sister had been at the party.'

'His name, do you remember it?' He pulls a handkerchief from his trouser pocket.

'Gareth, I think. A Welsh name but he was as Yorkshire as the rest of us.'

My knees give way and I hold myself upright with my palms on the table, locking my elbows to take the weight.

'She wasn't raped and didn't sleep with Toby. It was a drunken kiss and fumble at the party that Gemma put a stop to.' Mike nods in thanks.

'I should have believed her.'

'Yes you should have. And you should not have pushed her. Is there anything else you didn't tell the police? Do you have any idea what could have happened to Gemma?'

He shakes his head forlornly. 'No. Like I said, I thought she might have run off because of what I did. She was so lovely, nobody would ever want to hurt her.'

Apart from you, I thought. You weren't averse to giving her a good shove when your heckles were high.

'I'll call the police and tell them,' he says, as if he's doing me a favour.

'You do that. About time,' I reply and waltz straight out of his office as quickly as I came in.

The school and work traffic has subsided by now meaning that it only takes me about twenty minutes to drive to my next destination, the warehouse-like supermarket that nearly every town and city has in its environs. It's the first time I've visited but the layout is practically the same as every other one of its ilk.

I just miss hitting a bollard when I swerve into an empty parking space. My forehead feels like it's burning up and I'm finding it difficult to get my brain to action my thoughts. Get out of the car. Lock the door. Walk to the entrance. My legs feel heavy and putting one foot in front of the other takes all my concentration.

I head for the customer service counter and queue behind a woman who is trying to return a half-eaten packet of ham. Everything seems too loud and yet the noises are blurring into one making it difficult for me to hear what's being said. I only catch the odd word such as 'salmonella', 'off' and 'inedible'. Eventually she accepts a voucher and leaves. It's my turn, but before I can speak, the man behind the counter announces a two for one deal on pizzas over the loudspeaker.

'I need to speak to Gareth Mitchell, he works here. It's urgent,' I tell him as soon as his broadcast is finished. He replies that he'll call the office and see if Mr Mitchell is free. After a short conversation the man, whose name badge informs me is called Ronnie, says Gareth will be out in a minute.

It's a few minutes before Gareth turns up.

'Annie! What a lovely surprise! How was your shift?' He

leans towards me to kiss me on the cheek but I jerk back instinctively and he smooches thin air.

I sneeze loudly and Gareth looks concerned. 'Are you OK?' he says having quickly recovered his composure following my kiss dodge.

The urge to slap both of his two faces nearly overwhelms me but I remember Mike confessing he shoved Gemma and swear not to stoop to his lowlife level.

'We have to talk. We can do it here or in private. Your choice.'

He looks confused. 'I share an office. Where's your car? Perhaps we can talk in there?'

I stride ahead of him to my old banger, unlock the door, get in myself and wait until he gets into the passenger seat.

'What's wrong? Have you heard something more from the police?'

I let out a croaky ironic laugh. 'It's rather a case of me having something to tell them. You're a liar and a sick bastard. Are you a murderer too? Don't even think of laying a finger on me. There's CCTV all round the car park.' I hold my keys in my fist with the most pointed one ready in case I need it for a weapon.

'What are you talking about?' Is it my head or had he hesitated a bit too long before he answered me?

'Don't bother telling more lies. I know you stalked Gemma at school and Toby had to warn you off. I know you told Mike that Gemma slept with Toby at a party. Did you hurt my sister? Did you kill her?'

Gareth's composure has now well and truly slipped. 'No! I swear I know nothing about what happened to her. I thought

I'd find out from you. Look, Annie, I can explain, please let me explain, what you've been told, it wasn't like that.'

'No! You lied to me, you used me, you slept with me, and I'm not happy about it. At all. Why should I believe a single word you say? I'm going to the police, Gareth, and telling them what I know. They can find out who you really are.' A coughing fit overtakes me and I take a gulp from the bottle of water I keep in the driver side door compartment.

Gareth holds his hands up in the air then loosens his collar. 'I'm telling the truth, Annie. Yes, I did have a crush on Gemma at school and it was why I first approached you in the pub but I swear, everything else between us is real. I'm with you because I want to be, not because of Gemma. I didn't kill Gemma, I had a schoolboy crush on her, I'd never have harmed her.'

Was he spinning me more lies?

'Did you or did you not tell Mike that Gemma had slept with Toby?'

At least he has the decency to look guilty when I say this. He looks down at the floor where there are a few used tissues and an empty crisp packet.

'Yes,' he mumbles.

'What was that? Speak up!'

'I did, but I was only fourteen. I made a stupid mistake...'

'A stupid mistake? Like those you made as a grown man lying to me about your relationship with my sister? Lying about how you knew her friends? You know that the day you lied to Mike about Gemma sleeping with Toby was the last day she was seen alive? Maybe she went missing because of you! Maybe she's dead because of you!'

'I didn't lie about the party. My sister told me Gemma was locked away with Toby in the bedroom for ages.'

As if that makes a difference to me.

'That doesn't mean they had sex!' I interrupt. 'Don't try and wheedle your way out of it!'

'Annie, please,' he begs, 'believe me when I say I do really like you; ever since our first date I've wanted to be with you…'

'Then you should have been honest with me, Gareth.' Exhaustion floods over me. I don't have enough energy left to shout. 'I'm going to go to the police and tell them what I know. Get out of the car and stay away from me.'

He doesn't need telling twice. Gareth speedily opens the passenger door, says that he's sorry, and half-runs back into the store.

My fist unclenches around my keys and somehow, in between the angry sobs I find coming out of my mouth, I start the engine and leave the car park without hitting anything. The drive home is a blur of elation, fuzziness and gut-gnawing sadness.

I had liked Gareth. I had believed him. I had slept with the man who had stalked and betrayed my sister all those years ago, even imagined living in his house and sharing his bed every night. He may even be lying and have something to do with Gemma going missing. How stupid does that make me?

~ 28 ~

It is hot, so hot. I wind the front windows down in the hope that the breeze will cool my aching head. The drive home feels unreal, as if I'm riding on a dodgem or playing a boring computer game that involves getting from A to B without ploughing down a pedestrian. I'm on autopilot, my feet and hands are taking me where I want to go, cutting my conscious thought out of the equation. There's so much going around in my head that each thought is jumbling, swirling, fighting the others for attention meaning that I can't concentrate on anything at all.

All I want to do is lay my head down on my pillow and sleep.

After a moment, or three, of nothingness, I realise that my car is parked a couple of doors down from Mother's house. I don't remember searching for the space or parallel parking. Despite the breezes blowing in the car, and the autumnal weather, I'm still burning up. I twist the car key in the ignition to turn on the electrics, press the buttons to shut the front windows and will my body to get out. What's next? I shut my eyes and try to think in sequence. That's it, lock the car and put one foot in front of the other, unlock the front door then keep going up the stairs until I make it to my bed and oblivion.

A beep on my phone interrupts me after I've successfully completed step one. It's a message from Priti. I must have texted her this morning after confronting Mike.

What's happened? Please call, I'm v worried.

The screen also tells me there's a missed call from Gareth and a voicemail message. I plunge my mobile into my trouser pocket and pull out a used tissue to blow my nose with. That's the moment I notice, whilst trying to avoid getting a snot waterfall on my fingers, that there's loud music coming from next door and the front door is ajar. Bloody Reg. I need to phone the police, my pillows and duvet are calling me, I want the loo and the last thing I wish to do is have a confrontation with that creepy git; but then I think of how the music will be disturbing Mother and will put the kibosh on my wish for a peaceful slumber. Aunty Lena's words, about how we should show Reg kindness, battle with everything else in my head for top priority. They win. A quick minute and a polite request to turn the music down won't hurt.

I knock on the front door, not that he's likely to hear it above the 1970s rock blaring out (even his country and western music would be preferable to that headache-inducing cacophony of screaming and bass) and shout his name. No answer, so I gingerly walk into the hall, past the pile of old newspapers and empty bottles that have yet to make it into the recycling box and push the open door into what I presume is his lounge.

'Hello? Reg?'

The first thing I see is the huge stereo with a turntable, CD player, cassette decks and large speakers. I stride over and press the off button. Quietness at last, so quiet that I now hear a dull groan coming from inside the room. Behind me, slumped on the sofa, is a man's body, his hand clutching onto what looks like a brandy or whisky bottle. There's a vomit trail cascading from his mouth. Immediately I reach for my phone, dial 999 and ask for an ambulance. Then I put my basic first aid training from my hospital induction into action, try to clear the existing vomit from his mouth, check that he's breathing and slap him round the face for good measure.

To be clear, slapping isn't in the handbook. I want to rouse him to ask what he's taken and how much, but also I feel a flash of anger that he's made his problems mine. I don't need his cry for help when I have my own problems to deal with.

The slap works. Reg regains consciousness for a minute, a fact I gather by his shouting, 'Ow!'

'Reg, this is Annie from next door. I've called an ambulance. What have you taken? How much? Tell me, it's important.'

He moves a little and breathes out toxic alcohol fumes. The stink, mixed with the smell of stale vomit, is almost unbearable. 'Annie? Go home. Just let me die.'

'No. I won't.' I shake him gently by the shoulder. 'Sit up. Stay awake. What have you taken? How much of that have you drunk?' I say snatching the near-empty bottle from his grasp.

'Paracetamol. Whisky. Leave me be. I deserve to die.'

'That's not your decision to make. It's never too late to get help.' I pull him upright and haul him to his feet. 'Can you walk?' I don't know where the strength is coming from for me to do this. Once again, I seem to be on autopilot mode, my body ruling over my conscious thoughts. Reg takes a couple of steps leaning on me and then bends double to be sick. I plonk him down on the sofa and look for the kitchen. I find it in the room at the back of the house, just as dated and tired as my mother's but far dirtier, turn the plastic bowl in the sink upside down to pour the murky water down the drain, fill up a mug with cold water from the tap, grab the tea-towel hanging from a cupboard and then go back to the lounge, giving Reg the bowl to catch the rest of his vomit in.

Once he's finished, I pass him the tea-towel to wipe his mouth with and the mug of water.

'Swill your mouth out then drink some water,' I tell him. Where's the ambulance? Surely a good few minutes have passed since I rang the emergency services?

'Diana,' Reg says seemingly to me. 'I'm sorry, Diana.'

'I'm Annie,' I reply. 'Try to stay awake. The ambulance is on its way. Why did you do it, Reg?'

He tries to stare at me but his eyes aren't focusing. 'It was a split-second thing, I didn't mean to...'

I think that it must have taken longer than a second to neck all that booze and wash down the pills.

'You can get help, Reg. It's never too late.'

'What? It is too late.' He looks at me confused as his eyelids start to crinkle and droop, tempting him once again into the black realms of unconsciousness. I give him a good shake.

'You've got to stay awake, Reg. The ambulance will be here soon.'

I don't know if he hears because he passes out again.

Outside I finally hear ambulance sirens. I put Reg in the recovery position then head to the front door to show the ambulance crew the way. They double park and, in a flash, run into the house asking questions about Reg and what has happened. I tell them I'm his neighbour and I went in because he was playing loud music (did he do that because he wanted to be found, I wonder?) and his front door was open. I explain Reg said he'd taken paracetamol and whisky. I tell them he's been in and out of consciousness – all the things I think they'll need to know.

A police first-responder arrives to join the throng in the lounge and the team insert a cannula into his hand. Whilst they're working I notice an envelope on the sideboard. I try to make out, although my head is spinning, the spidery writing on the front. It's addressed to the police. I pick it up and see that underneath is another with a scrawl that looks like 'Diana' on the envelope. Without thinking I slip that into my back trouser pocket and mention the other to the police officer.

Reg is on a stretcher now ready to be taken straight to hospital. Will he recover? Time is of the essence the two paramedics say, but it helps that they know what he took. I give my contact details to the police and say I'm going home. I don't know whether they expect me to accompany Reg in the ambulance but the way I'm feeling that's a good Samaritan act too far. Besides, I tell myself, the NHS doesn't need my germs.

As I leave the room, the police first-responder picks up the envelope on the sideboard. A suicide note, I presume.

But if Reg's overdose was a split-second decision then how come he had time to write a letter? Perhaps he wrote it a while back when feeling suicidal and had never ripped it up.

I know I've started a healthcare job, but I wasn't expecting to have to deal with a serious incident like this so soon. Although my legs are shaking, my feet manage to carry me home. My aching hands unlock the door and I dash straight for the loo where I'm sick myself, a reaction to what I've just experienced and the pounding of my throbbing, scorching head. The next thing I know I'm in bed, fully dressed, the feel of the pillow on my temple providing a momentary cooling sensation.

Everything goes black.

~29~

I'm burning in hell, the flames lapping the bottom of my jeans and threatening to climb higher. However much I shake my legs I can't put out the fire that's creeping up my legs and burning my flesh, its acrid stench accompanied by crackling and the sound of manic laughter just behind my head. I can barely breathe – despite the flames I'm bathed in sweat but it's not enough moisture to stop the orange tentacles reaching out for my torso and my face. 'Gemma, Gemma, is that you? Help me!' I cry out but she does not come and the laughter continues. The flames reach my hair and I scream in pain before succumbing to the relief of nothingness.

Then she's there, right beside me, holding my hand and wiping my brow with a cold flannel. I'm five again and tucked up in my own bed. Gemma is looking down at me with compassion, her ponytail swinging as she moves her head to lean closer towards me.

'Thank you,' I say, feeling comforted. She smiles and brings her pale shiny lips towards my ear. 'You evil bitch. Dying is too good for you. I want you to suffer.'

I'm screaming again, back in the flames. Someone is trying to strip my clothes from me but I know that if they do the fire will sizzle my flesh and I lash out, kicking and pushing as much as my limited strength will allow. The person – or is it a being, a devil? – holds my two hands together whilst my trousers are pulled off. I know I'm going to burn on my own funeral pyre. Terror gives me one last impetus to fight but the other is too strong for me. 'It's OK, Annie,' says a voice, 'I'm trying to make you better.' I feel water on my lips, a glorious cooling sensation, and I gulp it down. There's something else in my mouth too, a pill maybe, and I swallow it along with the liquid, which forces the flames to back off and there I am, naked, no energy left to do anything rather than lie down and give in to whatever will come next.

Blankness and then I'm a little girl again, sitting at the top of the swirly carpeted stairs, listening to what the grown-ups are saying down below. My mother is sobbing, crying, 'Why, why, why,' over and over. 'My lovely Gemma, why couldn't Annie have died instead? She should have taken Gemma's place in the grave. Annie has always been a bad girl. Bad blood will out.' I clutch the top step with my fingers then push back violently, throwing myself forward, and I tumble in a forward roll down hundreds of stairs, a pain shooting through my body as I pass each step, going further and further into the black abyss but never reaching the respite of the bottom, no final crunch to signal the end of my ordeal. Just pain, never-ending pain, sobbing – is it coming from my mother or me? – and utter, intense sadness.

'Annie, it's me, I'm here. Just rest.' It's a woman's voice. I'm suddenly aware that I'm wearing fresh pyjamas though the sheet is damp against my unclothed feet. There's something at the back of my mind I need to think about but I don't know what it is, it's locked somewhere in a box with a huge padlock firmly locked. Where am I? I'm tired, so tired. More liquid to my lips but this time via a straw. It's fizzy and sickly but still I suck hard, filling my stomach as if it were to be my last drink. Someone takes my hand and squeezes it as I lie my head back again against the pillow. Then Gemma is there again, staring at me with her beautiful, unlined eyes. Behind her lurks Toby. She doesn't seem to twig that he is there. I try and cry out but cannot make a sound. My lungs hurt with the effort to try and scream. He is creeping nearer and nearer to Gemma, raising his hands towards her bare neck, reaching out with his fingers, clasping her flesh, squeezing, and I'm paralysed, can do nothing to stop him...

Darkness again. The sounds far off are of a car driving down the road and the squeal of a fox mating. I need the loo but can't move my heavy body far enough to get out of bed. My bladder burns with hot rage. The devil comes back. 'You're a dirty bully,' it taunts. 'A filthy, worthless, waste of space.' It punches my stomach, pounding and pounding. I try so hard not to let it win, but it keeps on tormenting me and punching until I release my bladder and feel a warm flow down my leg permeating the sheet and mattress. It's right. I am dirty. I'm a little girl again, outside in the garden, spreading soil across my face and messing up my gingham dress. There's Gemma, looking at me, judging me, when I so desperately want her to play with me, notice me. She turns her back in disgust and starts to walk away so I run at her, throw myself against her body to make her listen and she falls, far far down into an abyss I can't reach out and rescue her from.

Then I'm even younger, a baby in a pram my mother

has pushed to the park. 'Everything is all your fault,' she sings to me in a lullaby voice as she pushes the pram further and further into the lake. It's a tune I remember, though the words differ: 'Everything is all your fault, all your fault, all your fault, everything is all your fault, all day long.'

The water reaches my body and soaks the blanket I'm wrapped in yet I feel no cooler. It's rising higher, up to my head, my lips, but I can't cry out, can't scream, can't fight the sodden material I'm swaddled in. 'Goodbye, Annie,' Mother says as she gives the pram a final shove further into the lake…

With a shock I open my eyes, dragged up to consciousness by fear. I have the pins and needles of a dead leg, caused by lying awkwardly on one side, cutting off my circulation. My duvet is tangled around my limbs and I'm bathing in my own sweat. I sit up stiffly and push the covers back towards the end of the bed. The curtains are partially open and I can see it's daylight outside. Next to me there's a glass of water and a couple of biscuits. I realise I'm hungry, so very hungry, and devour the biscuits as quickly as possible. What time is it? What day is it? When I try and stand I feel inconceivably heavy on my feet, as if I've aged a couple of decades. My phone isn't where I usually leave it at night on the bedside table. I pull on a pair of socks and a hoodie from the chest of drawers then make my way to the bathroom, go the loo and wash my face with cold water. In the mirror above the sink I look blotchy, haggard, greasy and too thin. I must have been in bed longer than one night I think.

Coming out of the bathroom I hear voices downstairs. One is definitely a man's voice, although I can't make out what he's saying. The other, I conclude, must be my mother's. I'm so weak that instead of walking down the stairs I shuffle down them on my bottom. It's when I see the police jacket hung up at the bottom of the stairs that I remember what happened.

Reg tried to commit suicide. Did the paramedics manage to save him?

'Annie, is that you?' Mother says, walking into the hall from the kitchen. 'Thank God you're on the mend. Come and get some food, you must be starving.' She reaches out to me to help me down the final two steps then leads me gently into the kitchen where DI Glass is sitting at the table nursing a cup of coffee. He smiles and comments that he's sorry to hear I've had the flu.

They make small talk whilst Mother toasts some bread for me, brings me a glass of water and boils the kettle for a cup of tea. I've got too much of a head fog to say anything. It's only when I'm eating the toast that Mother starts to talk and tells me DI Glass is here to officially confirm that Reg has confessed to murdering Gemma. He told the police where he'd buried her, in woodland a few miles away, and the forensics team have recovered a body that they think further DNA tests will prove is hers. Her schoolbag was found with the remains.

It was Reg? He killed my sister and I'd saved his life? A tsunami of nausea and fury crashes over my head.

'So he's still alive?'

DI Glass replies calmly and professionally. 'No. He died this morning in the ICU of acute organ failure. But yesterday he was conscious long enough to confess to Gemma's murder and his words backed up what he'd written in a note to the police.'

Mother's face is ashen and her eyes are ringed with bright red sores. I try to swallow down the blend of sickness and sobs that my stomach threatens to heave up. DI Glass mentioned remains. I gulp down a glass of water.

'When did he do it? Why?'

'We don't know the motive as yet. All he said was that it was a moment of madness. Gemma came home from school the day she went missing – one thing we weren't aware of from the initial investigation – and entered the garden through the back gate. He killed her there after an argument.'

'In our own garden? But that doesn't make sense, I would have been at home that day. Why didn't I hear something?'

Mother stops me. 'It's me who should have heard something. You'd have been playing in the house, Annie. Reg told the police Gemma didn't come indoors.' I can hear the vitriol in her voice as she says our next-door neighbour's name. She'd lived next door to her daughter's killer all those years and never known. How must she be feeling? Hatred? Relief that she finally knows what happened? In one thought I'm glad he's dead then in another I wish he were still alive so I could have killed him myself with my bare hands.

DI Glass interrupts my stream of consciousness. 'Once our forensics team have finished their investigation and we have an official identification then Gemma's body will be released for burial.' He pulls a compassionate expression that I imagine must be well-used in this line of work. 'It's thanks to you, Annie, that we re-opened our investigation. We believe it was us interviewing Mr Swanson again that pricked his conscience and led to his confession.'

'Death is too good for him,' Mother replies. She's too

proud to let her tears fall in front of her guest. DI Glass leaves, saying he'll let us know as soon as he has more news with regards to identifying the remains. I slump forwards on the table with the weight of this new knowledge. Then I remember the letter Reg left for Mother. I reach for her hand and squeeze it.

'What did his letter say? Have you read it? I thought it was a suicide note when I picked it up. Did he confess to you as well?' The words come out quietly.

'What are you talking about?' she replies tersely.

'The letter addressed to you that I picked up in his house. Have you seen it? I put it in my trouser pocket.'

'What letter? I haven't seen one. I washed your trousers after Elaine and I undressed you when you were ill. There was nothing in the pockets.'

'But there was a letter for you from him. I picked it up, I'm sure I did.'

'Annie, you've been seriously ill with the flu, rambling like a maniac. I haven't seen a letter. Are you quite sure?'

'I think so... my memories of that morning are a bit hazy but I thought there was a letter for you. Maybe I dropped it in my bedroom? I'll go and look upstairs.'

Mother tells me not to because the police had searched Reg's house and didn't mention finding a letter addressed to her, plus she says I need to eat and drink some more then rest. I ignore her and slowly, shaking with each step, climb the stairs. Upstairs I search my room. The letter is not on the floor, on the bedside table or in my bag. In fact, it's nowhere to be seen. I don't have many possessions but I riffle through them all to find it, pulling clothes out of drawers and pouring the contents of my handbag onto the floor.

'You imagined it,' says Mother, who has followed me upstairs. 'You were in and out of consciousness for three days, hallucinating and talking rubbish about devils, flames and God knows what else. Annie, you had a severe case of flu. Elaine came round to help me nurse you, otherwise the doctor said he'd have had to take you into hospital.'

Good old Aunty Lena. But as for the letter, is it true I imagined it? I can't have done, can I? I think back to what I can remember from my bouts moving in and out of consciousness in my sick bed. The nightmares had seemed so real.

What I do remember with the force of a gut-punch is Gareth's betrayal. I suppose there's no point telling the police about it now. I find my mobile in my bag and the battery bar is red due to lack of charge. There are a few texts from Priti including one replying to a text I sent to her after the ambulance arrived that I don't remember sending. There are also five missed call alerts from Gareth. I don't want to listen to his messages so I delete them straight away. The last is a message from the HR department at the hospital confirming that Mother rang them to tell them I had flu and asking me to let them know when I'm fit for another shift.

I slump with the over-exertion. I'm hungry and dehydrated. Mum tells me to lie down and get some more rest. 'That evil man is an alcoholic who put this family through decades of misery. I hope he rots in hell. All this time he knew what had happened to Gemma, he lived next door and saw our grief but said nothing. Nothing!'

She sits down on the bed and takes my hand. 'You get some sleep. Elaine's coming round soon and bringing lunch for us. You've got to get well, Annie, that man robbed me of one daughter and I'll move heaven and earth so as to not lose you too.'

Mother draws me into a hug and, despite the shock of physical intimacy with her, I lean into it with physical and mental weariness.

Reg had confessed to burying her in the woods. That bastard is the reason we never knew what happened to Gemma and my parents could not find any peace. He ruined my childhood and took away the opportunity for me to ever know my sister properly. With a steely resolve, I decide I'm not going to let anyone hurt Mother ever again. Reg murdered Gemma. How could he have done that? How could he have buried her body that day and kept it a secret for all those years? It's far too soon for me to decipher my revulsion for him but what I do feel is the blunt force of reality. I've spent years assuming that Gemma is dead, being angry at her for spoiling my childhood and us not knowing the truth about why she disappeared. Now I shut my eyes and see the picture of her smiling face in the photograph taken in the park. She was so young. She really is dead, her body a dug-up partially decomposed corpse. How scared must she have been when Reg attacked her? I hope she didn't suffer. I desperately want to be able to hold her in my arms and tell her I'm sorry I've not mourned her, I'm sorry I've blamed my problems on her, I'm sorry we never got to be friends as adults and have the bond of confidences that only sisters can share. She might have been married with children by now. Tears start rolling down my face and I'm overwhelmed with more heartbreak than I ever had over the abortion, the break up with Shaun or Gareth's lies.

I've lost my sister forever. This is not a game of 'what if' anymore. She really is gone.

~ 30 ~

I take a fortnight to physically and mentally convalesce, gathering strength every day through lots of home-cooked food brought by Aunty Lena, short walks and lots of sleep. Before I caught the flu I never could have imagined that a person could naturally sleep so long.

Priti found out via the television news that a man had been arrested for murdering Gemma. The day I awoke after my phone had recharged I sent a quick text to reply to her messages and update her with the basic facts. She came as soon as she could to see me and braved the reporters who camped outside our house for a few days after the story broke. Mother and I stayed indoors and didn't reply to journalists' pleas for an exclusive interview or chance to tell our side of the story. I'd had my fingers burned with the local rag's previous slant on the police questioning Toby in prison. That didn't stop people I'd never heard of selling stories about Gemma to the tabloids, claiming to have known her well and be devastated at the loss of her. After the discovery of her body, Gemma instantly morphed from a troubled teen who may have run away to an angelic helpless victim of a depraved neighbour. Her story spent about a week repeating itself on twenty-four-hour news channels and spawning 'me too' tales in magazine and newspaper supplements: sorry real-life stories from other parents whose children had been murdered. Reg's ex-wife Karen, his son and his son's family apparently fled abroad to escape press attention only for stories to be printed about them holidaying in luxury in Spain whilst 'little Gemma's' (the phrase had become a tabloid favourite, even though Gemma was sixteen when she was murdered) family's hearts were shattered in the UK.

Ian and Jen have been a great help by extending the hand of friendship and explaining the legal side of things to Mother and me. He kept his word and didn't tell anyone else about the two threatening letters. Our only contact with the press was a public statement we released through Ian. It simply thanked the police and asked for us to be left alone to grieve Gemma in private.

Ian explained that as Reg is dead Gemma's case is now closed. By killing himself he escaped a sentence of between fifteen and thirty years in jail – not that far off the time Mother and I served not knowing what had happened to Gemma. Father, of course, went to his grave still in the dark.

No more threatening letters arrived. The police could not find proof as to who sent the first two. No cut up newspapers were found in Reg's house amongst his piles of unrecycled junk but that doesn't mean he didn't do it: presumably if he did write them he would have had the intelligence to get rid of the detritus, however pissed he was. DI Glass brought Robert Smith in, the most likely suspect, for questioning over the threats but didn't find enough evidence to charge him. He's a slippery man who knows how to evade the law. I guess I'll never know who the sender was, the coward who was too weak to confront me face to face. Still, occasionally my heart beats faster when I see a white envelope arrive in the post and I remember that someone out there meant me harm and is still hiding amongst the shadows in society.

Whilst I'm convalescing, Priti entertains me for a weekend with a stash of magazines, nail polishes, DVDs and a bottle of Prosecco that she calls medicinal, although she's not partaking herself because her big news is that she's six weeks pregnant. She'd kept that one quiet.

She says that the baby-to-be pleases her traditionally-minded husband more than her but I can tell that deep down she's thrilled at this life change. The Priti I know would never have sex without contraception if she didn't want to be a mother. I keep quiet about my abortion as it's not the time or the place to tell her. I doubt I ever will now. I'm thrilled about Priti's news but not sorry that I did what I did. I would have been heavily pregnant by now.

Priti asks me to be a secular godmother to her child. In the Hindu religion apparently there is no godmother equivalent but they do have a naming ceremony called the Namakarana. She says when she has a baby she's going to need her friends more than ever and if I'm godmother than I have no excuse not to spend lots of time with her. I strangely find myself looking forward to it, being a significant part of a baby's life but also having the ability to give him or her back to his or her parents. It's a new chapter for Priti and for me as well.

When I'm back to full health and the news story has died down, replaced by a seemingly-endless cycle of political scandals and other victims of heinous crimes, I go back to work. A while later, thanks to Una's advice, I get a place on an access to healthcare college course which, when I complete it, will mean I can apply to do a degree in nursing. I'm not sure yet what area I'd like to specialise in but, after spending so much time with Mother at the hospital, I'm drawn towards oncology. Mother's cancer is still at bay, although she still has to have regular check-ups. She'll never be cancer-free but the tumour thankfully hasn't grown again or spread.

The house next door is boarded up. Ian tells us that the garden and internal structure were pulled apart by the police to try to find forensic evidence and ascertain whether he could be linked to any other murder or serious sexual assault crimes. They find nothing. The house, however, is uninhabitable due to Reg's years of neglect and the police investigations. There's no one to put everything back in its place. The last thing I heard was that the bank had foreclosed on Reg's mortgage and planned to auction off the property to a developer.

It feels ghoulish to stay in this house, particularly when we know Gemma was murdered in the garden here. Mother decides to sell up and make a new start away from the bad memories. Even after the press lost interest we still had the odd person knocking on the door asking if they could look in the garden where the murder had taken place. They'd pretend to offer condolences but really we knew they were treating Gemma's death as if it were some form of entertainment, akin to visiting a village where a murder TV series was filmed or going round a haunted house at a theme park. Needless to say, no one ever made it across our threshold.

Before Mother puts the house on the market, we once again bring out the bin bags and cardboard boxes to declutter.

244

A housing charity takes all the furniture from Gemma's room and I whitewash the walls, turning it into a blank canvas for the next owner.

Thanks to a slightly below its market value asking price, the estate agents quickly find a buyer. It seems that a murder scene isn't off-putting to purchasers as long as the price is right. Mother makes an offer on a two-bed garden flat near the college, puts my name jointly on the deeds and says I can stay there as long as I want to. I certainly don't plan to stay forever, but am thankful to remain until I can afford to rent my own place or move in with a friend. We're rubbing along alright together now – she's the only family I have left and, at this point, what with everything that has gone on, we need each other.

And Gareth? He left a few phone messages and even came to the house with a bunch of flowers and a condolence card but we both knew there was no chance of getting back together. With a non-feverish brain I believe him when he said that after our first date it truly was me he was interested in rather than just wanting to find out more about Gemma. I still can't forgive him for lying to me, though, and for what he did to Gemma, yet with hindsight I rushed in too quickly, moved from Shaun to him to plaster over my loneliness as if being in a relationship could fix my troubles.

Knowing what I do now, I can't quite figure out what I ever saw in him.

Not that I've turned into a nun. I've been on a few dates since with a fellow HCA at work. This time I'm taking things slowly, seeing him about once a week. Who knows what will happen but right now having some fun away from the sluices, IVs and blood pressure monitors suits us both fine.

At last, Gemma's body is released by the coroner and we can plan her funeral. It takes place on a rainy day at the crematorium. Neither my family nor Gemma were religious but it feels right to lay her to rest with a Christian service. If anyone deserves the chance for eternal rest in heaven, after what Gemma suffered it is her. We pick a couple of hymns that Gemma would have known from school, 'All Things Bright and Beautiful' and 'Amazing Grace'. Aunty Lena, Den, Mother and I are the chief mourners and we support each other throughout the day. I can't help but wonder how a God could let a young girl die and her murderer walk free for so many years, but put those thoughts aside for another time. It's not the first time it has happened and it won't be the last.

Aunty Lena, Den and I help Mother write a speech for the vicar detailing Gemma's short life and what she achieved. I've since got to know Fiona quite well and she's told me lots of lovely stories about Gemma, including when they went to a pop concert in Sheffield and managed to push their way to the front. Fiona's snippets help me to form a better picture in my mind of my sister. At the pub after the funeral, she takes me aside to tell me how pleased Gemma was to have a little sister and that Gemma had once told her that she sometimes felt guilty for not giving me lots of attention but she was busy with her own life and resented every now and then having to do the childcare. I hold onto the thought tightly. It helps me to know that Gemma had once cared about me. If only Mother had explained her depression to Gemma and I all those years ago, if mental health hadn't been such a taboo, then maybe Mother and both daughters would have understood each other better.

Gareth comes to the crematorium and sits at the back, ignored by Fiona after a polite nod of recognition. Mike sends a condolence card apologising for his behaviour but stays away from the funeral. It turns out to be a packed affair. A lot of Gemma's school friends turn up along with my father's ex-co-workers, neighbours, DI Glass and a couple of colleagues, plus, I suspect, a few people I don't recognise who have turned up because of the notoriety of the case and don't stay for the refreshments afterwards so as not to be caught out. I take a deep breath in shock when I glimpse a confident teenager in black with dark hair swept back in a ponytail walk out of the church. From the back she could be Gemma. I later learn she's the daughter of one of Gemma's old schoolmates. If Gemma had lived, would I have been an aunty? Reg cruelly took that possibility away from her and me on that horrific day.

Toby, of course, still incarcerated in prison, doesn't come. The courts turn his appeal down. Whether that is because of the letter of the law or the decision was swayed by an online petition to keep him behind bars, organised by a group that supports female victims of domestic violence, I don't know. Over a hundred thousand people, including me, signed it. The publicity around the solving of Gemma's disappearance brought Toby's situation into the mainstream media. The attention that Robert Smith courted backfired on him. I like to think that Gemma's death may have prevented another woman suffering at Toby's hands. Certainly I imagine that Jasmine, his ex-wife, will sleep a little easier in her bed knowing he is to stay behind bars where he can't ever hurt her again. She has moved back to live with family in the Philippines and I hope that brings her peace.

We still don't know how or why Reg killed Gemma. Her body was too decomposed to analyse the cause of death but there was evidence of trauma to the ribs. We don't know whether, and I blanche at thinking this, he sexually assaulted her before or after. The police say there's no evidence to suggest he did but they can't rule it out. I clutch on to the belief that if she'd struggled or shouted out then someone in one of the houses nearby would have heard. Practicality-wise if he killed her in our back garden then he would have had a very short window of time to murder her and dispose of the body without being seen or heard from a neighbour's upstairs window. I want to believe she didn't suffer.

The police open a review of the handling of Gemma's case to see what lessons can be learned. Their records show that Reg was interviewed a day after Gemma's disappearance but nothing suspicious was found to follow up on. Father had told the police that Reg hardly had anything to do with Gemma and she had never been to his house alone. One thing that first police interview did record was the officer's recollection that Reg smelt of alcohol. Could he have been blind drunk the day before and killed Gemma in a fit of anger? Had he made a sexual move on her and she'd turned him down? Or, despite him saying it was a moment of madness, was he a psychopath, planning the murder in advance and seizing his chance when he found her alone in the garden? In the initial interview in 1989, he told the police he'd been working from home doing paperwork until mid-afternoon when he went, for his job as a sales representative, to visit two clients about forty miles away and ate dinner at a pub in between the appointments. His wife confirmed he was asleep when she got back with their son after they spent the evening with her mother to celebrate her birthday. The publican and two clients confirmed Reg's alibi. When he confessed to murder, all those years later, Reg changed his statement to say that after he killed Gemma he wrapped her body in an old carpet, parked his car at the end of the snicket behind our houses then carried the bundle to the boot of his Ford Sierra estate. He went on to say that he buried her in woodlands sometime that evening after his second business meeting then drove home, had a shower, put what he'd been wearing in the washing machine along with some other clothes and drank brandy to help him sleep.

Sleep? How could anyone sleep after doing what he did?

I go about once a week to put flowers on Gemma's grave. It's a quiet time, me telling her what I've been up to in the week and imagining the replies a big sister would give.

If only she could answer me back.

~ 31 ~

2020

The flat seems strangely cold and quiet as I turn the key and walk in. It's been a while since I was last here and the rooms have gained a fusty, unused odour. Priti follows behind me – her son Anuj is having a daddy day – and together we're laden with cardboard boxes, sticky tape, bin bags and a plethora of cleaning products.

Firstly I go into the lounge and draw the curtains wide open to let the light in and watch it reveal dust dancing in the air. One beam of sunshine highlights the embroidery hoop on the sofa with its half-finished pattern of colourful cross stitches. I can make out a nurse's uniform and the word 'congratulations' at the top. Mum had kept her present to me, a tapestry to mark my promotion to clinical nurse specialist in oncology, a secret when she was alive. It was on the sofa when Craig and I found her that evening we were invited round for tea, the evening when she didn't answer the door and I used my own key to let us in, expecting her to be in the loo or listening to the radio and not dead on the floor thanks to a massive stroke. She hadn't had a chance to squirrel the cross stitch away – hadn't known that she'd embroidered her last ever stitch.

Craig is coming to help later after his shift but this afternoon it feels right that it's just Priti and I sorting out Mum's clothes and personal possessions. She bequeathed the flat to me. Craig and I are yet to decide whether to move in ourselves when the notice on our rented one-bedder expires or sell it and buy somewhere else. Financially it makes sense to live here but right now my mind is playing tricks, imagining Mum has just popped out to the shops, is having a bath or will walk in and offer a cup of tea and a packet of digestives. It feels too soon, too raw to jump in and take what was hers, even though legally it is mine. I miss her so, something the younger me would have laughed out loud to hear.

We decide to start in Mum's bedroom. I pull the clothes out of the drawers and wardrobes whilst Priti chooses whether to send them to a charity shop or, for those garments well past their prime, to take them to a fabric recycling centre. I recognise many of the outfits having seen Mum most days after I moved out and into the nurses' home and then, a while later, in with Craig. The exception are the clothes from the past, from the 'lost years' as we called them, when I was in Leeds.

'Oh I like this!' exclaims Priti as she pulls out a red and orange blended silk (fake probably) scarf. She wraps it round her neck jauntily in a fashion I'd never have thought of. Since Anuj arrived, Priti hasn't had much spare money to treat herself what with giving up her job ('What a relief! Thank God for reproduction, I'll never have to enter a call centre again!' she beamed) to look after him full time. After he started school, she carved out a niche online as a British

Asian fashion and lifestyle influencer, although as yet her income is in the hundreds and not the millions, not that that has put a dampener on her business ambitions.

'Have it. It suits you.'

'Are you sure you don't want it?'

'I'm sure. If you don't take it it'll only go to the charity shop.'

Priti puts the scarf into her handbag. 'Thanks! Do you want me to make a start on those boxes?' She points to the shoeboxes at the bottom of the wardrobe. 'You know shoes are my speciality.'

'Stilettos not comfy pull-ons!' I joke, then busy myself folding the clothes into piles and the correct bin bags for their next destination. How strange it is to sort through someone else's possessions. I remember Mum and I doing the same thing with Gemma's clothes. Some day somebody will do it with mine.

Priti pulls out boots, espadrilles and sandals from the boxes. I smile as I see her examining the kitten heels I borrowed for the HCA interview six years ago. 'Nearly killed my feet walking in those!' They go in the charity shop pile whilst the old trainers go straight in the bin.

My back is turned to Priti when she says, 'This box hasn't got shoes in, Annie.' I turn round to see the box Mum had stopped me from seeing when I tried on her clothes for the interview. 'Oh, that's Mum's private stuff. Diaries and letters her counsellor told her to write about Gemma.' Whilst I'm very curious to read what they say I don't act on that thought. Mum has a right to her privacy in death. She'd been adamant that she didn't want me to read them.

'What shall I do with them then?'

'Tip them out in the bin bag for the rubbish please hon.'

I go back to my job of tying a knot in the full bin bags and labelling them with their contents. Behind me I hear a thump as Priti tips out the contents of the box. She sighs and I catch her hip click as she bends down.

'What's up?' I ask.

'One missed the rubbish bag. Hang on a minute, it's a letter.'

'It's probably nothing important.'

I nip to the loo and then go to the kitchen for a glass of water. When I return to the bedroom, Priti's ashen face looks serious and she's clutching a couple of A4 pieces of paper in a tight fist.

'What's wrong?' I ask.

'Nothing. Just a load of old rubbish.' She moves to rip the paper up but I grab her wrist to stop her, sensing something amiss. I can always tell when she's avoiding telling me something. 'What's going on? Did you read it?'

Priti replies in a rather-too-bright voice, her pitch far higher than usual. 'It really is nothing. Just forget it, Annie.'

'Have you read my mother's letter? What does it say?' I snatch it from her.

'Don't read it,' she begs, which of course makes me want to read it more.

I walk to the window, the acrid taste of adrenaline hitting my mouth. The letter is written in spidery writing, which I vaguely recognise, searching for a memory as to why. After five seconds it hits me. It's Reg's writing, the same as the letter to the police. My eyes skip to the top of the first page. I hold my breath as I read…

Diana, I know you never could or should forgive me for what I did. I am so sorry. Believe me I hate myself more than anyone else could. I cannot live with myself anymore. I deserve to die. Every second I'm awake I wish I'd made a different choice that day, called an ambulance or shouted for a neighbour. But you must believe me, Diana, I never meant to hurt Gemma. All I could think of was protecting Annie.

Thursday 4ᵗʰ May 1989. 4.16 p.m.

It was the thump Reg heard first, the onomatopoeic crump of a body hitting the floor. It sounded like something had fallen on one of the concrete paving slabs that meandered their way along the length of the otherwise grassy garden to the greenhouse at the end.

He'd been out in the garden having a smoke. Although he told Karen numerous times that he had given up, a sop to one of the many things about him she wanted to change, he still had a cigarette when she was out, relishing the fact he was sticking the proverbial two-finger salute up behind her back. They barely spoke any more when their son Scott, who was about to take his A level exams, wasn't in the room. Karen's disapproving looks said a thousand words on their own. They'd been happy enough when they set out on married life and he couldn't pinpoint the moment, or even the year, when love turned to affection and then to a bubbling-under animosity. But it did, it oh so did.

Today Karen was meeting Scott after she left her building society cashier job for the day. The pair of them were then going to see Karen's parents an hour's bus ride away for a meal to celebrate her mother's birthday, although it would have taken much less time if he'd have driven them in the car as Karen hadn't passed her test. Some birthday for his mother-in-law, he thought, when she had to cook her own dinner. There was no way he was going to take the pair: his present to her was not showing up, pleading prior work commitments. At least the two women could talk about him in the kitchen whilst Scott went to the pub for a drink with his grandad. He thought Karen was never happier than when discussing his faults.

Reg arranged with his boss to work from home every now and then to do paperwork and cold-calling companies for business. Today he had two thoughtfully-arranged evening sales appointments to go to.

Karen worked too far away to nip home for lunch and always took a homemade sandwich in with her. The boring minutiae of a stale marriage. Finally he was going to leave. Tonight, after his meetings, he'd tell her. He'd move out. She could have the house. Diana was less likely to get together with him if he were still living next door – she was a stickler about scandal and what the neighbours thought. Yes, she'd turned him down again earlier but he wasn't going to give up. Remembering that afternoon they'd spent together, reliving how she'd made him feel, that was all that had kept him going these past six years. It was those pills she took talking. They belonged together.

Karen would no doubt be relieved to be free of an out-of-date marriage without having to be the guilty party ending it. She would enjoy revelling in the attention of being left, her gripes and grumbles about her husband now proven ten times over. Scott was hoping to go to a polytechnic in Portsmouth to study engineering if he got his grades. His parents splitting up shouldn't affect him too much, Reg would still make the effort to visit him and give him as much cash as he could for his course. The boy has brains – surely his parent's divorce wouldn't come as too much of a surprise. The days when divorce brought shame on a family had long gone.

He wanted to wake up with Diana, rescue her, save her from a doped-up marriage after years of downtrodden misery.

He would go round tonight to Diana and Frank's to tell them he and Karen were splitting up. When Diana realises it's really happening she might be more likely to come with him. He'll have to look up B&Bs in the Yellow Pages, stay in one for a week or two until he can rent a flat. Somewhere good enough for a woman like Diana. It could be like when he and Karen were newlyweds, except with a different woman. He imagined cosy suppers, christening each room and a place full of laughter instead of permanent bone-chilling tension.

The thump tore him away from his thoughts. He'd been looking over the fence whilst he smoked and daydreamed. Minutes earlier he saw Annie was playing in the garden. Apart from the sound of Kylie Minogue singing 'Hand on Your Heart' on the radio a few doors down, hers was the only activity he could hear in the back gardens. Seeing her, the girl born nearly nine months after the afternoon Diana and he had made love, made him wonder and fantasise again about whether she was his daughter. He had never summoned the courage to ask and Diana never said but, holding the baby when he and Karen had visited with a bottle of wine to wet the newborn's head, he had wondered, he had somehow felt a connection. He'd looked at Annie and saw his father's eyes and his own stubborn resolve in the way she held her head. Plus, his mother had been a ginger, and neither Diana nor

Frank were. They say it can skip a generation in the family.

Before the thump, he'd heard the familiar squeak of next door's back gate opening and some heavier footsteps. As he took his last drag then crushed the cigarette butt underfoot, he heard Annie say, 'Oh! It's you.'

'What are you up to, ratbag?' Their voices were quiet.

'Playing. I'm floating in the sea. Come and play, I'll be the fish, you be the dolphin.'

'No.'

'Please…'

'No, I've got revision to do.'

'Why do you never want to play with me?'

'I've not got time. I've got revision to do.' Gemma's voice was cut off by a few quick lighter footsteps.

Reg took more notice of the squabble, ready to tell the girls to play nicely.

Annie ran over to Gemma and pushed her in the stomach, catching her unawares, before turning on her heel and running into the house through the back door.

One thump then silence. Reg looked over the fence again, saw Gemma lying contorted on the floor, her unbleeding head touching the edge of a concrete slab. Her fingers twitched and she let out a groan, as if she were trying to work out how to push herself upright.

Reg looked round anxiously for help but the back gardens surrounding him were softly quiet save the chirrup of a bird and the flaps of its wings. He should call an ambulance, but what if Gemma needed resuscitating? It could take too long to go into the house and ring from the landline. Decision made, he dashed out of his back gate and into the Towcester's, then tried to shake Gemma to rouse her from unconsciousness. If he were watching this on a television screen he would be yelling at himself to shout for help, unable to suspend his disbelief in his failure to do so. Yet what his inner instinct told him to do was check her pulse and her breath – the former faint, the latter non-existent. What came to him was a memory of learning CPR in the Scouts on a terrifying wax doll, concerned that his first kiss would be from rubber lips that had already been passed round the troupe.

She must have suffered a head injury when her skull hit the concrete. The pavement slabs were uneven: he hadn't seen fully but Gemma must have tripped over one when she tried to keep her balance. He rolled her on to her back, opened her airway, blew into it, then placed his two downward-facing clasping palms on her chest and pushed hard. Too hard. A human bust felt much different from the faint memories of the long-ago Resusci Anne. He felt cracks under his fingers and – was it two or three? – ribs give way. A faint groan escaped from Gemma's lips, and then nothing. Her eyelids didn't flicker. She stared at him glassily. There was no pulse nor breath. She was dead.

He panicked and looked round over the fences. There was no one there. Nobody else saw him or Annie. If he called the police now would they believe a five-year-old pushed Gemma? And if they did, what would happen to her? Her life would forever be marked. But also his fingerprints were all over Gemma's body. He'd broken her ribs. They'd say he hurt her, not tried to resuscitate her. He'd go to prison. If Diana knew he was involved there'd never be a chance of getting together with her. Reg couldn't think straight. It was as if his brain shut down and his body took over on autopilot. He found himself getting an old roll of carpet out of his shed, ducking down as he pulled it through to the Towcester's garden so as not to be seen over the fence.

Five minutes later, the garden was deserted, apart from a lone butterfly skitting amongst the buddleias.

Questions for Book Clubs

1. At the beginning of the novel, how justified do you think Annie is to hold a grudge?
2. Mental health is a key theme. How does Diana's experience in the 1980s compare with the present day?
3. How does Annie's character change throughout the novel, and why?
4. To what extent do you think Annie's financial circumstances contribute to her choices?
5. Gemma and Annie had different experiences of school. Are school days the best years of your life?
6. What could Diana and Frank have done to be better parents?
7. What was your impression of Gareth? Should Annie have forgiven him for his teenage actions?
8. Why does Priti tell Annie not to read the letter?
9. How culpable do you think Reg is?
10. Does Annie hold any responsibility for what happened to Gemma?

Acknowledgements

Firstly thanks must go to my husband, Chris, for his love and support and my parents, David and Beryl Batchelor, for raising me to aim high.

Thanks to my tutor, Tom Bromley, from the Faber Academy – I first began working on this novel when I took their six-month online writing a novel course – and my fellow students for their encouragement and feedback, particularly Paula Winzar, Carlos Enrique Meza and Sara Schneider.

Early readers Victoria Steyn and Denise Burrows gave invaluable feedback on the plot and Richard Greenslade helped with brainstorming ideas. Thanks also go to Catherine Stewart who suggested questions for book club group discussions, editor Laura Gerrard and cover designer Emily Courdelle.

You wouldn't be holding this book in your hands if it wasn't for the enthusiastic backing of Clare Christian's lovely RedDoor Press team and their belief in my story. I'm delighted to be one of their authors.

About the Author

Penny Batchelor is an alumna of the Faber Academy online 'Writing a Novel' course. She lives in Warwickshire with her husband. *My Perfect Sister* is her first novel and she is currently writing a second.

Web: www.pennybatchelor.co.uk
Facebook: @pennyauthor
Twitter: @penny_author

Find out more about RedDoor
Press and sign up to our
newsletter to hear about our
latest releases, **author events**,
exciting **competitions**
and more at

reddoorpress.co.uk

YOU CAN ALSO FOLLOW US:

     @RedDoorBooks

     Facebook.com/RedDoorPress

     @RedDoorBooks